A SYDNEY TAYLOR NOTABLE BOOK

"**For fans of Angie Thomas**'s *The Hate U Give* and Nic Stone's *Dear Martin*." —SLJ

"This **fast-paced** novel will keep readers thoroughly engaged." —*Kirkus Reviews*

"**A riveting, emotional read.** . . . A reminder of the responsibility we all have to call out injustice wherever we see it." —*Kveller*

"Based on an actual event, this gripping story will have a lasting impact. . . . **Highly recommended.**" —Jewish Book Council

"**Readers won't be able to resist putting themselves in the students' shoes** and thinking about when and where they themselves would draw the line, or if they would dare confront power at all." —Nancy Werlin, author of *The Rules of Survival*

"This **wise and nuanced** novel has loving arms that, while hugging two teens who must confront a popular teacher, also can reach all those who are belittled and unheard." —Thanhhà Lai, *New York Times* bestselling author of *Inside Out & Back Again* and *Butterfly Yellow*

"A riveting, important, and thought-provoking read. **Unputdownable and unforgettable.**" —Leah Cypess, author of the Death Sworn series

"This fast-paced, compelling story will inspire readers to stick to their principles and fight for what's right. **A timely and necessary read.**" —Kip Wilson, author of *White Rose*

"**Brave, breath-stealing, and bold.** A compelling and necessary read." —Gae Polisner, author of *The Memory of Things* and *Jack Kerouac Is Dead to Me*

THE
ASSIGNMENT

LIZA WIEMER

EMBER

Text copyright © 2020 by Liza M. Wiemer
Cover art copyright © 2020 by Jasu Hu

All rights reserved. Published in the United States by Ember,
an imprint of Random House Children's Books, a division of Penguin Random House LLC,
New York. Originally published in hardcover in the United States by Delacorte Press,
an imprint of Random House Children's Books, a division of Penguin Random House LLC,
New York, in 2020.

Ember and the E colophon are registered trademarks of Penguin Random House LLC.

Visit us on the Web! GetUnderlined.com

Educators and librarians, for a variety of teaching tools, visit us at RHTeachersLibrarians.com

The Library of Congress has cataloged the hardcover edition of this work as follows:
Names: Wiemer, Liza M., author.Title: The assignment / Liza Wiemer.
Description: First edition. | New York : Delacorte Press, [2020] | Audience: Ages 12 up. |
Summary: Standing in opposition to a class assignment to debate Hitler's Final Solution,
seniors Cade and Logan become embroiled in turmoil involving their teacher, principal,
Commissioner of Education, white supremacists, and their entire community.
Identifiers: LCCN 2019041073 (print) | LCCN 2019041074 (ebook) |
ISBN 978-0-593-12316-4 (hardcover) | ISBN 978-0-593-12317-1 (library binding) |
ISBN 978-0-593-12318-8 (ebook) Subjects: CYAC: Conduct of life—Fiction. | High
schools—Fiction. | Schools—Fiction. | Holocaust, Jewish (1939–1945)—Fiction. |
Antisemitism—Fiction. Classification: LCC PZ7.1.W4917 As 2020 (print) |
LCC PZ7.1.W4917 (ebook) | DDC [Fic]—dc23

ISBN 978-0-593-12319-5 (paperback)

Printed in the United States of America
10 9 8 7 6 5 4 3 2 1
First Ember Edition 2021

For all the young adults across the globe who have the courage to speak up against any injustice, even when you are afraid, even when others are against you, even when you have to confront those who should've been your role models.

You are lights illuminating darkness. The world needs you.

———————

To Archer and Jordan for being my inspiration.

———————

And to my lamplighters: Justin and Annabella, Ezra and Bracha.

What you're about to read is a fictionalized story based on an actual assignment given to students in a New York high school education program. It's an assignment that could be given anywhere.

Any country. Any town. Any school. Even yours.

THE ASSIGNMENT

CHAPTER 1

LOGAN

Are we supposed to pretend we're Nazis? The second Mr. Bartley turns his back to our class, I lean over to my best friend, Cade, and whisper, "What do you think?" I tap the assignment on my desk.

He lifts his hands, palms up, mirroring my confusion. "Weird, right?" He says it a little too loudly, drawing Mr. Bartley's attention.

I nod, face forward, and refocus on the assignment. I read it one more time, hoping that somehow I've misunderstood the instructions.

TOP-SECRET

MEMO TO: Senior Members of the Nazi Party

FROM: SS General Reinhard Heydrich, Chief of the Reich Main Security Office

SUBJECT: A FINAL SOLUTION OF THE JEWISH QUESTION: Your attendance is required for this critical meeting scheduled for 20 January 1942 at the Wannsee Villa in Berlin, Germany.

PURPOSE: As members of Hitler's elite Nazi leadership, our purpose is to debate a Final Solution of the Jewish Question and to share perspectives on how to resolve the storage problem of Europe's eleven million Jews.

POSITIONS:

Pro: Extermination

Con: Sterilization, ghettos, work camps

WHAT TO PREPARE FOR THE MEETING: As a Nazi, you must thoroughly research and analyze five reasons supporting your position of a Final Solution of the Jewish Question.

Research:

    a. The Nuremberg Laws

    b. Attitudes on religion and race

    c. Our policies on education, including who may attend or teach at primary and secondary schools and universities

    d. Economics, including our perspective on who has the right to own businesses and property

    e. Our leader's stance on Darwin and survival of the fittest

    f. How to increase our superior Aryan race by exploring key ideas such as emigration, expulsion, evacuation, and eradication to be *judenrein* (Jew-free)

Note from Mr. Bartley:

The Wannsee Conference was one of the most pivotal historical moments that had a destructive force on humanity in the twentieth century, one that continues to leave a profound mark on society today. As you complete the research for this assignment, it is important for you to know that the goal is not to garner support or elicit sympathy for the Nazi perspective. It is, however, imperative for you to understand the Nazi mentality, even if it makes you uncomfortable and is diametrically against your moral, ethical, and philosophical beliefs. Researching this historical meeting and your side of the debate allows you to broaden your points of view and develop critical thinking skills.

I flip the page, read through the requirements for our papers and how we're going to be graded on the debate. My stomach somersaults. Get an A by successfully debating reasons to put Jews in gas chambers versus torture them, starve them, force them to be slave laborers for profit until they're dead. Either way, Mr. Bartley is asking us to advocate for murder.

Everything in my body screams, *This is so wrong!* But do I say it to Mr. Bartley? Looking at the other sixteen seniors in our class, I don't see anyone other than Cade who seems uncomfortable with this assignment.

"One more minute," Mr. Bartley calls out. "Then I'll answer questions."

I have a question. *Is this a sick joke?* I can't bring myself to ask it out loud. Mr. Bartley isn't *any* teacher. He's a great teacher, my *favorite* teacher.

He must have a reason why he wants us to pretend we're Nazis. I reread his note. It makes me more than uncomfortable. For the first time ever, I'm tempted to get out of class by asking to go to the girls' bathroom or the nurse's office. I could say I have a pounding headache. Thanks to this assignment, I do.

Mr. Bartley leans against his desk, and when he notices me

staring at him, his warm smile fades. I pick up my pen and trace the blood-red "TOP-SECRET" that's stamped on top of the memo. I don't get it. Why would Mr. Bartley want us to keep this a secret? History of World Governments is the fourth class I've taken with him, and we've never had any assignment like *this*.

Soon after Mr. Bartley started teaching at Riviere High School my sophomore year, he became our most popular teacher. He has the kind of smile that makes you know you've been seen, that you matter. During lunch and his free periods, his room is always filled with students. I've liked him for bringing in guest speakers, for taking us on field trips, showing movies, and letting us decorate his papered walls with quotes, facts, and pictures for every new unit. I love to contribute quotes. He makes history exciting, interesting, and challenging.

I run my thumbpad over the silver bracelet my cousin Blair gave me for my seventeenth birthday and wonder what she would think of this assignment. I'm tempted to take a photo and text it to her, but I don't want to get caught with my phone and have it taken away.

Cade's bouncing knee catches my attention. He writes in his notebook, then flashes it at me. He's drawn an X over "Nazi" and written, "No. Freaking. Way!"

CHAPTER 2

CADE

The Allies defeated Nazi Germany during World War II. Why would I want to pretend I'm a Nazi? Mr. Bartley wants us to broaden our points of view. Really? How is it possible anyone would think murdering millions of people was okay? It's simple. Killing is wrong. Debate over. This is ridiculous.

Despise barely describes how I feel about this class and I have no one to blame but myself. I let Logan rope me into taking it instead of Advanced Web Design so we could spend more time together before we graduate. I look at my best friend and know it's worth it. She's worth it.

But this assignment?

It fills me with dread. My grandparents grew up in Poland and lived through World War II. Grandpa was fifteen at the end of the war. Nana was fourteen. They immigrated to the United States in the late 1960s. The one time I asked Nana about her family, she smiled and said, "I have you right here." Then she pulled me into her arms and squeezed me tight.

A memory returns to me. I was twelve. Nana and my parents were at church, and Grandpa and I were in his workshop. The smells of linseed oil and sawdust filled the air. We were elves, making puzzles for Santa to give to children on Christmas. As we sanded the pieces we'd cut from old drawers, I asked Grandpa what his life was like when he was my age. I remember Grandpa said he didn't like to talk about it, that lots of bad things happened in Poland during the war. His expression grew solemn. His tone was firm. "Promise me you won't ask Nana about her childhood, either. It will only upset her," he said.

I nodded.

We kept working, but then a little while later he said, "Other than your grandma, I haven't told another soul about my life in Poland. Not even your mom. But you're old enough to understand, and I'm growing old." He paused. "The story might frighten you."

I said I didn't care.

I can't quite remember. Something about watching his Jewish neighbors being rounded up by Nazis? I buried those stories when we buried Grandpa two months later.

Mr. Bartley plants himself in front of Logan's center row. A murmur goes through the room as if Mr. Bartley broke a silencing spell. He holds up a palm like he's a crossing guard halting traffic, and it's quiet again. "Questions?" he asks.

Logan's hand shoots up, but then she lowers it when Mr. Bartley aims his clicker at the Smart Board and brings up the assignment.

Kerrianne Nelson gets called on. "I'm confused. The Final Solution of the Jewish Question. Do you mean the Holocaust?"

Mr. Bartley says, "Exactly. The Final Solution was the plan and implementation of the Holocaust."

"Ah, okay. I thought so." She smiles at her boyfriend, Mason Hayes, but he's too busy picking at a thread on his hockey jersey to notice. When she sees me looking at her, she frowns. Like most of the people at our school, I've known Kerrianne since kindergarten. We always got along, but for some reason when Logan moved to Riviere and joined us in eighth grade, Kerrianne stopped sitting with us at lunch and started hanging out with the hockey players.

"Question, Spencer?" This is a surprise. Like me, Spencer Davis never raises his hand in class. If Spencer talks, it's to his hockey teammates or to the girls he deems worthy of his time and attention. He claims to have hooked up with at least a dozen. As if. Thank everything holy Logan isn't one of them.

"Can we get extra credit for dressing up for the debate?"

I turn around to see if he's serious. Oh yeah. Dead serious.

Mr. Bartley says, "Although I appreciate your desire for authenticity, Spencer, that does not extend to dress. No uniforms for this debate."

Someone whispers, "Damn." I glance around, but I can't figure out who it was.

"Excuse me, Mr. Bartley—" Logan breaks off when Mr. Bartley calls on someone else.

He answers a question about citing sources, then another on the structure of our papers that are due the same day as the debate. Moving over to his desk, Mr. Bartley grabs a paper bag and shakes it. He says, "Each of you will draw a number—either a one or two. Call it out after you pick. Mason, you start."

When it's my turn, I mumble, "One." Logan says, "Two."

"All the ones will take the pro side. Twos will take con," Mr. Bartley says. "You may work together to create your platform, but your paper must be your own. Your arguments should be based on the Wannsee Conference held on January 20, 1942. A week from this coming Monday we'll transform our room into the Wannsee Villa and hold our own top-secret Nazi conference to debate how to handle the biggest threat to the Aryan race— the Jew."

The Jew. The way he said it makes my skin crawl.

Mr. Bartley advances to the next PowerPoint slide. "These were the fifteen Nazi men who came together to address how to handle the storage problem of Europe's eleven million Jews. Adolf Eichmann is in the center because he was instrumental in implementing the Final Solution. He oversaw the deportation of Jews from their homes to ghettos to death camps. Tomorrow, we'll watch the movie *Conspiracy,* which reenacts the meeting with these men."

Men? More like monsters, I think.

"The movie will be a good resource, but I highly recommend you get a jump start tonight on your research to support your arguments."

"But they—they're . . . *Nazis,*" Logan stammers without raising her hand.

Mr. Bartley's stern expression cautions her not to speak out of turn again. "Yes, and your job is to understand their mentality. I know re-creating this debate is a challenge, but history is filled with many horrors and this is an impactful way to learn. Experience is always a great teacher." Mr. Bartley smiles. "Unless you'd rather memorize dates and facts and take multiple-choice tests like I had to in my boring high school history classes."

The room erupts with groans and "No thank yous."

Once again, Mr. Bartley raises a hand to quiet us down. "All right then. Back to the Wannsee Conference." He goes through several more slides. My eyes meet Logan's, and then hers dart over my shoulder.

She gasps. I twist in my seat to see why Logan's freaked out and my mouth drops open.

CHAPTER 3

LOGAN

Jesse Elton stands and snaps his feet together. He lifts his right arm and salutes like a Nazi. *"Heil Hitler,"* he calls out.

Several people laugh, and Jesse gives them an appreciative grin. Cade's stunned expression matches mine. Does everyone else find that funny? I look around. Revulsion flashes across Daniel Riggs's face, but it disappears so quickly that I question whether it was there to begin with.

Spencer holds out his fist to Jesse, then mimics the salute and says, *"Sieg Heil.* Hail victory."

This can't be happening here, in my favorite class with my favorite teacher.

And just as I wonder if Mr. Bartley is going to do something, he walks over to Spencer and Jesse. His tone is sharp as a blade cutting through metal. "Those actions are inappropriate. This isn't a joke and you are never to make light of the Nazi salute and the hate it represents. I expect you to take this assignment seriously."

Jesse drops his gaze, but not his smirk. Spencer shrugs his shoulders and looks at Mason, the RHS varsity hockey team captain and my biggest rival for valedictorian. Jesse and Spencer are his guys, his teammates, and for one second I hold out hope that maybe Mason will be the leader he's supposed to be, to say something, do something—even a look of disapproval. But he's not looking at them. He's not looking at anyone. He's picking at a thread on his jersey.

Another teammate, Reginald Ashford, however, shoots daggers from across the room at Spencer and Jesse. The muscle in his jaw tics. He's pissed. *Good.* There's always been a bit of a rivalry between Mason and Reg, and now I can't help but think Reg should have been team captain instead of the coach's son.

And then there's Spencer. He shrugs his shoulders when he sees me glaring at him. Disgusted, I turn back in my seat. It hardly matters that Mr. Bartley reprimanded them. This assignment is a green light for these guys to act like Nazis. I don't know if I'm more disappointed with Mr. Bartley or with Spencer and Jesse. Definitely Mr. Bartley. I don't get why he thinks it's a good idea to promote fascism by having us do an immoral debate.

Mr. Bartley says, "Let me be clear. I am *not* asking you to be sympathetic to the Nazis. Quite the opposite. This is a serious examination of a historical event. Let's learn from this moment and remember to be respectful." He looks pointedly at Jesse and Spencer.

"By examining these perspectives, this assignment gives you the opportunity to discuss and present a topic that will force you out of your comfort zone. Why is this important? It's important because there will be plenty of times in your life when you'll be in a situation where people will express ideas existentially and philosophically opposed to your own. It happens every day on the internet. You'll face it on your college campuses." Mr. Bartley looks at me. "The point is to understand all sides and be prepared to debate. I promise, after you complete this work, you'll have a better grasp on how to create and present compelling arguments."

"But, Mr. Bartley—"

He goes all traffic cop on me and I close my mouth. "Let me finish, Logan."

Kerrianne snickers. I so want to raise my middle finger and tell her to go perch on a building with her fellow gargoyles. Mason asked me to prom last year. Not my fault she was second choice after I said no. Ever since, Kerrianne has been nasty to me. You'd think after eleven months as Kerrison, she'd be over it.

I focus on Mr. Bartley.

He says, "We only need to look to Sudan and Myanmar, to name just a few nations, to understand that genocide is not history. It's a part of our modern society. We can turn to China and the reports of concentration camps holding up to a million Uighur Muslims. What is the excuse for this inhumanity? Power and politics!

"So, for this assignment only, I want you to walk in the footsteps of Nazis to gain insight into the Final Solution and their justifications for genocide. I look forward to reading your personal perspectives for your side of the debate and your point of view on the Holocaust in your papers."

When Dad and I lived in Milwaukee, we had Jewish neighbors. Mr. and Mrs. Simon treated me like another grandchild—babysitting whenever Dad's sister, Aunt Ava, couldn't, reading books to me, and bringing me birthday presents. Every time I saw Mr. Simon in our apartment building, he'd greet me with "Howdo, howdo? How's the sweetest girl on our floor today?"

They had a granddaughter my age, and whenever Gayle came to visit, the Simons always invited me over. During Hanukkah, Gayle taught my cousin Blair and me how to play a game with a four-sided spinning top called a dreidel. I cried when the Simons moved to California to be closer to Gayle. To this day, I miss them. I can't imagine anyone ever wanting to hurt the Simons for any reason, let alone because they're Jewish.

To my knowledge, no one in our school is Jewish, and I don't think there are any Jews in our town. But what if there were?

The sound of drumming fingers draws me out of my head. Mason's looking at me. He stops tapping his notebook. His other hand rests on his thigh, clenched in a fist. For a split second I wonder if he, too, is appalled by this assignment. But no. His gaze shifts to the clock, then settles on Kerrianne. Of course. He's probably counting the seconds until he can get his hands on her.

She is doodling in her notebook. *Ugh*. Hearts and stars when Mr. Bartley's talking genocide.

Cade catches my attention, flashes his notebook. "U ok?"

I feel ill. But Cade's concern helps make it bearable. I answer him with a nod.

CHAPTER 4

MASON HAYES

Mason notices Logan fidgeting in her seat and scowling, especially after his hockey teammates, Jesse and Spencer, stand and give the Nazi salute. Their actions are a violation of their team's code of conduct—all members must refrain from disparaging or disrespecting others—and it bothers Mason. To his relief, Mr. Bartley calls them out on it, puts them in their place.

Hell, as captain, he's tried.

Recalling what transpired after last Friday night's hockey game, Mason fists his hand against his thigh. They'd won by a single goal, and Mason's dad, Coach Hayes, had come down hard on all of them, pointing out mistakes that could have cost them the game. "I expect every one of you to think about what you did wrong. We got the win, but it wasn't enough. You can and will destroy the next team at regionals."

After Mason's dad left the locker room, Jesse, Spencer, and a few other teammates spouted racial slurs about a Black player on their opposing team—a player with more skills, more moves than

Jesse and Spencer combined. Mason stepped in and told them that they were way out of line and were better than that. When they didn't stop, he told them to shut the hell up, that they were jealous of the dude, and to worry about their own play.

Jesse lifted his hand, sarcastically saluted Mason, and said, "Aye, aye, captain," getting laughs from some of the guys. Spencer repeated it, then knocked his shoulder into Mason's. Things escalated from there. They trashed Mason, taunted him, told him he was gay like Daniel Riggs.

Thinking about it now, Mason still gets pissed off. He doesn't care about what his teammates say about him—he can deal with it. But when they make racist comments or talk smack about Daniel for being gay, it irritates him. It's cruel. Why do they have to be that way?

Mason glances at Daniel. He's hunched over, looking at his phone under his desk. Whatever is on the screen has his full attention. Daniel keeps to himself, never bothers anyone.

Although they've gone to the same school since kindergarten, Mason has never been friends with him, mainly because Daniel has never been interested in hockey. Mason got his first pair of skates at two and started youth hockey at four. So did Spencer, Jesse, and Reg, and they've been friends ever since. For Mason, being on the ice is as necessary as breathing air. When his team voted him captain, Mason had earned it.

Still, Jesse, Spencer, and some of the other guys thrive on giving Mason hell. Last Friday night, they went too far. Mason lost it and threw Jesse into a locker. The fight ended when their teammates pulled them apart.

Clenching his teeth, Mason replays his dad's reaction. Coach Hayes called him into his office, ordered him to close the door. He pointed to the cold metal chair. The second Mason sat, his dad lit into him. "You're going to apologize to the team. I won't tolerate that behavior from anyone. Not the team captain, and certainly not my *son*."

Mason knew better than to talk back to his father, but he couldn't help it. "Then why am I the only one here, *Dad*? They're racists, and if someone recorded it—"

Coach Hayes cut Mason off. "You lead by example, and your behavior crossed a line."

"Nearly every day they cross that line. They violate the athletic code we all had to sign, and you do nothing," Mason seethed. "One word from you and they'd stop. *I* put them in their place and I'd do it again. I won't apologize."

"Then you're benched."

"Great." Mason stood.

"Sit down!" his father roared.

Before turning around, Mason wiped the grim smile from his face. He knew Coach Hayes wouldn't bench him. No way would he jeopardize winning regionals and their chance at the state championship.

His father clasped his hands. "Mason, they were letting off steam. Some of this stuff you have to let go or it distracts the team from doing what they need to do. Keep the boys focused on the game. That's it. Besides, this never would have happened if you had played better, if you hadn't missed that goal . . ." He went on and on, picking Mason apart until Mason wanted to shrink into his chair just like his mother did at home when the criticism was aimed at her. Mason stood and walked away under a barrage of threats and curses. He knew all too well how his father let off steam.

Punching Jesse had felt good, *too* good, and that realization gripped Mason with fear. *I will never become my father,* he vowed. *I will never become that violent, horrible man.*

Later that same night, when he and Kerrianne were in her bedroom, she asked him what was wrong. He told her about Jesse's and Spencer's slurs. "They're just jealous of you," she said. "They do it because they know it annoys you. You can't let them get to you. If I let everything get to me, I'd crawl into a hole and die. Come here. Kiss me and forget about them."

Looking over at Kerrianne now, Mason admits to himself that he doesn't love her. After Logan turned him down for prom last year, Kerrianne was an easy, uncomplicated yes. They were friends, and even though she'd hooked up with a few of his hockey buddies the first semester their freshman year, she hadn't been with anyone else. She stopped drinking, she stopped hooking up, but she didn't stop hanging out with the team. And because Mason didn't drink, either, they bonded over their alcohol-free red Solo cups, their love for hockey, and country music. Since prom, they've been a couple.

So what if he occasionally fantasizes that Kerrianne is Logan? He feels guilty about that, and because of it, Mason knows he should break up with Kerrianne, especially since she talks about a future with him. He wanted to tell her it was over weeks ago. He couldn't. Not with Kerrianne on the Snow Ball dance committee, planning tomorrow night for the past two months. What kind of jerk breaks up with his girlfriend after she's bought a midnight-blue strapless dress? (Yeah, she texted him a photo of the wrist corsage she said would complement it best.)

Mason realizes he needs to focus on Mr. Bartley. He's at the Smart Board. A picture of Hitler fills the screen. Sick. Mason lives with a brutal dictator in his father and coach. He certainly doesn't want to advocate for one at school.

Out of the corner of his eye, he notices Logan running her fingers through her short choppy hair, gripping it like she wants to tear it out. When Mr. Bartley says, "Examine if there is any legitimacy for the arguments on your side of the debate," Logan looks like she wants to strangle him.

Mason's right there with her. Half the assignments he gets—including this one—are a waste of time. But there's college, and he's always known that if hockey isn't his ticket out of Riviere, his grades have to be. He has both. Besides, he likes battling it out for valedictorian against Logan.

Again, he glances toward her, then refocuses on the evil dictator with the bad mustache. Mr. Bartley says, "History is one of our best teachers. Unfortunately, this assignment will show you that society hasn't learned much at all."

Who wouldn't agree with that?

CHAPTER 5

CADE

As Mr. Bartley drones on about Nazis, snippets of the old story Grandpa told me in his workshop flash into my mind. I try to piece them together like the jigsaw puzzles we made. I know my grandpa told me he grew up in Poland on a farm with fields of wheat and apple trees. There was a barn filled with cows and a horse, goats and sheep. A river ran through their property, and he used to follow its bank to get to the nearest town. If he said the name, I don't remember, but it was in Poland.

I glance out the window. Big flakes of snow fall diagonally, swirl in gusts of wind, adding to my deteriorating mood. It means more work for me and my family's inn. I mentally add "shovel and salt the parking lot and sidewalks" to my to-do list. With a wedding party checking in tomorrow morning, I expect a late night, and instead of listening to Mr. Bartley, I go through everything I'll need to do when I get home—extra touches to get ready, like arranging champagne, glasses, and Nana's homemade chocolates for the bride and groom.

Mr. Bartley steps in front of my desk and frowns at my blank notebook. "Disappointing," he murmurs, and continues down my aisle. I pick up my pen and glance at Logan to see if she heard. She's glaring at Hitler's image and has a full page of notes. On my right, Spencer flips his notebook up, showing me lines of text with red swastikas for bullet points. The word "Jew" has a red slash through it. He's also drawn gallows. Stick figures wearing Jewish stars hang from ropes. I shake my head in disgust and mumble "asshole" under my breath.

I try to focus on what Mr. Bartley's saying about the Final Solution, but Spencer's gallows spark another memory. Grandpa had talked about gallows. I close my eyes, picture sitting with him in his workshop surrounded by wood shavings, sanding toys for Santa.

Grandpa told me that the Nazis were rounding up the Jews. A truck had stopped at their farm, checked their papers. The SS officers took their food, then warned his family to stay away from town. But Grandpa was worried about his Jewish friend. He wanted to find him. Even though his parents forbade him to leave the house, Grandpa snuck out after they fell asleep. He saw hundreds, maybe a thousand Jews in the town square forced to stand silent as several Nazis selected six boys for no reason and hung them from gallows. The rest of the story floods back into my mind like a tidal wave. I know what happened to his friend. I know what happened to the people in the town.

The memory leaves me shaken as Mr. Bartley scans the room.

"A demonstration," he says. "I'd like those of you with blond hair and blue eyes to please stand up next to your desks."

Pretty much everyone twists in their seats, checking each other out. Jesse Elton and Allie Fitzpatrick stand immediately. Allie has the most beautiful eyes, a deep turquoise blue the color of a calm Lake Ontario on a sunny day. In the front row, last seat on the left, Heather Jameson hesitates, but with everyone's attention on her, she slides out of her chair and stands. She smooths back strands that escaped from her ponytail, then crosses her arms over her chest. Like Kerrianne, I've known Heather since kindergarten. She's tiny, barely five feet, and looks more like a sixth grader than a senior. Like Logan, she loves to read. Heather always has a novel open, even in class. I think books are her way of avoiding people—armor—especially after her older sister was arrested in Riviere's biggest drug bust. It happened during our freshman year. Heather's sister ended up in juvie. Unlike Logan, who has a singing voice that makes dogs howl, Heather has a voice that could make angels weep.

With all this attention on her, she looks like she could weep now.

Mr. Bartley does another quick scan of our class, then addresses Jesse, Heather, and Allie. "Again, this is strictly a demonstration. If you feel uncomfortable, you do not need to remain standing."

Speaking to all of us, he says, "Under Nazi Germany, blond-haired, blue-eyed characteristics were considered ideal for their Aryan race of superior human beings. Jesse, if you lived under Hitler's rule, by appearance alone, you would have been considered a potential candidate for the SS." He faces the rest of the class. "Other requirements included being at least five foot eleven, physically fit, and in excellent health. However, candidates needed to provide proof that their lineage had no Jewish blood going as far back as one hundred fifty years."

"I'm pure." Jesse grins and flexes his muscles, getting a sprinkle of laughter. Mr. Bartley ignores him. Logan's disgust mirrors my own.

A photo labeled "Heinrich Himmler, the commander of the SS, with his daughter" fills the Smart Board. She, of course, has blond hair, blue eyes.

"Heinrich Himmler started a program called *Lebensborn,* or 'Spring of Life,' in order to accelerate their Master Race. It is believed that over a twelve-year time period, up to twenty thousand children were born under this program. That doesn't include the two hundred thousand or so blue-eyed, blond-haired children who were reportedly removed from their parents in captured countries to be raised in German homes. Take a look at the screen. I need a volunteer to read out loud part of this October 4, 1943, speech that Himmler gave to SS officers." A few hands go up. Mr. Bartley calls on Kerrianne.

"One principle must be absolute for the SS man; we must be honest, decent, loyal, friendly to members of our blood and to no one else.

"What happens to the Russians, what happens to the Czechs, is a matter of utter indifference to me. Such good blood of our own kind as there may be among the nations we shall acquire for ourselves, if necessary, by taking away the children and bringing them up among us." Kerrianne's voice cracks and when she continues, it's in a much softer tone. "Whether the other races live in comfort or perish of hunger interests me only insofar as we need them as slaves for our culture; apart from that it doesn't interest me."

Mr. Bartley continues. "Under *Lebensborn,* Himmler highly encouraged his elite SS officers to procreate with racially pure single women deeply devout to Hitler's principles. The women included in this program had to believe in the ideals and pledge their fidelity to Nazism. They, too, had to prove that they had no Jewish blood."

Heather braces herself on her desk and stares down at her boots.

I look at Allie. Pink splotches dot her cheeks and neck. I've never given much thought to genetics, but I'm suddenly grateful for my reddish-brown hair and hazel eyes.

"Nice!" Jesse smirks.

"Knock it off," Mr. Bartley booms, glaring at Jesse. "Not nice at all, Mr. Elton. But I'm happy to give you extra credit if you do additional research on this subject. I'm certain you would not find Himmler to be a respectable role model. Please read the next quote from that same speech, Jesse."

With the smile wiped from his face, Jesse begins. "We shall now discuss it absolutely openly among ourselves, nevertheless we shall never speak of it in public. I mean the evacuation of the Jews, the extermination of the Jews.

"It's one of those things that's easy to say. 'The Jewish race is to be exterminated,' says every party member. 'That's clear, it's part of our program, elimination of the Jews, extermination, right, we'll do it.'

"And then they all come along, eighty million good Germans, and each one has his decent Jew. Of course the others are swine, but this one is a first-class Jew. Of all those who talk like this, not one has watched, not one has stood up to it.

"Most of you know what it means to see a hundred corpses lying together, five hundred, or a thousand. To have gone through this yet—apart from a few exceptions, examples of human weakness—to have remained decent fellows, this is what has made us hard. This is a glorious page in our history that has never been written and shall never be written." Jesse blinks at the screen.

Heather slides into her seat, and so does Allie, who looks a little green. Jesse remains standing.

"I don't get it," Heather says quietly. "We're not smarter or better than anyone else. Himmler's speech, the Nazis' treatment of human beings, is appalling."

Mr. Bartley leans against his desk. "Excellent observation, Miss Jameson. And through our enlightened perspective, I completely agree with you. I look forward to you sharing why you find it appalling in your paper. For the sake of the Wannsee Conference reenactment, however, our purpose is to understand the Nazi perspective on superiority and how it fueled their inhumanity."

Logan's hand shoots up. When Mr. Bartley calls on her, she says, "The problem is there are people who still believe in a superior race. They believe what the Nazis did was okay." Her eyes dart to Jesse. "It's wrong. What is there to debate?"

The end-of-the-day bell rings and the room erupts with the

sounds of chairs scraping against the linoleum, cell phones being turned on, backpacks being zipped.

Mr. Bartley raises his voice above the noise. "That's exactly why it's important for us to learn about this, Logan. When you're at Georgetown, you'll think back to this assignment and appreciate this challenge."

Logan opens her mouth, but then Spencer approaches Mr. Bartley and he gives Spencer his attention.

Jesse walks over to Heather. She ignores him as she sticks her latest novel into her backpack. He drapes his arm over her shoulder. "We should call ourselves the Aryans," he says, a small smile playing on his lips. "You, me, Allie, and the rest of the blue-eyed, blond-haired beauties of Riviere High School."

Heather shoves his arm off her, spins, and power walks out the door. Logan and I follow, but I lose sight of Heather as students pour out.

Logan grabs my hand, pulls me off to the side. "I'm not comfortable with this assignment," she says. "This is wrong for the very reason I said. Some people still believe in white supremacy. Look at the violence that happened in Charlottesville, Virginia, when the white supremacists held their rally. A woman was killed."

Goose bumps rise on my arms. I step closer to Logan and keep my voice low. "I can't do it. My grandpa saved a Jewish boy, and now Mr. Bartley wants me to argue in favor of murder? I can't—" I cut myself off.

"Wait, back up. Your grandpa did *what*?"

"I shouldn't have said anything."

"Why not?"

The revelation weighs heavily on my shoulders. I trust Logan. If I share Grandpa's story, she'll take it to her grave. But I gave him my word. I don't have the right to tell Logan, especially when Mom doesn't even know.

"I can't. I promised."

"Your grandpa?"

I nod. "Before he died. He told me true stories, Logan, horrible stories. Until recently, I'd forgotten about them. What the Nazis did to his Jewish neighbors—" I swallow.

Mr. Bartley enters the hallway clutching his computer bag handle as if he's carrying government secrets. Logan straightens, backs up a few steps until she touches the wall. He lifts his chin to acknowledge us. "Have a good evening, you two."

"You too," I mumble as he passes.

We track his steps, and only when he begins the descent to the main floor and disappears from view, does Logan speak. "I don't understand the purpose of this assignment. I heard Mr. Bartley's explanation, but it's not right. Role-playing or not, history or not, an assignment requiring us to defend Nazis is wrong. Why would he want any of us to act like that?"

Nazis. I can still hear the bitterness in my grandpa's shaky voice when he talked about Nazis. The way his mouth pinched, the pain that crinkled his brow when he told me the story of how he saved his Jewish friend. During one emotional moment, he stopped, struggled to maintain his composure as he gripped the sand block he was using.

This is not how I want to remember Grandpa. I try to conjure

26

images of him standing behind our reception desk and welcoming guests, dancing with Nana with her hands covered in flour, or taking an early-morning walk together on the inn's beach to watch the sun rise. But each one fades. I look at Logan. "We need to do something about this assignment."

Defiance blooms in her eyes. "Damn right. What do you think we should do?"

CHAPTER 6

LOGAN and BLAIR

Video chat:

> **BLAIR:** (on her smartphone, sitting in her beat-up car in the parking lot of JustaDollar, where she works as a cashier) Wow, Logan. I'm telling you, that assignment would never fly at Glenslope.
>
> **LOGAN:** (on her laptop, sitting at her rummage sale desk she painted sky blue) You sure? This is a history class—
>
> **BLAIR:** Hell *yes,* I'm sure. A billion percent. I don't know how many Jewish students we have, but there are enough that we get a day off for Rosh Hashanah and Yom Kippur. Half of our school is POC. If a teacher at our school gave out an assignment like that, I'm certain the majority of students and their parents would storm administration and get that racist antisemite fired.
>
> **LOGAN:** We don't want Mr. Bartley fired.

BLAIR: (surprised) Why not?

LOGAN: We only want the debate canceled. Mr. Bartley's not a white supremacist. Normally, he's a great teacher.

BLAIR: A good teacher would never give that assignment. I don't get why you're defending him. How well do you really know him?

LOGAN: (frustrated) I'm not defending him or the assignment, okay? Good people make mistakes. We want to give him the benefit of the doubt. He'll listen to us. I know he will.

BLAIR: If you say so. But maybe you can get other students to go with you? Anyone Jewish at your school? There's no way he could let this assignment stand if he has to justify their murders.

LOGAN: (shakes head) No, I don't think so. One sec. (gets last year's yearbook from her bookshelf, flips through it) If there are any Jewish students, I wouldn't know. Last year, we had six hundred students and the only POC were two junior exchange students from Japan. Our school is pretty much all white-bread. (turns to the pages with clubs) We don't have an LGBTQIAP+ club, either. Compared to Milwaukee and your school, there's hardly any diversity here. Other than Cade and me, I highly doubt any students or parents would storm our principal's office because of this assignment. (pauses) Any of your neighbors hanging Confederate flags from their porches?

BLAIR: You're kidding?

LOGAN: No. On my drive to school, I pass at least four homes with those flags, and the last time I was on Main Street, the resale shop had one in its display window.

BLAIR: I repeat, are you kidding me? Logan. That's— I don't even know what to say. Seriously, I can't imagine being surrounded by that kind of hate. At my school, some Muslim students wear hijabs and some Jewish students wear kippahs. No one blinks an eye. I walk down our hallways and every day I see interracial couples holding hands. Same with girls and girls and boys with boys and, at least with my friends, no one thinks twice about it. Glenslope has problems, but not *your* problems. I'm worried about you. If you and Cade are going to take on your teacher, you need a plan.

LOGAN: We have one. We're going to meet with Mr. Bartley before school and present him with a list of reasons why he needs to cancel this assignment.

BLAIR: (turns the key in her ignition, starting the engine to heat up her car) But, didn't you once tell me that Cade doesn't always come to school on time?

LOGAN: So?

BLAIR: Do you have a backup plan?

LOGAN: I don't need one. He promised, so he'll be there. And you know Cade never promises, because—

BLAIR: —the inn always comes first. That's why I asked if you have a backup plan. Even with his promise, things come up and I don't want you talking to your teacher alone. Why don't you have your dad go with you?

LOGAN: I haven't told him about the assignment, yet. Besides, would you want your mom marching into school to talk to your teacher?

BLAIR: Point taken. Still, with everything you just told me, favorite teacher or not, why would Mr. Bartley listen to just you?

LOGAN: (sighs) You're right. I'll figure it out.

BLAIR: Of course you will. Listen, I gotta go. Mom wants me to pick up Culver's.

LOGAN: One more thing I miss from Wisconsin.

BLAIR: (grins) Deep-fried cheese curds, butterburgers, buffalo chicken tenders, topped off with melt-in-your-mouth chocolate custard. Hmmm.

LOGAN: Great. Now I'm craving Culver's. So mean.

BLAIR: Yes. Yes I am. Text me the minute you're done talking with Mr. Buttley, 'kay?

LOGAN: Bartley.

BLAIR: (smiling) Love you.

LOGAN: Love you, too, cuz.

CHAPTER 7

CADE

"Cade, I need you to double-check the bathrooms. Make sure they're spotless," Mom says as I finish dusting the parlor. She leans over the reception desk, eyeing the room I just cleaned as if she could spot a speck of dust from this far away.

"I'll take care of it," I say, knowing ten hours ago—the last time I'd gone through each guest room—everything was perfect.

"Mikayla, don't nag the boy," Nana says, coming through our apartment door. She sends me a sympathetic smile, then turns to Mom. "Give him a few minutes to have a snack. From the second he got home, he's been working. There's plenty of time, and if necessary I can scrub a toilet." The lilt of her Polish accent thickens with irritation. "I'm not an invalid, you know."

"Ma, of course not. But no one in this family can make your pies, so let us worry about everything else."

"*Ach.* That's my point. You worry too much."

Nana's so right, but I keep my mouth shut.

The brewing argument is my cue to escape. As I reach our

apartment door, Nana steps in my way, takes my hands, and turns them over in hers. "Nice strong hands, perfect for kneading dough. Maybe it's time for me to pass on all my baking secrets to you, hmm?" She narrows her eyes at Mom. "Before I become too old to do anything around here."

I gently squeeze her hands. "You're not old, Nana. Besides, we need you. Our best reviews always mention your cooking."

"Humph." She lowers her voice, but it's still loud enough for Mom to hear. "I put aside some *rogaliki* in our secret place so your dad won't eat them all. Now give me a kiss and go enjoy your treat."

"Thanks, Nana."

I make my way into our small kitchen, take the pasta box out of the cupboard, and head into my room. Kicking my door shut, I set the box on my nightstand, which Grandpa and I made from repurposed wooden crates.

The smells of powdered sugar and strawberry jam fill the air, making my stomach growl and my mouth water in anticipation. I plunge my hand through the pasta box flaps and draw out a piece. The small crescent-shaped pastry melts in my mouth. I eat one after another until the box is empty. Setting it aside, I pick up *The Tenant of Wildfell Hall,* a novel I promised Logan I'd read. Eventually.

The book reminds me of the first time Logan came bouncing through the inn's double-arched doors, drenched from a downpour. Her dad, Professor March, scowled at the puddles as they walked to the reception desk to check in. I smiled, welcomed them. Logan smiled back, and said, "I'm so sorry we're dripping all over the floor. If you get me a rag, I'll clean it up." I refused, told her it wasn't a problem.

The next day, she wouldn't let me make her bed or give her fresh towels or vacuum the carpet. Before I could move to the next room, she asked if she could tag along. Her dad was at an interview for the Dean of Mathematics position at SUNY-Lakeside. While I did my chores, she asked me questions about the inn, Riviere, and my family. She was good company, and with her dad's extensive interviews, Logan had plenty of time to hang out with me as I cleaned rooms. By the third day, she was restocking the bathrooms and mini-refrigerators and emptying trash with me.

That afternoon, she came around the reception desk, leaned against our closed apartment door, and started talking again. This time, it was her love for all things history, particularly English history. She rattled off English authors she loved, like Jane Austen and the Brontë sisters. One part of me was impressed. None of the twelve- or thirteen-year-old girls in my grade were quite like her—bright, spunky, ballsy, interesting, worldly. Half the things she talked about were new to me. I liked listening to her, but the other part of me wondered when she would pause so I could tell her she didn't belong behind the counter.

When she did take a breath, her eyes grew wide, and I thought that she finally realized she'd crossed that invisible barrier between guests and innkeepers. But no. Not Logan.

She pivoted around, taking everything in. "You're so lucky to live here. It's beautiful."

"We don't exactly live here," I said. "We live in the old servant quarters." I pointed to our apartment door, then swept my arm in front of me. "The rest is for guests." I had hoped she'd get the hint. She didn't. Not even close. She hopped up and sat on the desk!

A minute later, she followed me into the parlor. As I straightened magazines, she brushed her fingertips over the leather chairs, the stone fireplace, the wood coffee table, and even the stained-glass lamp, as if taking it in by sight wasn't enough. She went to the bookshelves, ran a finger over the spines, scanning the titles. She removed Anne Brontë's *The Tenant of Wildfell Hall.*

"Have you read it?" She said it with so much hope, I was tempted to lie. I shook my head. "You must!" She tucked it under her arm. "Of all the Brontë sisters' novels, it's my favorite."

I learned a valuable lesson about Logan that day. My mumbled *yeah* was interpreted as "Yes, Logan, I'd love to read *The Tenant of Wildfell Hall.*" Twice a year since, thanks to her calendar app, she asks how far I've gotten.

Okay, I fully admit, a year ago I thought I'd get away with watching the BBC miniseries, but Logan wasn't having it. "Nice try, Crawford. But the series decimated Helen's strength of character and it failed to mirror the authenticity of Anne Brontë's revolutionary feminist novel." She waved the book at me. "Read it, then we can talk about it."

I pick up my pen, open my copy to the bookmarked page, and begin to read.

Two minutes later, my flip phone buzzes with a text. I hate

texting on this thing. It's a tedious pain in the ass, but it's all our budget could afford.

> **LOGAN:** Well? What did your mom say?
> **ME:** Haven't asked
> **LOGAN:** It's important.
> **ME:** I know. Gtg

It's been over a month since we had guests stay at the inn. Our upstate New York town during winter doesn't attract many vacationers. This wedding party is a big deal. I never should have promised Logan I'd meet her before school tomorrow to speak with Mr. Bartley. But what choice do we have? There's no way I'm going to present arguments in favor of murdering Jews. If we can't convince him to change the assignment, I'll take an F.

I glance at the photo sitting on my dresser in a frame Grandpa made. It's of the two of us outside the inn. His arm is over my shoulder and he's smiling at the camera. I'm looking up at him.

Nana always says that I'm the spitting image of Grandpa and that we're a lot alike. Would I have had the courage to hide a Jewish boy, help him escape, when I was twelve?

A sharp rap on my door makes me jump.

"Cade?"

"One sec, Mom." I brush the crumbs off my shirt and scramble to open the door.

She shifts a laundry basket in her arms, bracing it on her hip. "Would you fold these? I need to cancel and reorder items for the Stoke bridal shower next month. I swear Mrs. Stoke is going to drive me to drink with all her changes."

I take the laundry basket from her and set it on my bed.

"Thank you." She breathes a sigh of relief. "One more thing. I checked the weather report. Another foot of snow is expected overnight. It's supposed to stop by six a.m., so hopefully it won't delay the wedding guests." Her voice is tight with worry. "I'll need you to clear the parking lot and the sidewalks before school tomorrow."

Inwardly, I groan. "Can't Dad do it? I'm meeting Logan early. We have to talk with Mr. Bartley about an assignment."

She slumps against the doorjamb. "He strained his back at work today. If he gets laid up and isn't able to finish the dry-walling job, we're going to be in trouble. We're lucky he has the work. I'd do it myself, but I'll be up all night sewing the curtains for Mrs. Hager's living room."

Resigned, I give my standard answer. "I'll take care of it." I pick up my alarm clock and set it for 4:00 a.m.—two hours earlier than on days we have no guests. If I'm going to meet Logan at school on time, I'll need every minute. I look up. "Anything else?"

She hesitates, and just when she's about to say something, a loud *ting* from the reception desk bell gets our attention. Her face lights up with her guest smile. She dashes toward the lobby. A few beats later, I hear her guest voice. "Welcome! How can we help you?"

"Our flight's been canceled. Instead of drivin' in this mess, we were wonderin' if you had a couple rooms available with king-size beds?"

"We sure do. Where you folks from?"

Texas, I peg.

"Houston," the woman says.

I smirk. *Grandpa would be proud,* I think, and it squeezes my heart. Guessing where a person was from based on their accent was our thing. He was the master. Until I was eight, I was in awe of his accuracy. Then I realized our reservations listed guests' addresses. When I called him on it, he nailed every walk-in's place of origin for a month. He loved entertaining guests by doing impressions of actors, presidents, and cartoon characters. Compared to Nana, he barely had a Polish accent. Only when he spoke Polish or shared his childhood stories did Grandpa speak with a heavy lilt.

The conversation at our reception desk regains my attention. "We'll do whatever we can to make your stay comfortable," Mom says. "What time do you expect to check out?"

"We'll have to leave by six to make our flight."

In a blink, my morning plans evaporate. Not only does Mom promise we'll have a basket with Nana's cinnamon rolls ready for their early departure, but our guests choose our two best suites with fireplaces and Jacuzzis. By 6:05 a.m. I'll be turning the rooms over so they'll be ready for when the wedding party's out-of-town guests check in by ten.

I grab my phone and text Logan. "Sorry. Can't meet before school."

Without waiting for a response, I power off my phone, then head to the lobby to offer to carry the guests' luggage to their rooms and kindle fires in their fireplaces.

CHAPTER 8

LOGAN

What am I doing?

I've asked myself this question a hundred times since I crawled out of bed at four a.m., got dressed, and drove to the Lake Ontario Inn. My debate in favor and against barging in on Cade could fill dozens of notecards. Even as I trudge through knee-deep snow toward Cade's lit first-floor bedroom window, there's still no clear winner.

I've never shown up at his house this early, which is why I didn't knock on their apartment door. I stop in my tracks, glance over my shoulder, and follow my trail past their entrance and the inn's parking lot. There's still time to flee. Cade never needs to know I was here.

My indecision is resolved by a bitter wind that blasts me from behind and pushes me forward. *Okay, I'm going.* I pull off my gloves, take my phone from my coat pocket, and text Cade. "Open your blinds. I'm outside."

I watch for a shift of light, a sign of movement. Nothing.

No surprise since my calls have gone straight to voicemail and my texts from last night have gone unanswered. Stepping forward, I tap his windowpane. My heart drums against my ribs as I wait and wait and wait for Cade. I hunch down so close that my breath forms ice crystals on the glass. A bent slat gives me a narrow view into his closet-size bedroom. His open bottom dresser drawer touches his footboard. The sheets on his twin bed are twisted into a mess. Did he sleep as badly as I did? Half the night, I went back and forth between worrying about the assignment and rehearsing what we would say to Mr. Bartley.

Now I'm worried Cade won't return to his bedroom and I made this trip for nothing. Leave or stay? As I debate the merits of both sides, Cade strolls through his door wearing only a towel around his waist.

I'm frozen in place. Cade stops, scans his room. Did he hear me tapping on his window? He rubs his eyes, confirmation he didn't sleep well.

Cade's broad shoulders relax. He takes two strides to his dresser, pulls out boxers, jeans, and a sweatshirt. He really looks incredible in that towel. *Look away,* I tell the voyeur. And just as I turn, he drops the towel and I get a fine view of his firm butt. I scramble backward and tumble in the snow.

Several seconds later, Cade yanks up the blinds. Kneeling on his bed, he cups his hand over his eyes and presses his forehead to the windowpane. He's not wearing a shirt, but he has jeans on.

"Cade!"

"Logan?"

"It's me," I say, getting to my feet.

He unlatches the window and lifts the sill. "You scared the crap out of me. What are you doing here?"

"Making snow angels and freezing my butt off."

He laughs, and it warms me to my toes.

He motions toward my path. "I'll meet you at the back entrance."

As I retrace my footsteps, I try to convince myself that the shiver that ran down my spine had nothing to do with seeing Cade in a towel. Suddenly, I'm much too hot in my winter coat. Who am I fooling? Best friend falls for her best friend. I am such a cliché and I hate clichés. I so need to shut this down. Besides, I'm pretty sure Cade doesn't feel anything more for me than friendship. If he did, wouldn't he have made a move ages ago?

I take a deep breath and let it go, watch the steam float away. The moment I reach the apartment door, Cade opens it for me. He's fully dressed, including his rare Dimple Zone smile. I melt right there.

"So, you came for breakfast?"

He's teasing. I've never come over for any meal uninvited, even though I've been told I'm welcome anytime. I pull off my hat and gloves. "I got your text last night and I texted you back. If you'd had your phone on, you'd know why I'm here." To punctuate the point, I spread my arms wide, then hang my coat on a hook as I inhale heaven. "Oh man. Nana made cinnamon rolls?"

"Fresh out of the oven." His eyes shift to my hair, then back to my face. His lips twitch like he's trying not to laugh. I reach up, smooth down the strands as tiny sparks of electricity make

41

my palm tingle. He shoves his hands in his hoodie pockets and leans against the wall. "What did the text say?"

I sigh dramatically. "It said that I emailed Mr. Bartley and asked him to meet us before school to discuss the assignment." I reach into my coat pocket and once again check my email. Mr. Bartley still hasn't responded.

"It said that whatever chores you had to do this morning, I'd help. We're in this together, a team, and I'm not talking with Mr. Bartley about the assignment without you." I take a gulp of air. "What should I do first?"

He doesn't say anything, just stares at me.

"What?"

"You know it's four-thirty in the morning, right?"

"Really?" My voice is thick with snark. "I had no idea."

"How many cups of coffee have you had?" There's that grin again. He knows me so well.

I give him a playful shove, then march to the Crawford kitchen to get a cinnamon roll and my third mug of the morning.

CHAPTER 9

CADE

For the past ten minutes, I've leaned against the wall outside Mr. Bartley's locked classroom and watched Logan circle around like a caged lioness. We finished everything I had to do at the inn so I could be here with her. Every so often she checks her email, sighs heavily, then resumes wearing down the linoleum.

No response from Mr. Bartley. I mentally make a list: four possible reasons why Mr. Bartley isn't here: (1) his internet went down in last night's storm; (2) he didn't check his email; (3) he read it but wasn't able to come to school early (then why didn't he respond?); (4) he was abducted by an alien nation in need of a History of World Governments teacher (if only we were so lucky). Logan reverses directions. Her fingers tap against her hip like she's keeping time to music only she can hear. After a few more circles, she stops in front of a poster-size sign promoting tonight's Snow Ball dance. She waves me over.

"Your parents' first date was the Snow Ball dance, right?"

"A couple centuries ago."

A long awkward silence falls between us. Usually I don't have any trouble reading Logan, but the way she's staring at the couple slow dancing in the center of the winter wonderland, I can't help but wonder if she feels like she's missing out. Neither of us has ever gone to a school dance, and when she turned down Mason's invitation to prom last year, I was relieved. Despite all the rumors at school, however, Logan and I will never be more than best friends. From the day she moved to Riviere right before eighth grade, she was destined to leave. I, on the other hand, was born to stay.

Logan turns away from the poster and starts pacing again.

"Do you want to go?" I blurt out, instantly wanting to stuff the words down my throat.

She stops. Surprise or maybe horror fills her face. "To the Snow Ball dance?"

"Yes. No." I shake my head. "Of course I don't want to go. It was— Never mind. This morning, before we left, Dad gave me the night off." I shrug. "It was just something to do."

Logan frowns. "But you hate to dance."

"Yup. No moves." I shuffle like a robot. "Forget I mentioned it." If only the floor would open up and swallow me whole. Freshman year I told Logan that I didn't dance, but that's because she thought Kerrianne wanted me to ask her to homecoming. Not in a million years. There's only been one girl I've ever wanted to dance with, and that's Logan. "I should really be home anyway. With the wedding guests, there will be plenty of things for me to do around the inn."

"Oh no. Definitely not. You're taking the night off, with me,

44

and that's final. And since we want to have fun, that rules out dancing." She smiles.

"No dancing. Got it. We can see what's playing at the Riviere Marquee?"

"A movie is boring and ordinary."

"What else is there to do in Riviere?"

"Leave it to me." She sets her hands on my shoulders and gives me a shake. "I can't believe it. You have a Friday night off! Why didn't you tell me? We should throw a party, except I hate parties with people. What to do? Cade Crawford has the night off. How did this happen? Tell me everything. What did your dad say?"

I'm not going to tell Logan what he really said, which was that I should ask Logan to the dance. "We're just friends," I'd responded. To which he'd said, "Nothing wrong with going with a friend. Your mom and I were friends."

Inwardly, I groan. I look at Logan. She's waiting for an answer. "There's not much to tell. He said I've worked hard and deserve a night off from the inn."

She slaps a hand over the slow-dancing couple and places the other over her heart. "I, Logan March, solemnly promise to arrange an unforgettable, amazing night filled with adventure that doesn't involve dancing. It'll be a night we'll remember years from now, like the kind some old people get nostalgic about when they long for the wild times they had in high school." She beams at me.

I raise an eyebrow. "Have I mentioned that getting arrested is not my idea of fun?"

She winks. "Duly noted." Her gaze shifts to the wall clock, then toward the main stairwell leading to the first floor. With a huff, she asks, "Where is Mr. Bartley?"

"Maybe the snow delayed him. We could come back at lunch?"

"But there will be dozens of students in his room." She goes back to pacing.

I want to bang my head against a locker. Why did I bring up the dance? I can't believe Dad suggested it. Worst of all, I can't believe I'm actually disappointed. Doing something tonight is a bad idea. I'm tired of dwelling in the Friend Zone. I'm tired of pretending I don't want more with Logan. I gotta figure out a way to cancel. Inn emergency? But then Logan might show up to help. Fake fever? Maybe . . .

Logan regains my attention with her mumbling. ". . . why . . . absurd . . . Mr. Bartley . . . fake . . . challenge . . . test, assignment, debate." None of it makes much sense to me.

She comes to an abrupt halt. The happiness radiating off her is nuclear. Her backpack slips from her shoulder and *thunks* onto the floor. "I got it!" At first I think she means our plans for tonight, but then she says, "I have a theory about why Mr. Bartley gave us the assignment." She gives me a playful shove. "There isn't one. There can't be an assignment because there is no legitimate debate. He's waiting for someone to prove it. It's a test on making moral decisions and how they impact humanity."

"A test."

Some of her conviction slips when she registers my skepticism. She unzips her backpack and pulls out the assignment. "You know those elaborate riddles that go on and on, twisting you up with too many details that you don't see the simple solution?"

46

I nod. Logan loves riddles, like the one about the plane crash-ing halfway into Canada and halfway into the United States with 283 passengers on board. The twisty tale ends with *If there were 283 passengers and 5 crew and they all died, how many survivors died in Canada?*

The answer is zero. Survivors live.

Logan waves the paper. "That's what I believe Mr. Bartley did with the assignment. I bet he wanted to make it look legitimate, creating detailed instructions to get us to think. I bet he's waiting for someone to say it's morally wrong.

"Let's look at the facts." She ticks them off on her fingers. "One. We've never had an assignment even remotely like this, so that sets it apart. Two. He's a brilliant teacher, and he's fair. Three. Giving a fake assignment is totally something he'd do. His lessons are sometimes unconventional. Four. It's top-secret so that he can teach this lesson again next year."

Logan's theory sounds thought-out, but improbable, at least to me. If she's right, Mr. Bartley sure went through a lot of trou-ble to teach a moral lesson. Sterilizing an entire people is evil. Ghettos are evil. Genocide is evil. How hard is that to figure out? But I get it. I get Logan. She needs an answer.

I have my theories, too, and as I prepared for our guests last night, one question kept popping into my mind: *Could Mr. Bart-ley secretly be a member of a white supremacist group?* My conclu-sion: possible, but highly unlikely. But it seems more plausible than some elaborate moral test. And horrifying, so I haven't men-tioned it to Logan.

"Well? What do you think?"

"I hope you're right."

"Of course I'm right." But her voice is laced with doubt, and her glow has dimmed like a dying flashlight on the verge of blinking out. I feel responsible for it. I open my mouth, but I'm not able to give any reassuring words.

The bell rings. I take a step, but Logan grabs my hand. There's desperation in her eyes. Once again, I get it. I get her. Mr. Bartley didn't show up. He didn't respond to her email. Someone else would brush it off, let it go, and move on. But not Logan. It cuts.

"There's no way he believes the Final Solution is defensible."

"Well," I say, picking up her backpack and swinging it onto my shoulder, "I really do hope your theory is right because it'll be the easiest A I've ever earned."

CHAPTER 10

LOGAN

Two hours after school started, Mr. Bartley answered my email: "Sorry for the delay. Didn't get your note until now. Let's talk after class." I would have forwarded the message to Cade, but since he doesn't have a smartphone, he wouldn't have seen it until he got home and logged in to the computer. So before History of World Governments, I met him outside the boys' locker room. When I told him what Mr. Bartley said, he nodded. His expression was pensive, and he stayed quiet the entire time we walked to class.

Sitting at my desk, I glance over at him. He's hunched forward, legs stretched out, sketching in his notebook.

I blew it. I blew it, I blew it, I blew it. Why didn't I just say we'd go to the dance? Since Mr. Bartley isn't here yet, I pull out my phone and, for the hundredth time, I text Blair.

ME: He's barely said six words. What if I ruined everything?

BLAIR: You didn't. And six words from Cade is his normal. Stop obsessing.

ME: I'm not. You didn't see his face. He looked like I kicked his dog.

BLAIR: He has a dog?

ME: NO!

BLAIR: You'll fix it. Good luck talking to Mr. Barfly! Gtg my teacher's glaring

ME: Bartley!

I slip my phone into my backpack pocket and look at the clock. Mr. Bartley's now five minutes late. Most of the class has earbuds in, listening to music or watching YouTube videos on their phones. Heather is reading. Mason is talking to Kerrianne. Daniel has his head down and might be sleeping, and Cade is still sketching. I tear a corner of my notebook, roll the paper between my fingers, and shoot the ball at his paper. It bounces off his ear and onto the floor. He turns his head, his eyes full with questions. I plaster on a contrite smile, form a heart with my hands, flash it his way, and stick out my tongue, curling it into a U.

He shakes his head, and just when I think all is lost, his lips twitch.

Under his desk, he does something completely unexpected. He raises his pinkie, pointer finger, and thumb and bends his other two fingers down into his palm. Sign language for "I love you."

Wow.

Then he crosses his eyes and sticks out his tongue.

I laugh.

He smiles, and my world is back on its axis. This is us: best friends.

Mr. Bartley walks in, hits the lights. The windows let in the late-afternoon winter sun. "Sorry, people. Let's get started." He picks up his clicker, fast-forwards through the beginning of *Conspiracy,* and pauses on an image of Nazis arriving at a mansion.

Mr. Bartley says, "To prepare for your assignment, we're going to watch this reenactment of the Wannsee Conference, which was held at a villa in the Berlin suburb of Wannsee. Reinhard Heydrich, one of Hitler's most powerful and highest-ranking officers, arranged the top-secret conference.

"As you'll see, the discussion becomes intense. Take notes— pros and cons—on how the Nazis propose to deal with the Jewish problem. Remember, this is 1942 and you need to think not from your modern perspective, but from theirs."

I open my mouth to object, but the words don't come. Should I stand up and reveal my theory?

Mr. Bartley continues. "A little background. By 1942, Jews had already suffered under the Nuremberg Laws, which were enacted on September 15, 1935. The laws forbade Jews from marrying or having sexual relations with Germans. Previous intermarriages were declared invalid. The laws took away German citizenship from Jews. They were banned from teaching or attending German universities and schools, from practicing medicine and law, from government positions. No Germans could conduct business with Jews, forcing many Jewish businesses to close or to sell at prices way below value. At first only Jews were targeted, but eventually the laws included others—Roma, criminals, people with physical or cognitive disabilities, and anyone else the Nazis saw as undesirables. Who can tell me why the Nazis did this?"

Prepared to answer and to also share my theory, I raise my hand. Mr. Bartley calls on Reg.

"Non-Aryans were considered inferior. The Nuremberg Laws promoted racial purity and were meant to protect German citizens."

"Correct. And because of those laws, some German Jews chose to leave, but many who wanted to escape didn't have the financial means to do so. Even if they fled to another European country, their safety wasn't guaranteed. By 1942, Nazi-occupied Europe had already rounded up Jews, forcing them into ghettos and concentrations camps. Genocide was already underway, but at this point, it had barely addressed a Final Solution of the Jewish question. The Wannsee Conference brought various branches of the Nazi government together in order to expedite the destruction of the Jewish people.

"Our debate will reenact this historical event, but you may also incorporate other authentic perspectives appropriate to the position you were assigned. Research the Nuremberg Laws. Though the Nazis' actions were abhorrent—and I use this word purposefully—it's important for you to examine their arguments."

I had been so certain the assignment was a moral test, but after Mr. Bartley's speech and with *Conspiracy* ready to be viewed on the screen, my courage to speak up fades. I rack my brain, trying to find some logic in Mr. Bartley's reasoning. Something I learned in my sociology seminar triggers a thought.

Maybe this assignment is symbolic of how easy it is to persuade us to follow orders?

It's another theory based on the famous 1961 Yale University Milgram experiment on obedience to authority figures. Milgram's students willingly inflicted increasing levels of *pain* on others because their instructor ordered them to. They lost their moral compass. Mr. Bartley isn't asking us to inflict physical pain, but he is asking us to do something reprehensible—justify systemic hate, racism, and murder. Is he trying to be Milgram?

I look around and decide to keep quiet for now.

"Pay attention to the actors' body language as well as their words. Get into their mindset."

Cade's hand shoots up.

"Mr. Crawford, can your question wait?" Mr. Bartley asks. "I want to get through this today."

"Is the assignment a test?" Cade blurts out. "I'm wondering if what you're asking of us—with this debate—if it's a moral test?"

Mr. Bartley's startled expression says it all. "I appreciate your question and am happy to discuss this further after class."

I mouth *thank you* to Cade. He shrugs.

Mr. Bartley hits play.

Over and over again the actors give the Nazi salute and call out, "Heil Hitler." *Is Mr. Bartley expecting us to do that for the debate?*

Sitting around an oval table, fifteen Nazis introduce themselves. The actor playing Reinhard Heydrich says, "We have a storage problem in Germany for these Jews." He continues on, explaining that the Nazis "have created a Jew-free society and a Jew-free economy." He adds, "We have indeed eliminated the Jew from our national life. Now, more than that, the Jew himself must be physically eradicated from our living space."

My gaze flickers to Cade. He sits with his arms folded over his chest, watching the screen.

As the movie continues, Heydrich explains that the Nazis' aggressive emigration policy for the Jews failed. "Who would take more of them. Who would want them was the policy's ultimate limitation," he says. "Every border in Europe rejects them or charges outrageously to accept them."

I am shocked to learn countries expected compensation, but I'm not surprised when the Nazis comment that even America turned them away. A while ago, I listened to a podcast about the MS *St. Louis*, a ship filled with about nine hundred Jews fleeing Nazi Germany in 1939, a half-year after *Kristallnacht*, the Night of Broken Glass. In an organized vicious attack throughout Germany, Nazis descended on seven thousand Jewish businesses, shattering storefront windows, destroying equipment and merchandise, torching over a thousand synagogues to ash. The German Jews on the MS *St. Louis* sought sanctuary in Cuba. For most, it was a temporary solution until their US visa applications were approved. When the ship arrived in Havana, however, the Cuban government refused entry to 97 percent of the passengers, even though the refugees had proper documents issued by a Cuban official. The captain had no choice but to sail toward Miami, hoping the United States would welcome the remaining refugees. But the US Coast Guard stopped the ship at sea. Some sent pleas to President Roosevelt, but the president never responded and the US government held fast to the strict immigration laws. With no safe haven, the ship was forced to turn back. Several Western European countries took in the refugees, but for nearly a third of the Jewish passengers, it was a death sentence.

How many more times has the United States turned away innocent people, forcing them to return to certain death?

Bile rises in my throat.

I return my attention to the movie. The Nazis debate the absorption of two and a half million Jews in Poland, discussing them as if they were rabid rats that needed to be exterminated from the planet.

How do you do that? With bullets. With poison. Carbon monoxide. Zyklon B.

I think about Cade's grandparents. They came from Poland. His grandpa saved a Jewish boy, and though I don't know the story, as I look at Cade, I see that this part of the movie has him riveted to the screen.

CHAPTER 11

CADE

No wonder why my grandparents didn't want to talk about life in Poland during World War II. The Nazi leaders are callously discussing how to murder Jews like they're herding eleven million broken horses and sending them to the slaughterhouse. These are human beings they're talking about. I can't wrap my head around this. *Conspiracy* may be a movie, but Mr. Bartley said it's considered an accurate account of what transpired during the Wannsee Conference.

I'm overwhelmed by disgust as some of the Nazis in the movie describe Jews as:

- Inferior subhumans
- Sublimely clever
- Arrogant
- Self-obsessed
- Calculating
- Rejecters of Christ

These are outrageous reasons to justify genocide. *I'm* supposed to use these to support my position? No. Freaking. Way. My theory that he's a part of a white supremacist group is beginning to take hold.

This much I've learned, and I want to shout it to the world instead of in my head: THERE ARE NO DIFFERENT RACES OF HUMAN BEINGS! The idea of inferior or superior races is a human construct. It's made up. It's false. It's a lie! But people use this bull every day to justify hate.

My eyes meet Logan's. Her face is deathly pale. I lift my chin, motion toward the door, but Logan shakes her head, picks up her notebook, and shows it to me. She's been busy taking copious notes.

Why? When we're not doing this assignment?

I drop my pencil, cross my arms across my chest, and send her a look letting her know I'm not pleased, but I'll stay. For her. And then I get a glimpse of Spencer's notebook. Across an entire page he wrote in black ink: *Filthy Jewish pigs must die.* He's not quoting the movie. Those are his words.

I glance around, hoping Logan and I aren't the only ones appalled by the Nazis on the screen. Daniel is a strong contender. He's slumped low in his seat and has his hoodie up, shielding his eyes. Reg has AirPods in and doesn't seem to be paying any attention to the movie. Kerrianne is texting under her desk. Heather keeps twisting locks of her hair around a finger and is focused on the screen. Jesse seems to be taking notes or doodling. Mason taps his pencil against his thigh, and every so often his eyes flash toward Logan. Why does he keep looking at her?

Finally, the lights come on. "We'll stop here," Mr. Bartley says. "The rest of the movie focuses on the men leaving the conference. I hope you have a solid foundation for your side of the debate. Next week, you'll have time to partner up and go over your arguments. Happy Friday, and those of you going to the dance tonight, I'll see you there." The screen holds the image of two SS officers giving each other the Nazi salute.

The bell rings.

As people head to the door, I bolt over to Mr. Bartley. "This assignment is immoral." He looks up from his desk, surprised, probably since I never speak up in class. "I won't advocate for murdering innocent people."

Logan comes to my side with her notebook. "I'm not doing this assignment, either. No one should. It's offensive and reprehensible."

Mr. Bartley picks up a stuffed folder and puts it in his computer bag. "Offensive. Reprehensible. Immoral." He ticks off each word with a finger. "I agree. But this is not only *history*, it's our contemporary world. Along our own border with Mexico, our immigration officers separated children from their parents. They were locked up and deeply traumatized, not knowing what would happen next or if they would be reunited. Our own government violated basic human rights. For some, the result was death. We haven't learned from history. In one form or another, human beings continue to show their ugliness."

"That's exactly our point," Logan says. "Those kinds of actions take place when people care more about policies than human beings. That happened in Nazi Germany. You watched the movie. There was no debate. Heydrich made it clear that the goal was to exterminate every Jew. He brought those Nazi leaders together to ensure their compliance." She consults her notebook, then looks up. "Kritzinger was the only one who seemed to object to murder, as if starving Jews in ghettos or working them to death was a better option, but he was swayed. By giving us this assignment, you're asking us to legitimize the Nazis' reasons for genocide."

Mr. Bartley tilts his head side to side, as if we're a pain in his neck. He stands and walks over to his closet, and says, "Don't be naive."

"Seriously?" Logan's voice squeaks.

He looks at us with pity as he takes his coat off the hook. "Genocide takes place every single day. People justify their position of hate every. Single. Day. In their minds, they have legitimate reasons. My job as a history teacher is to expose you to different perspectives. Throughout your lives you'll face opinions opposite to your own. I am preparing you to respond. This is a safe environment to explore and debate these issues. You find genocide offensive? Good! This assignment should make you uncomfortable. Life is often uncomfortable."

Anger crashes down on me like an avalanche. I set my hand on Logan's wrist to let her know I have something to say. "Mr. Bartley, history or not, you're wrong! This assignment fuels intolerance and hate!"

"Lower your voice, Mr. Crawford." His nostrils flare as his chest rises, falls, rises, falls. He puts on his coat. When he looks at Logan, his voice is controlled and resolute. "Re-creating history does not in any way give it legitimacy. If anything, it illuminates the sins of the past. Think of it like you're putting on a play." He points to the Smart Board with the two SS officers saluting one another in the movie. "You're actors. They're actors. You can get into your roles without personally supporting your characters' beliefs. How is this assignment any different from those actors playing Nazis?"

I struggle to find a response. Logan's eyes are on the screen. Mr. Bartley goes to his computer and the screen goes blank.

"I have never been unreasonable with the work I've given my students. I understand you don't like it, and that's okay. We need to agree to disagree. That's life. I expect your best work."

Logan's lips part, but no sound comes out. I press my arm against hers. She's trembling. I look at Mr. Bartley. "Fine," I say. "I'll take an F." And I follow Logan out the door.

CHAPTER 12

LOGAN

Who was that teacher? What happened to Mr. Bartley?

As I walk out of his room, the shock of his response morphs into fury and indignation, propelling me like a lit fuse burning through gunpowder. It takes all of my willpower not to explode. I stalk through the hallway, dodge and weave around the Friday after-school rush like a taxi in New York City traffic.

Blair's words come back to me. Students and parents would storm administration if a teacher had given this assignment at Glenslope High School.

"Where are we going?" Cade asks when I pass our lockers. He leaps over a backpack and nearly collides with my AP Lit and Composition teacher, Mrs. Ingram. I point toward the office where Principal McNeil reigns over our school.

I wrench the door open and barely register Mason and Daniel standing at the counter. They turn and stare. Our school secretary, Miss Wather, holds out her jar, which is filled with Valentine's Day candies. Her smile drops the second she sees us.

"What's wrong?" she asks, setting down the jar. Her hand flutters to the vintage butterfly brooch she always wears.

If I open my mouth now, I'll explode and I need to save it for Principal McNeil. I round the counter and storm to his office. Cade shoots Miss Wather an apologetic smile, but thankfully, stays at my side because there's no way I could do this alone. I lift my hand to knock on Principal McNeil's door, but Cade beats me to it.

"Come in," Principal McNeil says.

Neat piles of papers and files sit on his large wooden desk along with a computer, several textbooks, and a papier-mâché can filled with pens and pencils. A shade covers the only window in the room, blocking out nearly all of the late-afternoon sun. On one wall, he has photos of every graduating class from the past twenty-some years.

I push aside one of the two chairs Principal McNeil has in front of his desk and stand before him. Cade rests his hands on the other seat back. I motion to him with my thumb and announce, "We have a problem."

Principal McNeil grabs two water bottles from his mini-fridge and hands us each one. His gaze bounces between Cade and me. He points to Cade. "Why don't you start."

Cade's first few sentences have more *uhhs* and *umms* than words, but then his nerves settle and he does an amazing job presenting our position. "We told Mr. Bartley we won't do the assignment," Cade says, winding down. "We'd like you to have him change it."

Principal McNeil picks up a pen. "Are you saying Mr. Bartley asked you to sympathize with the Nazis?"

Cade hesitates, then shakes his head. "Not exactly. He did say their actions were abhorrent."

I jump in. "But plenty of people in this world are antisemitic. This feeds right into it. Several students did the Nazi salute and said, 'Heil Hitler.'"

Principal McNeil's brow furrows and his wrinkles are so deep they look like someone carved them into his skin. "I completely agree with your position on genocide," he says. "Thank you both for bringing this to my attention. I will speak with Mr. Bartley. Since we are now into the weekend, let's discuss this further on Monday." He steeples his fingers. Neither Cade nor I move. "All right?"

I guess it has to be. Cade and I nod.

"Good. Will I see the two of you at the dance?"

Cade's eyes flicker to me. "Uh . . . we're not—"

"Going," I finish. "We have other plans."

Principal McNeil smiles. "Well then, enjoy your evening."

* * *

Principal McNeil Friday, 4:52 p.m.

To: LoganMarch@rivriereschools.org,

CadeCrawford@rivriereschools.org

Re: Assignment

Thank you for coming to speak with me regarding your concerns about your History of World Governments assignment. Mr. Bartley and I would like to meet with you on Monday before school at 7:00 a.m. to discuss this further. If you are unable to make it, please let me know immediately.

Principal McNeil

There's something about Principal McNeil's email that's unsettling. I shove aside the pile of clean laundry I dumped on my bed, flop down on my stomach, and reread it slowly, trying to decipher the message behind the message. He didn't say Mr. Bartley would retract the assignment. But he did say we would "discuss this further." My gut tells me Principal McNeil isn't siding with us. Just because they're in a position of authority shouldn't mean we have to accept this flawed assignment, right? Yeah, right.

Frustrated, I pick up my phone to text Cade, then chastise myself for forgetting how much he hates texting on his flip phone.

I dial his number.

When he finally answers, he sounds breathless.

"What are you doing?"

"I just hauled a couple bags of salt from the shed. Can't have ice on the sidewalks or parking lot. What's up?"

"So I'm guessing you haven't seen the email?"

"What email?"

I go to my desk and read Principal McNeil's message to Cade. "Something about it bothers me."

"It doesn't say much of anything."

"That's the problem."

"I'm not following you."

I get up and walk into the hall. "It's more of a gut feeling. I'd say we have a slim to no chance this is going to go our way. We need to be ready." I trail my fingers along the wall, stop, and straighten a photo collage I made Dad for Father's Day.

"What do you think we should do?" Cade asks.

"I'm not sure. I need to think about it."

I wander into the living room and look out the front window. Across the street, Kyle and Myles are building a snow fort. Police officer Shawn Sullivan and his wife, Wendy, recently told me that I'm their eight-year-old twins' favorite babysitter. Myles starts a snowball fight, and I'm tempted to go outside and join them.

Cade brings me back to reality. "I said I'd take an F. But what about you? You have a lot to lose."

An F will definitely impact my GPA. For sure, Mason would become valedictorian. I could live with it. But what about Georgetown? Could there be ramifications? Ironically, it was Mr. Bartley's glowing letter of recommendation that helped get me into their Early Action program. I swallow the lump that forms in my throat and say, "We're in this together. If there's no alternative, I'll also take an F."

Alternative. It sparks an idea. "I've got it! We need to present an alternative assignment, not just for the two of us, but for everyone. We need to walk into Principal McNeil's office Monday morning with a detailed outline, expressing our arguments and offering a better assignment that fulfills Mr. Bartley's requirements."

For a few beats, Cade doesn't say anything. I check my phone to make sure the call didn't drop. "Cade?"

"I was just thinking. I have to work tomorrow and Sunday. But I guess we could start on it tonight. What time?" I hear resignation and disappointment in his voice.

"No. We're going out. I promised you amazing and tonight is

65

going to be amazing." I bite down on my tongue. I have no idea what we're going to do.

"You made plans?"

"You'll just have to wait and see." I pick up a throw pillow from the couch and bang my head with it, then gaze out at the twins. They're back to building their fort. Its walls are nearly as tall as them, at least four feet.

"So, when are we doing this research?" Cade asks.

"I'll come over with my laptop early Saturday and Sunday morning or after work. Maybe both." *Whatever it takes. However long it takes.* I expect it will take every free minute we have this weekend, but Cade doesn't need to know that. "I'll need coffee, and if you save me two of Nana's cinnamon rolls, I'll type the whole thing."

"Only two?"

"I didn't want to be greedy."

"Well, in that case, I'll also save a couple pierogies for you."

I'm one of Pavlov's dogs. I even sit. "Potato and cheese?"

"Yup."

"I might have to kiss you." I slap a hand over my mouth, then grab the throw pillow and whap my head with it. Die, just die.

"Well then, I just might let you."

"You might—?"

He's laughing. Oh. The heat that spread from my head to my toes dissipates. My smile turns into a grin, and I'm laughing, too, until it floats away. "So," I say, drawing it out.

"So, what are we doing tonight?"

"Nice try, buddy." Silence pours out the phone. I pull it away from my ear, checking to make sure I didn't accidentally hang up. Nope. Cade lets out a long sigh.

Ugh. *Buddy.* Sometimes I don't know what to do with myself or Cade.

I flip around, kneel on the couch, and watch the twins smooth snow over their fort's walls. It gives me an idea. If I can pull it off, I can give Cade that adventure. I get up, open the front hall closet door, and grab my coat. "I'll pick you up at seven," I tell Cade. "Dress warm."

CHAPTER 13

CADE

"We're here," Logan finally announces, pulling into an empty snow-covered parking lot.

A sign reads: "Welcome to Fort Ontario. Closed for the season."

"Why exactly are we here?" I ask, since it's only open to the public May through October. We have Fort Ontario brochures at the inn, and I recommend it to guests who love historic sites. The only time I came here was on a bus for our end-of-the-year sixth-grade field trip. Until now, I haven't returned.

Logan laughs, pops open the trunk, and climbs out of the car with her backpack swung over her shoulder. She removes a thick, coiled rope and stuffs it into her backpack. Burrowing under a blanket, she pulls out two sets of snowshoes. She hands me one set.

"We drove forty minutes to go snowshoeing? Couldn't we have done that in Riviere?"

She hip-bumps me. "This will be fun. I promised amazing, and I will deliver."

"Right. And why do we need a rope?"

"If you don't stop asking questions, I'm pulling out the duct tape and I will enjoy using it on you." She pats her backpack.

"You know, kidnapping is a felony."

"So is breaking and entering." She grins wickedly.

I clamp my mouth shut. She can't be serious, right? I follow in her footsteps, leaving a trail through the pristine snow surrounding the massive stone walls of Fort Ontario. With each step, I seem to grow smaller like an ant at the base of a canyon. The stone walls are at least three times the height of an ordinary chain-link fence. We'll need more than rope. We'll need a cannon or two. Or a catapult. I could totally see Logan launching me over or making me climb a tree, except I don't see any trees close enough to the fort. We're the only ones here. I'm not sure what Logan's up to, but I don't exactly have a good feeling about it.

To slow her down, I scoop up snow, pack it into a tight ball, and aim for a low-hanging branch of a birch tree some twenty feet in front of us. I nail it, sending an explosion of snow over the ground.

"Bet you can't do that again," Logan says.

"What will you give me if I do?"

"That depends on what you want?"

You. It's the first thing that pops into my head, but since I'm not a fan of self-inflicted torture, I keep my mouth shut. I take my time answering. I could ask to find out where we're going, but that's hardly a reward. Nothing special comes to mind, at least not anything I have the guts to ask for. Then it comes to me, and if I hit the target, I'll win the biggest stuffed bear at this carnival. "Sometime, someday, I want to know what you're thinking. And when I ask, you need to tell me exactly what's going on in your head."

She digs her snowshoe into the fresh powder and kicks out like a punter. The spray blows back into her face, and she laughs. "Okay. If you lose, same goes."

"Done." I take off my glove and extend my hand. Skin to skin, we shake on it, and then I nail that spot not once, but twice.

Logan stares at me, wide-eyed, mouth gaping. "How did I not know you could do that? You should be playing baseball for the Riviere Rockets."

I shrug. "I played in elementary and middle school, but after Grandpa died, we couldn't afford to hire summer help. Practices and games were during our busiest times. So I quit."

"But didn't you love it?"

The tiny fissure scarring my heart aches. I can't afford to let it matter. I keep my voice steady and expression neutral because my answer isn't only about baseball, it's also about *her*. "I've wanted a lot of things I can't have. It's how it is, Logan. I try not to think about what I can't do or what I can't have because it doesn't change a thing." Sympathy fills her face, and that only makes things worse. I've shut down every fantasy I've had of having more than just friendship between us for so long, that this feels dangerously close to a confession. I can't have that. I form another snowball and aim for another branch, then say, "Giving up baseball wasn't a huge sacrifice. I love the inn more."

She nods. It's slow and contemplative. "Sometimes I envy you. How settled and sure you are of your future. I don't have that. Studying history at Georgetown is just something to do until I figure things out."

Logan's right. Since I was a little boy, I've imagined growing old like my grandparents and running the inn with my own family. More recently, that dream has included her.

I shut that thought down and say, "It'll work out, and whatever you choose will be amazing."

"You're sure about that?"

I smile. "A hundred percent."

She starts walking and once again I trail behind. She turns away from the fort, and I breathe a sigh of relief as we trudge along a plowed road. We pass three old brick-and-stone buildings that Logan tells me were built in 1905 and were originally used for army provisions and for baking bread. Given her love of all things history, it's no surprise she knows these details. When we approach a fourth, smaller building, Logan shuffles up a snow-covered ramp, then removes her snowshoes. She motions for me to do the same.

The building is dark. I try the door, but it's locked. "What is this place?" I whisper, not out of reverence, but because I'm 99 percent certain we shouldn't be here. What is Logan up to?

She whispers back, "Welcome to the Safe Haven Museum and Education Center."

A museum. From the outside, it doesn't look much bigger than a nice-size house. We have brochures for it, but it has never crossed my mind to visit. "And, again, why are we here?"

Logan pulls off a glove and riffles through her small backpack pocket. "You'll see."

"Logan." I lean against the door and stuff my gloved hands in my coat pockets as if we have all night. Maybe we do?

"Sometimes you're such a pain," she says.

"And sometimes you're a bigger pain." I grin at her.

"Fine." She makes a sweeping motion with her arm. "Many people don't know that Fort Ontario was the *only* place in the United States during World War Two to house European refugees."

I shrug. "Okay."

"This is the museum for that temporary refugee center."

Like in a game of Clue, I put it together. *World War II. The assignment. Research. Adventure.* This is so Logan. Of course she would figure out a way to incorporate the assignment into our night.

"I've never been to a museum when it's been closed before. We're not breaking in, are we?" I let out a short laugh, but I'm only half joking.

"Not exactly." She holds up a set of keys. "One of these should work."

"Wait, what do you mean by 'not exactly'?"

"I borrowed the keys."

"How? From who?"

She inserts one key after another and comes up short. "Sometimes the less you know the better."

She tries a fourth key. The lock gives way and she pushes the door open. I nearly have a heart attack when the alarm starts flashing and screeching, but Logan sprints to the lit panel and pushes a sequence of numbers into the keypad. The incessant noise stops along with the blinking lights. I stand statue-still like the cutout figures I notice along the sidewall.

Turning to me, she lifts her arms in victory. "Genius. I gotta say I'm a genius."

I pull off my gloves, stick them in my pockets, and unzip my jacket. I rub the ache in my chest. "More like a genius criminal. In case we get arrested, I'm testifying that you were the mastermind behind this . . . whatever this is."

"Come on, Clyde. If we go down, we go down together."

"I hate to say it, Bonnie, I could do without this kind of adventure, but props for unforgettable."

"Admit it, you love this. I know you do."

"I love something," I mumble, jerking back a little. To my relief, Logan's several feet away, far enough that it's a safe bet she didn't hear me. Her focus is on the first in a series of black-and-white photographs along a sidewall.

With my eyes adjusted to the dim light I take in more of the room. We're in a lobby with a small gift shop filled with books and T-shirts. There are easels with paintings, a piano, maps, and a large diorama in the center of the room. I take a few steps closer to the diorama. It shows the entire layout of Fort Ontario and all the buildings.

Logan motions me over. She holds her phone's flashlight up to the first photo. "Imagine we're those two." She points to an emaciated young man and woman standing in a large crowd. "By some twist of fate, after surviving unimaginable hell in different concentration camps, we escaped. We found each other in a forest. 'I'm Hannah,' I said. 'And I'm Josef,' you said. And from that moment on, we traveled together, hiding from Nazis and scrounging for food and shelter."

The back of my hand brushes Logan's, sending sparks to my fingertips. For a few seconds, she doesn't move away, and then I follow her to photo number two.

The caption says: "The USS *Henry Gibbins*: The Ship That Brought the Refugees from Naples, Italy, to America. July 21, 1944, to August 3, 1944."

The ship's deck is packed with refugees, some still wearing the striped clothes of prisoners from concentration camps.

Logan continues. "We made our way to Naples because we heard there would be a ship bringing refugees to America. Freedom! And again by some miracle, out of three thousand desperate people, we were two of the nearly one thousand lucky chosen to go on the journey."

Logan's arm presses into mine, our hands dangling at our sides. I inhale, slide my fingers between hers, and exhale.

Photos three to six: "Life on the USS *Henry Gibbins*."

With our hands clasped together, Logan continues. "Our first meal, there was so much food! I ate and ate until my stomach hurt. We watched, helpless, as crew dumped leftovers overboard. All those starving people we left behind."

She squeezes my hand.

Photo seven: "Nazi Bombers and U-Boats Scouting the Mediterranean Sea."

"One night, the angel of death came, hovered as fear spread among us. The ship's engines stopped dead. The air raid alarm went off, men ran to guns, and black smoke filled the air to shield us from the enemy. The drone of Nazi warplanes above left us paralyzed with fear. No one made a sound, not even the babies held tightly in their mothers' arms. We barely breathed until they disappeared. Disaster averted. The angel of death left empty-handed."

Photo eight: "Lady Liberty Welcomes Refugees."

"After so much misery and loss, can you imagine what it must have been like to see her?" Logan asks. The hairs on my arms stand on end.

We move from photo to photo. Logan continues to narrate a tale of hope and despair. Once in the United States, the refugees were tagged like luggage and transported on trains that, for some, triggered terrifying memories of German cattle cars. When they arrived at Fort Ontario, the barbed wire surrounding the fort sent another fissure of fear. "Many locals were kind and generous. They tossed clothes, toys, and candy over the fence to the refugees." One hollow-eyed boy holds a brand-new pair of sturdy shoes to replace the scraps on his feet.

"They were safe and well fed, received medical care, learned English, gave concerts and plays, learned trades, attended religious services. The children left the fort every day to go to local public schools. But the refugees also called the fort their golden cage, since they weren't free." Logan leans in to get a better look at one of the last photos, then lets out a breath. "Here we are again."

It's the two people from the first photo—now a somber bride and groom.

She releases my hand, walks over to her backpack, picks it up, and sets it on a table. I curl my fingers into my empty palm, wondering if I'll ever get to hold her hand again.

She uncaps a water bottle, drinks deeply. "So, what do you think? We can pull this off, right? I thought we could do an alternative assignment on US immigration policy during World War

Two and the Fort Ontario Emergency Refugee Shelter. All the research we need is right here."

I glance around. I'm standing in the middle of a museum. I could have been at the Snow Ball dance shuffling my feet and hating every minute of it, except for being with Logan. "What do I think? I think you're a genius."

She grins. "Thanks, Clyde." With a flourish, she produces two notebooks and pens from her backpack.

I can't help it. I laugh. "Why the rope?"

"To throw you off." She sets the notebooks and pens on a table. "I bet you thought we were going to break into the fort, right?"

"Maybe," I concede. "One more question. Someone gave you the keys and the code, right?"

Logan saunters over. "You gotta admit it was a rush."

"My heart's still pounding."

"Mine too." Our eyes lock. She's standing inches from me and I'm barely breathing. Adrenaline pumps into my blood like high-octane fuel. For nearly five years I've fought to keep this friendship a friendship. I want to reach out and pull her in. Her breath mingles with mine and I can almost taste the mocha truffles Nana made special for Logan. A lifetime passes in a blink of an eye. Holding her hand, being here with her, adds fuel to this slow-burning fire. But just as I lean in, Logan steps back and turns to the table. "All right, Clyde. We have work to do." And she hands me a notebook.

CHAPTER 14

LOGAN

Just like in a debate competition, I had told Cade we needed to dress up and make an impression on Principal McNeil and Mr. Bartley. We'll make an impression, all right. But this isn't *quite* what I had in mind. I take in Cade's church clothes—white oxford and pressed black chinos—then appraise my untucked fitted white dress shirt I borrowed from Dad and my black pants. I swear Cade and I didn't plan it this way. Even our black Converse high-tops match.

Cade shakes his head and laughs, shuts his locker, and joins me at mine as I arrange the papers we need for our meeting with Mr. Bartley and Principal McNeil.

Cade says, "You want me to change into my gym T-shirt?"

"And spoil our fun?" I say in jest.

"You're sure? I could run to the locker room. It'll take two minutes. Five max."

"I'm sure," I say, lying through my teeth. But it's better for us to be a bit early than late.

We're not a couple, but we look like one and I'm even more self-conscious. At the museum, I had wanted to kiss Cade. I had wanted him to kiss me. I think he was going to, but I panicked. We spent the rest of the night keeping a safe distance from one another, pretending like we'd never held hands and that everything was status quo between us.

The way we're dressed is definitely not status quo. We look like one of those couples. If I saw a couple dressed like this, I'd make a sarcastic comment about it to Cade, have a good laugh over their color-coordinated coupledom, and maybe make gagging noises once they were out of earshot. Why didn't I wear my red or purple Converse? At least that would have given me some individuality.

Cade leans in and whispers, "We've got this."

When we reach the office, Cade opens the door for me. Miss Wather takes us in from head to toe and smiles. "I'll let Principal McNeil and Mr. Bartley know you're here, dears. Have a seat." She motions to the chairs outside Principal McNeil's office. Cade takes the middle. I sit on his left and clutch our presentation in both hands.

Ten minutes pass, and every person who has come into the office has noticed our coordinated outfits. Or maybe they've wondered if we're in some kind of trouble. Or maybe I'm reading too much into their smirks, raised eyebrows, and curious glances? I don't think so.

Why is Principal McNeil making us wait?

The anticipation is killing me. Cade and I spent every spare minute of the weekend preparing and practicing our presentation. I can't think of anything more we could have done.

I rub my palms on my pants, then tuck my hands under my thighs. Cade bounces his knee. I slide my foot next to his, getting his attention. Our eyes meet. We have a conversation without saying a word. *We will not back down,* he says. I tap my fingertips against our presentation and nod. *We got this!*

Finally, Mr. Bartley opens the door, ushering us in.

"Have a seat," Principal McNeil says from the chair behind his desk. He sounds pleasant enough, but his body language is dismissive, putting me even more on edge. A copy of the assignment covers most of his tabletop calendar. The blood-red "TOP-SECRET" pops among the stark white papers and dreary textbooks.

Mr. Bartley takes a few long strides and stands next to Principal McNeil like a sentry guarding a king. I read their body language like a book. Spoiler alert. Cade and I, the protagonists, are about to be hit with a metaphorical freight train.

"So," Principal McNeil says, bracing his elbows on his desk and lacing his fingers together. "I've thoroughly reviewed this lesson and the assignment and support Mr. Bartley one hundred percent. Studying the Final Solution and understanding the Nazis' actions and motivations are important parts of fighting racism, antisemitism, and hate. And I see nothing wrong with historical reenactments. In fact, I believe they're great teaching tools. Mr. Bartley has made it very clear that this activity is to help you and your classmates understand the mindset of the Nazis and what led to the most destructive acts of antisemitism in modern history."

He taps his copy of the assignment. "Furthermore, Mr. Bartley told me that he expressed his strong opposition to the Final

Solution and agreed with you that all genocide is immoral. Is this statement correct?"

I glance at Cade. Reluctantly, we both nod.

Principal McNeil smiles. "Excellent. We have no doubt you'll do a fine job presenting the Nazi points of view, and then write outstanding papers expressing how you strongly oppose their actions."

Cade speaks up. "With all due respect, we won't do this assignment. It's not just that the Nazis' actions were immoral. This *assignment* is immoral. We want it canceled."

"Excuse me?" Mr. Bartley says.

As we rehearsed for this scenario, I hand copies of our presentation to Principal McNeil, Mr. Bartley, and Cade. Cade's hand shakes as he takes his copy from me.

"What is this?" Principal McNeil flips through our eight-page document.

"Cade and I spent many hours researching and putting together our arguments against this assignment and creating alternatives." I hold up my copy.

"We've been asked to debate the Final Solution of the Jewish Question, but the Wannsee Conference had ultimately one purpose: to discuss how to implement the systematic murder of the Jewish people. That was confirmed in *Conspiracy,* the movie our class watched this past Friday. If you look at our document, we have included additional source material from the United States Holocaust Memorial Museum's website supporting this fact."

I focus on Mr. Bartley. "Furthermore, you compared our assignment to acting. Actors choose their roles. Everyone knows it's pretend. But by having us re-create the Wannsee Conference, you are forcing us into the Nazis' shoes, rationalize their actions, and justify their thinking. This assignment allows for the possibility that the Nazis were right."

Waves of frustration or resentment or both roll off Mr. Bartley, but he hasn't uttered a word since I handed them our document.

I straighten my posture as if I'm standing in front of the judges for one of my debate competitions. "As you know, the purpose of a debate is to persuade others that your position is correct. In order to be persuasive, there must be legitimate arguments. How can anyone justify starving people to death in ghettos? How can anyone legitimize enslaving people for the sole purpose of profit, abusing them until they're dead? That's murder. How can you ask us to justify genocide? We can't debate two evils. Asking us to do so normalizes the Nazi perspective. It dehumanizes the Jewish people. We shouldn't be asked to support systematic annihilation of *any* people, whether it's a historical perspective or not." I pause for their reaction, but from their silence it's clear I haven't convinced them.

I forge on. "After World War Two, the results of the Nuremberg Trials prove our position. The defense attorneys argued that these Nazis were only following their superiors' orders. But the International Military Tribunal concluded that under international law, morality overrode any order from a government or from a superior. Again, what the Nazis did was pure evil. There is no debate. Morality overrides this assignment!"

In need of support, I reach for Cade's hand. He laces his fingers with mine and holds tight. For two long beats, silence suffocates the room. I look over at Cade. It's his turn to speak.

81

CHAPTER 15

CADE

Logan squeezes my hand. My mind is as blank as an erased whiteboard. I can't remember one thing we wrote out on the notecards. I glance out the window, then focus on Principal McNeil. I pick up Logan's thread as best as I can. "I'm not in Debate. This isn't— Look, we're not Jewish. To our knowledge, RHS doesn't even have any Jewish students. But let me ask you, if there were Jewish students in our school, would you have us look them in the eye and deliver reasons to kill them? I don't think so."

I shift my gaze to Mr. Bartley. Swallowing hard, I say, "If we look at the broader picture, this assignment promotes intolerance and hatred not only toward Jews, but toward people of color, our LGBTQIAP+ community, people with disabilities, to name just a few. It feeds into white supremacist beliefs that exist today. Would you ask us to argue in favor of slavery? Would you ask us to advocate for the actions of school shooters? What about the terrorists who murdered three thousand people on 9/11?" I shake my head. "No. I'm certain you wouldn't. So why would this assignment be okay?"

Mr. Bartley's mouth is flat, like the line of a heart monitor hooked up to a dead patient. Neither he nor Principal McNeil responds. I don't get it. Do they seriously have nothing to say?

Gently, I tap Logan's foot, needing her to take over. I can't dislodge the lump pushing against my windpipe, making it nearly impossible to speak or breathe. I release the second button below my shirt collar.

Logan's eyes flash with concern, but I bump her knee and she gets the message to continue. "Cade and I visited the Safe Haven Museum and Education Center. It held nearly a thousand Jewish and non-Jewish European refugees.

"In contrast, the US government brought over 425,000 German POWs. Many stayed in this area. Instead of saving some of the millions of innocent people, we welcomed, housed, and fed the enemy. As an alternative assignment, we propose a field trip and paper on the Fort Ontario Emergency Refugee Shelter and US immigration laws during World War Two."

Principal McNeil stares at us.

"We'd appreciate it if you'd review it now," Logan says.

They turn the pages, taking their time reading the material.

Mr. Bartley's expression gives nothing away, but I notice his tight grip on the papers and his white knuckles.

A few minutes later, Principal McNeil sets down his packet. Looking from Logan to me, he asks, "Anything else you would like to add?" He purses his lips like he's annoyed.

Have we made any impact? I'm not sure.

When Logan and I prepared for this scenario, we agreed I would deliver our ace in the hole only if needed. I reach for her hand, squeeze it, letting her know I'm going for it. If this doesn't convince them to change the assignment, nothing will.

Immediately, my throat tightens up. "Principal McNeil, I found out that in 2013 an Albany high school English teacher gave her students an assignment kind of like this one. They were told to imagine that their teacher was a member of the Nazi government. They had to write a persuasive paper to—and I quote—'argue that Jews are evil.'" I swallow hard. "It was all over the internet. The teacher was put on leave."

There's an awkward pause.

"We're not here to make trouble. All we're asking you to do is cancel the assignment. Let everyone do the alternative." I glance at Logan. "That's it. That's all we have to say."

Principal McNeil flattens his palms on his desk and stands. "This is very impressive work. It's clear you put a tremendous amount of effort into it." He picks up a pen and uncaps it. "I'd like to speak with Mr. Bartley for a few minutes."

He walks around his desk and ushers us out.

CHAPTER 16

PRINCIPAL ARTHUR MCNEIL

When Arthur McNeil hired Joe Bartley three years ago, he was pleased by the prestige Joe brought the school. The year before, Joe had finished his twentieth year teaching in Maryland. Because of his innovative ways of teaching history, Joe had received the Maryland Teacher of the Year Award. Arthur had milked it for all the positive publicity the school could get. He even felt that it helped motivate new families to move to Riviere. And now Cade and Logan dangle a veiled threat over their heads, comparing Joe's thought-provoking debate to the essay given by the teacher who was put on leave in Albany?

He motions for Joe to sit, then opens a desk drawer and removes a bottle of acetaminophen. From a small refrigerator, he grabs two water bottles, giving one to Joe. He pops three pills and washes them down.

Picking up the teens' document, he admires their hard work. For that alone, he'd give them an A. Begrudgingly, he has to admit they have some valid points, but they also overstepped student boundaries by telling them what should and shouldn't be taught.

Still. He doesn't want trouble. He wants this to go away.

On a frustrated sigh, he says, "Nothing's changed, Joe. I support you one hundred percent. You work to engage these students and help them think outside the box and, like you, I see nothing wrong with your students reenacting this historical event. Your students need to understand how ordinary people were brainwashed to dehumanize the Jewish people. It happens every day."

"Exactly."

"You go above and beyond to help these kids in every possible way, Joe. I see how you've made a huge difference in our students' lives. So I'm going to ask you to bend a bit here. I don't want this molehill to turn into a mountain. Let's take care of it now."

Joe scrubs his hands over his face. "What do you have in mind?"

"Let them do the alternative assignment on the refugee shelter and immigration laws. It's a brilliant idea, wouldn't you agree?"

Joe nods.

"Make the same offer to the rest of your students."

"What? Why? No one else has an issue with my assignment. You don't have an issue with this assignment. I've done what you asked. You said to challenge my students in a creative way. I've done that. But to offer an alternative to everyone?"

"You've exceeded my expectations. But by offering everyone the same opportunity, you're treating everyone equally. If no one else takes you up on the offer, then it'll send Logan and Cade a clear message. You understand?" Arthur leans forward.

Joe nods again.

"You win, they win, and this will be over."

"Okay."

"Call them back in."

CHAPTER 17

LOGAN

As Cade and I step out of Principal McNeil's office, we're greeted by the astonished faces of Mason, Kerrianne, and Spencer. Kerrianne's been an office assistant since we were freshman, so it's no surprise she's in Miss Wather's chair. Mason and Spencer flank her sides. What I'd love to know is what they're doing on the computer. Mason does his chin lift/nod. I nod back, relieved no one asks why we're here. Cade and I take our seats.

I pull my phone from my pocket. As I scroll through Instagram, Kerrianne whisper-shouts, "They're the Olsen twins. Hey, Spence, which one do you think is Mary-Kate and which one's Ashley?"

"Cade's definitely Ash. He's shorter."

"So mature," I mutter under my breath. (What I don't say is that Cade and I are the same height: five feet, ten inches.)

"I take it back," Spencer says. "Logan's the evil twin." Being quite the comedian, he begins reciting twin jokes from his cell phone. Kerrianne lets out an obnoxious snort.

With his voice low, Cade says, "Wow, maybe he should audition for *SNL*?"

"Or clown school," I whisper back. "But I think he'd scare small children." When Cade's smile reaches the Dimple Zone, I have a hard time appreciating it. I glance at Principal McNeil's closed door. Why is it taking so long? What is there to discuss? We nailed our presentation. It *has* to go our way.

Spencer walks over and stands in front of us. His eyes make a slow perusal over my body. The slime. Cade kicks out, forcing Spencer to jump back. Spencer curls his lips into a sneer and motions to McNeil's office. "Suspended or expelled? I vote expelled."

"Shut up, Spencer," Mason says. "Just back off." For some reason, Spencer listens. But when Spencer returns to Mason and Kerrianne, he whispers something to them. Kerrianne laughs, and Mason balls up his hand. The look that Mason gives Kerrianne, then Spencer, is murderous.

"Hey, I'm sorry." Kerrianne says it more to Mason than to us. "But—"

"But what?" he chides. She closes her mouth.

Principal McNeil's door opens. Cade and I stand. Mason says, "I'll see you later." I have no idea if he's talking to all of us or only to Kerrianne and Spencer because Mr. Bartley ushers us back in.

CHAPTER 18

CADE

Before Logan and I can take our seats, Principal McNeil pushes away from his desk and stands like he's on his way out. "We were impressed with your presentation," he says, "and appreciate your hard work and diligence."

I hear a "but" coming, and my heart sinks faster than a rock tossed into Lake Ontario.

"I'm happy to say we've reached a reasonable compromise. Everyone in class will have the option to either proceed with Mr. Bartley's debate and opinion paper or they can research the Fort Ontario Emergency Refugee Shelter and immigration laws alternative. Mr. Bartley will announce this in class today and have the requirements prepared in a handout."

He smiles at us. It's not friendly or kind, but oozes authority and confidence. "I'm certain you'll both do an outstanding job on the assignment." He motions for Mr. Bartley to open the door. "We've kept you long enough. Thank you for coming in to discuss your concerns."

Logan and I don't move. Her jaw drops.

Principal McNeil steps forward, gestures for us to leave. "I hope you'll have a great rest of the day."

Dismissed.

No more discussion.

Final decision.

Done.

Stunned, we silently shuffle out. My head throbs. This is so surreal. Compromise? No, that was to get us to shut up.

As we enter the hallway, Miss Wather approaches us. "How did it go?"

Dazed, Logan continues walking down the hall. I can't find my voice. Miss Wather studies my face. "Are you okay?"

"Yeah." But I'm not. I fold my copy of our presentation into fourths, shove it into my pocket, then hurry to catch Logan.

She fumbles with her lock combination, spinning the dial with a vengeance.

I lean against the locker next to hers.

"After everything we did, after everything we said, they still didn't get it. How could they not get it?" she asks, yanking on her locker handle. "*Argh!*" She gives the bottom end panel a kick.

I step in, enter her combo. The door pops open. "Maybe if I hadn't gone off script? I was so nervous—"

"You did great. I was proud of you. I'm proud of us."

I laugh bitterly. "Well, so is Principal McNeil. He *thanked* us for our diligence." I make air quotes around "diligence."

Logan pages through our presentation. "Yet, for some reason, it wasn't enough to cancel the debate."

I unzip my backpack, take out what I need for my morning classes, then stash my bag in Logan's locker. "What else can we do?" I ask.

Her eyes shimmer, and when she speaks, her voices cracks. "Would it seem ridiculous if I said I'm still hoping Mr. Bartley will see reason and change his mind? I'm hoping he'll read through our presentation again, recognize we're right, and have the guts to cancel the debate. *That* guy isn't the Mr. Bartley I know." She stops, swallows hard.

I look at our matching clothes. "Maybe it's his evil twin brother?" My attempt at humor falls as hard as a boulder tumbling down a cliff. She fights back tears. I take her hand and link our fingers together. I can't think of a thing to say to cheer her up.

"I'm going to make a pit stop before class." She motions to the girls' bathroom, slips her hand from mine.

"You gonna be all right?"

She nods.

I turn to go and nearly smash into Daniel. "Sorry."

"No. My fault." He shuts his locker, which is only a few feet from Logan's. Has he been eavesdropping?

"Hey, Daniel?"

His hair flops into his eyes. "Yeah?"

"What do you think of Mr. Bartley's debate?"

"It's pointless. The Final Solution is evil," he adds sheepishly.

"Yes! Exactly. Logan and I think Mr. Bartley should change the assignment."

"Oh. I started this weekend and finished my paper."

My heart sinks. "Okay. I understand."

"Do you need help? I did a ton of research."

"No. Thanks, though. I'll see you later."

As I head to English, I stop near the girls' bathroom, wondering if I should wait for Logan. I spot Heather and call her over, "Will you check to see if Logan's inside?"

Ten seconds later, Heather's back. "Nope. But I have class with her next period. You want me to give her a message?"

Logan must have exited while I was talking with Daniel. I shake my head. I consider mentioning to her what happened in Principal McNeil's office, but before I can decide, Kerrianne swoops in, loops her arm with Heather's, and starts telling her about the Snow Ball dance.

Walking away, I try picturing Mr. Bartley changing his mind. Based on what I saw in Principal McNeil's office, I highly doubt it. I try to imagine others choosing the alternative assignment. With the way so many of our classmates laughed when Jesse and Spencer gave the Nazi salute, I don't see that happening, either. But for all our sakes, especially Logan's, I hope I'm wrong.

CHAPTER 19

LOGAN

Together, Cade and I walk into History of World Governments and take our seats. Mr. Bartley's not here yet.

Nervous and hopeful, I look around for potential allies. Most of our classmates have their phones out, music playing through earbuds. Heather's long blond hair curtains her face and the book she's reading. Daniel's seat is empty. Mason, Kerrianne, Reg, Jesse, and Spencer huddle together around a tablet perched on Mason's desk. No surprise, they're watching a replay of the boys' last hockey game. All day, it's been playing on monitors in our lunchroom and hallways. Incentive, I guess, to get us into the team spirit and cheer on our Riviere Rockets for Saturday's regionals. Posters fill nearly every RHS wall. The team's lockers, inside and out, are decorated from top to bottom. To show support, we're encouraged to write positive messages. Some of the girls put lipstick on and leave their marks. I won't be doing that.

The bell rings and Mr. Bartley comes in and shuts the door. He sets a small stack of papers on his desk, then calls out, "Settle down. I have an announcement to make." He moves to the front of the room, clasps his hands, and waits for everyone's full attention. It doesn't take long.

"Regarding the Wannsee Conference and the Final Solution debate assignment. I believe you're mature enough to research the Nazis' perspective, reenact this historic event, and come to a logical conclusion."

Logical conclusion? *Logical?* Why is he assuming everyone is against Nazis? Every day the news is filled with hate crimes. I wonder if I should raise my hand and mention the mass shooting at that Pittsburgh synagogue or the massacre at the Black church in South Carolina? I remember reading that the guy was a white supremacist. Sometime before the shooting, he took a photo with a Confederate flag. There are people in this community, in this room, with Confederate flags. I look at Jesse. Who else?

Mr. Bartley continues. "If we don't fully understand the opposition by putting ourselves in their shoes, how can we truly formulate our own opinions?"

I blurt out, "What about putting ourselves in the shoes of the people *murdered*?"

He looks at me. "As we've discussed, that's a perfect argument to include in your papers." Turning away, he says, "I recognize some of you may be uncomfortable with the Nazis' point of view and find this assignment challenging. If you feel this way or have another valid reason why you don't want to do this assignment, you have the option to do an alternative. At the end of class, there will be time to speak with me about that option."

He steps forward. "I warn you now, the alternative assignment will not be easier. I have the same high standards and expect quality work—exactly what is expected of you for the Wannsee Conference debate. Are there any questions?"

Throughout his speech, there's a hint of admonishment, judgment, in his tone. I can't help but feel it's directed at Cade and me and anyone else who might question the assignment.

A murmur goes through the room and I hear someone say, "Why would anyone have a problem with the assignment?" I dig my fingers into my thighs. I can barely breathe. "Because they're whining babies," someone mumbles. If Mr. Bartley heard, he doesn't show it.

* * *

With ten minutes left of class, Mr. Bartley powers off the Smart Board. He says, "Anyone interested in the alternative assignment, this is your opportunity to speak with me. Otherwise, you may use this time for research or quietly discuss with other classmates your side of the Final Solution debate."

Reg gets up, and my heart takes a big leap of joy, then crashes when he wanders over to the pencil sharpener.

I dust myself off when Daniel slides out of his chair. He has papers in his hand. I can't help but watch as he approaches Mr. Bartley's desk. Mr. Bartley's surprise morphs to neutrality. He extends a piece of paper to Daniel. In bold letters it says, ALTERNATIVE ASSIGNMENT: Fort Ontario Emergency Refugee Shelter and WWII Immigration Laws. Daniel shakes his head. "I finished my research and paper over the weekend," he murmurs. "I can't attend the debate."

He can't? Maybe he has a doctor's appointment?

Daniel slides his assignment over to Mr. Bartley, leans forward, whispers something I can't hear. He stands in front of the desk and waits, shifting his weight from one foot to another. Mr. Bartley flips the paper over and nods.

"I need to go to the bathroom," Daniel adds.

Mr. Bartley hands Daniel a hall pass, and the moment Daniel steps away, Cade gets up and defiantly walks over to Mr. Bartley's desk. In a second, I'm at his side. The hairs on the back of my neck rise like soldiers preparing for battle.

"So, you want to do the alternative assignment?" His voice is so loud I'm surprised there isn't a bullhorn against his mouth.

"Most definitely," I say.

We take our copies. It's exactly what we presented, plus some specific instructions regarding the paper we're to write, similar to what was on the original assignment. Mr. Bartley says something, but I tune him out. I'm listening to some of the arguments my classmates discuss. It's like I'm in a room filled with white supremacists.

"Hitler said, 'It's either victory of the Aryan, or the annihilation of the Aryan and the victory of the Jew.' Are we going to let the Jew destroy us or are we going to destroy them?" Even though my back is to the class, I recognize Reg's voice.

Oh. My. God. My head is spinning.

Someone else says, "Survival of the fittest. The Nuremberg Laws made sure pure blood wouldn't mix with tainted blood . . ."

And another voice. "Jews aren't the only inferior race. According to this site, Africans, Slavs, Roma, Poles, people with physical or cognitive disabilities, Jehovah's Witnesses, homosexuals and prostitutes—"

I tune into Jesse, who says, "Genetically, Jews are predisposed to greediness, deception—"

Heather Jameson interrupts. "You seriously cannot believe there's a gene . . ."

"Logan?" Mr. Bartley draws my attention back to him. "Same due date. I look forward to reading your papers."

"Do you hear what people are saying?" I ask.

"Logan." Mr. Bartley's tone conveys frustration. He stands. "Question, class. Raise your hand if you personally support and believe in the arguments for your debate position." He pauses, scans the room. "Raise your hand if this reenactment has turned you into a Nazi." Again, he pauses. "Anyone?" Mr. Bartley refocuses on us. "So, there you have it. There's no need to worry. Let's put this behind us." It's not a question.

The bell rings and, as our classmates leave, Cade and I get some dirty looks. Jesse gives Mr. Bartley a military salute as he exits the room. Mason makes his way over to us, and whispers, "You didn't deserve that," then heads for the door. Kerrianne doesn't meet my gaze.

I want to say something to Mr. Bartley but have no idea how to stop this train wreck.

Cade and I walk out together. Never could I have imagined being singled out this way. Never could I have imagined Mason looking at me with so much pity. And never, ever could I have imagined that my favorite teacher would make an absurd and horrifying endorsement for intolerance and follow it up by humiliating us in front of the entire class.

CHAPTER 20

CADE

Logan and I don't say a word as we walk to our lockers, collect our things, and head to her car. Roadkill pretty much describes how I'm feeling right now. I buckle my seat belt, shift to face Logan, and ask the one question stuck in my head since we left Mr. Bartley's classroom. "Now what?"

"*Aaaaaahh!*" Logan's scream turns into a moan. "I don't know. We can't let him intimidate us. We're not wrong, are we?"

"Hell no." I unzip my coat, but it doesn't do much to relieve the pressure on my chest. I drop my head against the headrest. "We were sucker punched. And we can't let Mr. Bartley and Principal McNeil blur the line with their compromise. I haven't talked to my parents about it, but I can't help but think my grandpa—"

"What?"

"Over and over again, I've asked myself what he would do in our shoes. Is offering the alternative assignment enough or would he push forward and stop the debate? I hear his voice in my head, and I know there's only one answer."

"What does he say?"

She's not at all concerned about my sanity, and I love that. "'When it comes to life, you can be in the audience and watch. You can be one of the actors in the spotlight or you can be the person who shines the spotlight on the stage. The trick is knowing what role to play and when.' That's it."

"Are we the actors or the ones shining the spotlight?" Logan asks.

"Well, according to Grandpa, we need to be all three. If we're going to stop this debate, we have to be all three."

CHAPTER 21

LOGAN

"Dad?"

Silence.

"Dad?"

"Hmm?" He doesn't look up from his book, absently taking bites of the baked ziti I made for dinner. I sit kitty-corner from him at our kitchen table and drag my fork through the tomato sauce, making figure eights on my plate. I press harder, and the high-pitched *screee* finally gets Dad's attention.

His head snaps up. "Logan, that's really annoying."

"Sorry, but I need to talk with you."

"Oh." He shuts off his tablet, sets it aside. "Everything all right?"

I shake my head, and when his timid smile falls away, I clarify. "Everything's okay. I mean, I'm okay, but something's going on at school, and Cade and I aren't sure what to do about it."

At the mention of school, he relaxes a little, probably because anything academic is usually in his wheelhouse. But this? I doubt he's run across anything like this in the math department.

Dad sips his water, sets his glass on the table. "What's going on?"

I hand him copies of the assignment, the document we shared with Principal McNeil and Mr. Bartley, our notes from that meeting, and what's transpired in Mr. Bartley's class. He pages through while I explain in detail. When I finish, I ask, "Well, what do you think?"

He scrubs at his graying five-o'clock shadow. "You did the right thing. I'm proud of both of you."

Relief washes over me like I got an A on a difficult test. Until I notice his frown. "But?"

"But you're my daughter. I can't help but worry that taking this further will cause problems."

"What kind of problems?"

He folds his reading glasses and lets them dangle by the chain around his neck. "No authority likes to be challenged."

"We get that. But, Dad, this isn't right. I'm sure they think they're being reasonable by offering the alternative assignment to everyone, but it's not enough."

"Let me explain. You stand by your position, correct?" I nod. "Well, so do they. They believe they resolved the issue. You pursue this, there is a good chance they'll perceive you as being *un*reasonable and difficult. They're bound to be defensive." He makes two fists and holds them out six inches apart. "This is you and Cade." He lifts his left fist. "And this is Mr. Bartley and Principal McNeil." He knocks his knuckles together like two rams butting heads.

"Yeah, but—"

"Hear me out. You go further with this, it's possible—no, highly probable—they'll dig in. Based on what you've told me, they see themselves as experts. You, as students, can't possibly be right. At least that's my take on it. In my twenty-five years of experience, I've had my share of teachers who don't want to listen to students or be told how to teach."

"Are you telling us to forget about it?"

"Absolutely not."

"Speaking up for what we believe is important, right?"

"A lot of people have strong convictions, yet do nothing."

"But—"

"Are there other students in History of World Governments who feel the same way you and Cade do?"

"Maybe?"

"Why didn't they speak out? They've had the same opportunity to go to Mr. Bartley and express their objections. What stopped them?"

I hesitate, then say, "Well, if there are others, then they're definitely in the minority. We felt intimidated, so I'm guessing they're probably too afraid to go against Mr. Bartley." I think of Mason and what he said when the bell rang. *You didn't deserve that.* No, we didn't. It would have been nice if he'd said it to Mr. Bartley.

Dad rubs his eyes, and when he drops his hands, they're a sea of emotion. "Here's the question you really need to think about. If you let this go, could you live with it?"

My instinct is to say no. But I stay silent, glance out the window. Every second I've spent arguing with Mr. Bartley about this debate has been uncomfortable at best. Most of it's been hurtful and humiliating. Still . . .

I turn to Dad. "Do you remember our Jewish neighbors in Milwaukee, Mr. and Mrs. Simon, and their granddaughter Gayle?" He nods. "Since we got this assignment, I've thought about them a lot. If someone tried to hurt them, we would never stand by and do nothing. If we saw a *stranger* on the street being attacked, we wouldn't stand by and do nothing. How would I live with myself if I didn't pursue this? I couldn't."

My dinner sours in my stomach. "I've been trying to understand how Mr. Bartley could give this assignment, see this from his point of view. I can't. I've been trying to understand how anyone could advocate for murder. How was it that millions of people either actively participated or passively did nothing during the Holocaust? What happened to their humanity, morality? How could they watch and do nothing, turn their Jewish neighbors over to the Nazis, or worse—become Nazis and be part of murder or commit murder themselves?"

"I don't know and I have no answer, Logan."

"I've imagined what it would be like if we'd been dragged from our home at gunpoint, made to dig our own graves, and then forced to kneel at the edge. What if Mr. Bartley had us reenact *that*? There would be such an uproar!"

"Logan, don't."

"We have to, Dad. Because no one else in our class is saying this is wrong. These Nazis started out as regular people and became monsters. They had wives, husbands, sons, daughters, parents. They laughed and danced and celebrated birthdays. They went on picnics, walked dogs, and read bedtime stories to their kids. And yet they didn't hesitate to put a bullet into a neighbor's head and go on with daily life. They had to be so brainwashed or filled with hate to bear looking at themselves in the mirror.

"When Cade and I researched the alternative assignment, I stumbled upon a *60 Minutes* interview with Father Patrick Desbois. He's a French Catholic priest who's spent twenty-plus years trying to understand how the Holocaust could happen. His grandfather was a prisoner of war in a Nazi camp in the Ukraine and refused to talk about his experience. So Father Desbois traveled to that village, then throughout Eastern Europe and the former Soviet Union, to get answers. He and his team recorded over four thousand eyewitness accounts of Jews being rounded up from their homes and shot in massive graves. They've found many of those graves."

I choke back tears, but I have to continue.

"These witnesses saw everything, described it in detail. They were children and teenagers, so what could they do against Nazi soldiers? But the adults? They did nothing! Maybe they were afraid they would be murdered, too? Except Father Desbois heard firsthand accounts that after the Nazis left, the graves shifted and writhed for days and people did nothing to help the victims. Even worse, they searched the bodies and stripped them of watches, money—any treasure."

A tear trickles down my cheek. I pick up my napkin and wipe it away.

"Dad, Father Desbois's mission in life has been to let the world know how dark humanity can be. Most of my classmates are good people. Yet, they're doing nothing to protest this absurd assignment. If they had lived in Nazi Germany or in one of those countries Father Desbois went to, would they have stayed silent as their Jewish neighbors were murdered? Would they have turned them in and stolen their belongings?"

Dad clutches the edge of the table. "I honestly don't know."

"Cade and I have to do something about this. Maybe then others will, too."

"I'll support you and Cade in every way I possibly can." He pauses. "We've done all right, haven't we? You and I? Without a mother in your life, I've worried about you."

"We're good, Dad. Really."

He looks at me and asks, "You're sure?"

"I'm sure. I have you and Aunt Ava and Blair. I have Cade and his family."

I know my parents' story. They were never married, just lived together. When I was three, my birth mom packed up her things and walked out of our lives to be with another man. I don't remember her and I've never had a need to find her. Dad was awarded full custody. She simply gave up her parental rights. Maybe I should miss having a mom, but I don't. I never knew her. She's my egg donor, that's all. Whenever I've needed a mom, Aunt Ava has always been there for me. I'm so lucky my dad's sister loves me like she loves Blair. The hardest part of my life was when Dad moved us away from Aunt Ava and Blair to Riviere. I thought I'd fall apart.

I got lucky again with Cade's parents and his nana. I went from being a guest to being a part of their family. Although I love them all, Nana has a special spot in my heart. The week Dad and

I stayed at the inn, I asked Nana if I could bake with her. I woke super early and joined her in the kitchen. We laughed, listened to oldies playing on the radio. She gave me an apron and I helped her mix the dough for *chruściki,* a fried Polish pastry shaped like angel wings and dusted with powdered sugar. Nana called me her breath of fresh air. Later, Cade told me that Nana doesn't share her baking secrets, not even with him, and that in the six months since his grandpa had died, it was the first time he'd heard Nana laugh. When Dad and I checked out, Nana hugged me like she never wanted to let go.

In need of a hug now, I get up and walk over to Dad. I open my arms. He rises and hugs me close. For a few moments, even though I'm three months shy of eighteen, it feels so good to be his little girl.

I let go, pick up our plates, and bring them to the sink. Over the sound of running water, I ask, "So what do you think our next step should be?" I turn off the faucet and face him.

"I'm not sure." He comes to my side. "There is a rabbi on campus, and now that I think about it, a few years back he received some threatening messages. There were other incidents, but I don't remember the details. An organization called Humanity for Peace and Justice helped. Maybe HPJ could give you advice or you could talk with the rabbi?"

I unplug my phone from the charger. There's a missed text from Blair:

"OMG your day sounds like the worst! I DESPISE Mr. Bigotley! CALL ME! BTW, I got the part of Sandy in our school production of GREASE! Can't wait to tell you about it. Love you."

Grinning, I text her back, "Congrats! ☺ So proud of you!"

I go online and search for Humanity for Peace and Justice. Their site comes up immediately. The first line of their mission statement says: "To seek justice and provide support for those targeted because of religion, race, gender, or sexual orientation."

"Got it." The nearest office is in Albany. "I'm going to call Cade." When I reach the bottom step for our back stairway, I turn around. "Thanks, Dad." I smile. "Not just for this, but for being my dad."

CHAPTER 22

LOGAN, CADE,
LISSA CHEN, Education Director at
Humanity for Peace and Justice

Monday, 8:49 p.m. Three-way phone call:

LISSA CHEN: (in her home office, sitting at her desk with Cade and Logan's email on her laptop screen) Thank you for getting in touch with me. I must say I'm deeply impressed by your documentation and detailed account of what has transpired.

LOGAN: (sitting at her desk with her laptop ready to take notes) Thank you. Can you help us?

LISSA CHEN: I'll do my best. I have this job because these situations are so much more common than you'd think. Many of these incidents don't hit the media. We're able to deal directly with the school and take immediate corrective measures quickly and quietly.

CADE: (closes the door of the bridal suite he's cleaning) Do you think that could happen with this assignment?

LISSA CHEN: Absolutely. Recently, a teacher had her students read *Anne Frank: Diary of a Young Girl.* When they finished, she asked her students to pretend they were the Gestapo who captured the Franks, the Van Pels, and Fritz Pfeffer. The students were supposed to explain their actions. She thought it would help her students be sensitive and sympathetic to Holocaust victims. Not only was this misguided, but several of her seventh graders targeted a younger Jewish student, saying that she and her family deserved to die. We received a call from the parent and together we spoke to the teacher and principal. The principal was horrified. Instead of punishing those students, we brought in a Holocaust survivor's son and provided effective restorative justice activities. They're currently in the process of revamping the curriculum.

CADE: (sits on the stone hearth in the suite's bedroom) And it worked?

LISSA CHEN: We believe so. In your situation, I feel it's best for me to email your principal. I'll let him know you have the full support of HPJ and will explain our concerns and give suggestions on how to alter this assignment. There is nothing wrong with learning about the Wannsee Conference and the Final Solution, but it's completely inappropriate to ask students to represent Nazis and defend the indefensible. People can contort the truth to justify atrocities. Make excuses for the inexcusable. No matter what they conjure in their minds or how society turns away, they're still responsible. Just like your teacher is responsible for this assignment. Your class could have been researching how the Nazis' actions were based on pseudo-science, propaganda, lies, and antisemitism.

LOGAN: Exactly. What if Principal McNeil refuses to change the assignment? What will the next step be?

LISSA CHEN: We contact the press. (pauses) Neither of you mentioned your parents. Do you have their full support or support from other adults on this?

LOGAN: My dad was the one who suggested we contact you.

CADE: I haven't told my parents yet. Do you really think it's necessary?

LISSA CHEN: I highly recommend you let them know what's going on, Cade. We never know how these situations are going to turn out. It's important to have their support. If you'd like, I will be happy to speak or meet with them.

CADE: (blows out a breath) I'll talk with them tonight.

LISSA CHEN: Excellent. I'll email you all my contact info. As soon as I receive a response from your principal, I'll follow up with you. If you have any questions or if anything comes up, please don't hesitate to get in touch with me day or night.

CHAPTER 23

CADE

After Logan and I hang up with Lissa Chen, I head downstairs to talk with Mom and Dad about the assignment. But when I reach the last step, I hesitate.

Gripping the railing, I glance back toward the messy honeymoon suite, then shift my gaze to our closed apartment door. Twenty minutes ago, I left my parents at the kitchen table, going through receipts from the weekend and this month's bills.

The honeymoon suite wins.

I put on the latex gloves and give the four-poster king-size bed a hard shove, shifting it back against the wall. I strip the sheets and duvet and stuff them into my laundry bag. I drop the two empty bottles of champagne into the recycling bin and search for the two glass flutes I delivered Saturday night along with a bag of Nana's homemade chocolate fudge. Kneeling, I lift the dust ruffle and instead of finding glasses, I'm gifted with underwear. Why oh why is it never a twenty-dollar bill? I gather them up, pull off my gloves, and dump it all into the garbage.

Cleaning these rooms, it's impossible not to think about what happens in these beds, and it's moments like these that I think about Logan. But this time, instead of fantasy, my mind wanders to that moment when our eyes locked at the museum. We've both done a spectacular job pretending it never happened. But what *did* happen? I wanted to kiss her and I'm almost positive she wanted to kiss me. I'm not imagining it. Am I?

It doesn't matter. Anything other than friendship with Logan is doomed. But I wish there were some magical incantation that would stop me from wanting her.

I move into the bathroom and crack open the window. As I scrub away a bright yellow film from the Jacuzzi, I rehearse what I'm going to say to my parents about the assignment. By the time the bathroom sparkles for our next guests, I still don't feel ready, but I've put it off long enough.

Bills, checkbook, receipts, and parents are not at the kitchen table. Nana is in her room with the door closed. From the sound of it, she's watching another one of her cooking shows, most likely dozing off in her recliner. I check the office, then knock on my parents' bedroom door. They're nowhere in the apartment.

The lobby is empty. When I get to the first-floor hallway leading to guest rooms, there's a chill in the air. I call out, "Mom? Dad?" No response. I walk to the end, checking guest rooms. When I get to the last one, their muffled voices drift through a vent near the basement stairwell. I open the door and their voices grow louder.

"Can you fix it?" Mom asks.

"I'm doing what I can," Dad says. "I'd hoped the pilot light had gone out, but that's not the problem."

In the furnace room, Dad's kneeling in front of one of the

113

boilers' small doors. Mom's crouching next to him, holding a high-powered flashlight aimed at the coils inside.

"What's the matter?" I ask, startling Mom. The beam hits my eyes.

Dad scoots back and pushes up onto his feet. "The boiler for the first floor of the inn isn't working," he says, sounding stressed. "It's not the pilot or the fuse."

"Then what is it?" Mom asks.

Dad closes Grandpa's toolbox. "It's either the pump or circuit board. Neither one is a cheap fix."

"Are you sure?"

"Mikayla, I'm not an expert. So no, I'm not sure of anything," Dad snaps. His gaze shifts to my grandpa's closed workshop door, and I wonder if Dad's thinking what I'm thinking. If Grandpa were still alive, he'd know how to fix it. From the time my parents started dating their senior year, Grandpa took Dad under his wing and taught him about home repair—things my mom has little interest in. Dad grew up in foster care and knew nothing about his birth parents. He struggled, but my grandparents have always loved Dad like a son. His role models, he's always said.

"I'll call Zeke and ask him to take a look." Dad wipes grime on his jeans.

"We can't afford this now," Mom says.

Dad cups her face. "Please don't worry. I'll see if I can barter my labor for his. One way or another, we'll figure a way to work it out."

Not wanting to get dragged in, I hustle upstairs to our back door, take my coat off the hook. The second I step outside, I'm blasted with the bitter cold. I run to our woodshed. As Grandpa always said, it's important to be prepared. The nylon straps bundling the firewood cut into my palms. I hurry inside, and when I finally set the wood onto the fireplace hearth, red, painful lines dent my palms. I flex my fingers and it brings back a memory. Grandpa had a habit of holding up his callused hands and examining them as if they were a wonder to behold. *It's a miracle I didn't lose them,* I once heard him say as Nana rubbed her homemade cream into his palms. The pungent smells of ginger and chili pepper temporarily filled the air.

As I finish restocking the firewood in our parlor, my parents come down the hall, talking about credit cards and taking out a second mortgage. They turn the corner without noticing me. Dad straightens a landscape painting near the reception desk, and then they go into our apartment, shutting the door behind them.

I should tell them about the assignment. But tomorrow before school is soon enough. Or after. *Better after,* I think, since Nana will be baking at the crack of dawn, Dad will be leaving early for work, and Mom will be sewing or preparing for the monthly Riviere Junior Women's League meeting we host in the community room. I stock wood in that room's fireplace, too, bring out the lectern, and rearrange the tables.

With no chores left, I shut myself in my bedroom, plug my headphones into my dad's old Discman, and crank up some classic Queen, my dad's favorite band. I take out my calculus homework, but it's hard to focus. *Why should I say anything about the assignment?* Logan and I aren't in any trouble. It's being handled.

We don't need my parents' help. Most likely, they'll tell me to work it out. With HPJ involved, I'm certain Principal McNeil will cancel the debate.

I really hope so, because these reasons are not why I can't tell my parents. All my life I've been told not to make waves, to do whatever I can to resolve guests' issues as quickly as possible because our reputation means *everything*. Will my parents see protesting the assignment as making waves? I'd say there's better than a fifty-fifty chance. And now that Logan and I are doing the alternative assignment, would my parents want us to continue the fight to get the assignment canceled if Lissa Chen isn't successful? I'm not sure.

If I tell them everything and they ask me to let it go, what will I do? I can't imagine not standing with Logan when I know our position is right and Mr. Bartley is wrong. Unfortunately, I can only think of two options: Drop it or defy my parents. I don't like either one.

CHAPTER 24

LOGAN

From the moment we walk into History of World Governments, Mr. Bartley's gaze passes right through us, yet he acknowledges others with a nod, a smile, or a hello. Not once does he make eye contact during his discussion on the alliance made by Italy, Nazi Germany, and Japan to form the Axis powers. Not once does he call on me when I raise my hand to answer his questions about the propaganda posters used during World War II. Even when my hand is the only one to go up, instead of calling on me, Mr. Bartley answers the question himself as if it were rhetorical. But I know better, and so does everyone else in class. I've caught their pitying looks.

I'm 99 percent sure I know why Mr. Bartley is ignoring us. Principal McNeil must have received the email from Lissa Chen at HPJ and shared it with Mr. Bartley. Did I expect him to be upset? Yes. Did I expect him to act like a jerk? No.

We haven't done anything wrong, and that's what I have to remember. Still, I'm struggling. I don't want Mr. Bartley to hate us.

Wanting to disappear, I slump in my seat. For the next three questions, even though I know the answers, I keep my hands in my lap, wishing for a way to get out of class. I touch my forehead. Maybe I have a fever?

The weight of Cade's gaze forces me to glance over at him. He forms a tight fist, sending me a message to stay strong.

Another image fills the Smart Board. It's a Nazi poster showing a huge crowd of smiling people, saluting Hitler. "Yes! Leader, we will follow you!"

When Mr. Bartley asks for an analysis, Cade surprises me by raising his hand. It's the second time this entire year. The first was a few days ago when he brought up my misguided theory that the assignment was a moral test. What is Cade up to? But Mr. Bartley angles away from us so it's really easy for him to pretend he doesn't see Cade. I don't buy it for a second.

He calls on Heather Jameson.

"The image promotes absolute trust in Hitler," Heather says.

"How so?" Mr. Bartley asks.

"Look at how he's standing," she says. "He's on a stage way above the crowd with one fist propped on his hip and the other clenched at his side. He holds his head high. His back is to the people, commanding authority and strength. He's huge compared to the smiling, saluting people standing below." Heather adds, "It's psychological warfare on the masses."

Mr. Bartley nods, asks Heather to explain "psychological warfare." As she does, I accidentally on purpose elbow my notebook. It *thumps* onto the floor. Almost everyone turns their eyes my way, except for Mr. Bartley.

Yup. I'm invisible to him now.

Advancing the screen, he brings up an official US Army poster.

"This was produced and distributed by our government. Take a good look and think about its message."

The poster is a black-and-white drawing of Japanese soldiers leading American soldiers in chains, beating them. One prisoner is on his knees, the butt of the Japanese rifle poised to bash in the American's face. On top, the poster reads, "What are YOU going to do about it?" "YOU" is in red, reminding me of the red "TOP-SECRET" used on our assignment.

Mr. Bartley asks, "What impressions does it give you? How do you think it impacted Americans during World War Two?"

My hand shoots up. He looks right through me. Half the class is ready to answer. Dejected, I lower my arm, and that's when I hear "Yes, Logan?"

I'm so surprised Mr. Bartley chose me, my brain turns to mashed potatoes. Heat rises to my face. "Uh, I—uh—"

Mr. Bartley repeats the questions and, thankfully, waits for my answer. I launch into my analysis, stating that the poster was propaganda promoting hateful treatment toward Japanese Americans, turning public opinion against innocent people. "Even though it tells Americans to stay on the job until the enemy is wiped out, the line 'What are *you* going to do about it?' can be interpreted by the masses that they have blatant permission to take action into their own hands. This is extremely dangerous language, and—"

The bell rings.

Mr. Bartley holds up his hand, halting a few students who were ready to sprint out the door. "Logan's assessment is spot-on. By today's standards, it's *highly* offensive, but during World War Two this was the norm. Antisemitism was also prevalent and, in many crowds, socially acceptable." For a second, he holds my gaze. "You are dismissed. We'll continue this conversation tomorrow."

My head spins from Mr. Bartley's comment. I understand we need to examine propaganda and behavior based on the time period. But from my perspective, his point is another failed attempt to justify the assignment.

When Cade and I reach my locker, he says, "Glad that's over."

"Understatement of the day. Was Mr. Bartley ignoring us, or is my perception off?"

"Oh, he definitely was ignoring us."

"Good."

"Good?"

"Yeah. It beats the latter."

Heather walks by with Jesse at her side. He slings his arm onto her shoulder. "We're forming an Aryan club at school and I really think you should join us," he says.

She shoves him hard, and he stumbles. "Get off me. Don't you dare put your hands on me," she says. "If you do it again, I will report you to Principal McNeil." She storms off.

Jesse's laugh stops her. "I was just messing with you. It was a joke. Lighten up."

Heather spins around. There's venom in her sky-blue eyes. "I really used to like you. But now?" She lets out a sound of disgust. I move toward her, but the crowd sweeps her away.

A stunned Jesse stares after her and, for a few moments, his face reveals raw emotions I'd never expect to see from him—

confusion, regret, and sadness. They disappear when Reg and Spencer and a few other hockey players call Jesse over.

I look at Cade. "I think we could use some ice cream."

"It's twenty degrees and you're thinking of ice cream?"

"A hot fudge sundae, emphasis on hot fudge. And warm caramel. After all, this is a celebration. We need to go all out."

"And what exactly are we celebrating?"

"You raised your hand in class. *You* raised your hand."

He grins, full-blown Dimple Zone. "The sacrifices I make to help prove a point."

Damn. I really love this boy. If only he knew.

CHAPTER 25

CADE

"You get to decide, but since your principal refuses to cancel the assignment, I see no other choice but to take this to the press," Lissa Chen says through my phone's speaker. "The story could go nowhere or it could attract national and even international attention. We just never know."

Nervous, I glance around. This isn't a conversation I want everyone in our school parking lot to hear. I motion to Logan to unlock her car doors. As soon as we get inside, Logan asks Lissa, "What would we have to do?"

"My contact at the *Lake Towns Journal* will want to interview you. You can remain anonymous, but given what's transpired at school, people there will most likely speculate that you're the source."

"Logan and I need a minute to discuss it," I say.

"Take your time. I can wait."

I cover the phone's speaker with my hand. As Grandpa said, sometimes, even when you don't want to, you need to put yourself into the spotlight. "Logan, if Lissa thinks this is the only way, we have to do this. Trying to deny an anonymous tip, especially at school, doesn't feel right. We have to own this. What do you think?"

"Agreed."

I remove my hand and say, "We'll go on record and do the interview."

"Excellent. It's the right choice. I'll also give a statement, which will add weight to your position. Let me contact the reporter now and I'll call you right back. Hold tight, okay?"

Ten minutes later, my phone rings. But it's not Lissa. "Cade?"

"Yes?"

"This is Bethany Beshett. I'm the education reporter for the *Lake Towns Journal.* Lissa gave me your phone number. Is Logan still with you?"

"She is. I have you on speaker."

"Hi, Logan. I'm looking forward to meeting you both. I just happen to be in the area and was wondering if you could meet at the Riviere Public Library today. I could reserve one of the study rooms. Would four o'clock work?"

That's thirty minutes from now. Logan nods. "Sure," I say.

After I hang up, Logan says, "You drive. I want to research Bethany Beshett."

* * *

On the way to the library, Logan reads several articles written by Bethany Beshett, but I'm only half listening. My thoughts drift to the last moments I had with my grandpa before he died in my arms.

It was a Sunday a little over five years ago. Nana, Mom, and

Dad were at Mass. Grandpa and I were serving our guests coffee and tea and refilling the brunch buffet in the community room. Grandpa moved from table to table, telling jokes, impersonating actors, and making people laugh. Suddenly, his voice cut out. He swayed and collapsed to the floor. I remember running to him. I remember kneeling by him. I remember Grandpa clutching his chest. Someone called 911. Grandpa's breath wheezed in and out. He tried to talk. A tear rolled down his cheek. *Hold on! Hold on!* I begged, holding him tightly. His eyes were fixed off in the distance; then they went vacant like an abandoned motel. By the time paramedics arrived, Grandpa was gone. He died from a massive heart attack.

At the red light, I raise my eyes to the cloud-filled sky, wondering if Grandpa would want me to give this interview.

The story he told me replays in my mind. Months had passed since Grandpa witnessed the Nazis' liquidation of the town's Jews, and every day he worried about what became of them—most of all, his friend Yankel. One morning when Grandpa went to feed the animals in the barn, there was Yankel, filthy and not much more than skin and bone. He told Grandpa about what it had been like living in the ghetto—in a space fit for two people, there were fifteen, crumbs of bread or no food at all. Typhus swept through, killing his mother, his father, his neighbors. Piles of corpses filled the cemetery, which was too small to provide a proper burial for many of the dead. In the graveyard, Yankel, along with two other boys, used the mound of corpses as a shield to dig a hole under the fence. They escaped under the cover of darkness.

For several days, Grandpa hid Yankel in the barn, sneaking him morsels of food. On the fourth night, his mother discovered them. Grandpa begged her to help Yankel, and finally they came up with a plan. They bleached Yankel's brown hair so it looked blond, gave him a family Bible and a cross to wear around his neck. They told him what Catholic prayers and passages to memorize. They gave him bread, an apple, and a coat my grandpa had outgrown.

That night, as Yankel said his goodbye, Grandpa gave Yankel one more gift: his identification paper. *Your name is Waclaw now.*

At first, Yankel refused to take Grandpa's identity. But my grandpa insisted, pushing him to leave. *There can't be two of us here. You have to go far away and never come back.* Yankel promised that if he got caught, he would say he stole the paper. He promised never to betray my grandpa or his family. He kept that promise. My grandpa never saw Yankel again.

CHAPTER 26

LOGAN

Cade parks my car in the Riviere Public Library lot. Twenty minutes to spare. I unbuckle my seat belt and shift to talk with him. "You weren't listening, were you?" It's not an accusation, but a statement of fact.

"I was half listening. Sorry. Want to share the highlights?"

I unlock my phone and bring up Bethany Beshett's Facebook profile, which is mostly private except for a few photos and articles she's had published. "She has a degree in journalism. Last May she started interning at the *Lake Towns Journal*. All her articles focus on education. She's a good writer," I say. "And it seems like she sticks to the facts."

"Okay," he says.

I scrutinize his face. "You're nervous?"

"A little. I've been thinking about my grandparents. I wish I knew what happened to their families in Poland during World War Two."

"Did you ask your mom?"

"A long time ago. She said Nana and Grandpa never wanted to talk about it, so she stopped asking. She knows less than I do." He rubs his hands over his thighs.

"Cade. Is that one of the reasons why you want to do this interview?"

"It won't help me get answers, so no." He fixes his gaze on me. "I want to do this because it's the right thing to do."

CHAPTER 27

CADE

"Cade!"

What does Mom want now? I glance away from our moon-lit beach toward the limestone cliff and the stairs that lead to the inn. Waves slap against the ice, spraying cold water onto my jeans and jacket. I wanted five minutes to figure out how to tell my parents about the interview with Bethany Beshett, but even here I can't have peace.

I check the time on my phone. Twelve more hours until the article goes live on the *Lake Towns Journal* website.

I hear Logan's voice in my head. "That was amazing. *We* were amazing!" After the interview, I stood on the sidewalk in front of the library, looking up at Logan dancing on the top step, pumping her fists in victory. My grin hid the dread churning in my stomach, and even her hug goodbye when she dropped me off wasn't enough to vanquish it.

"CADE!"

"I'm coming," I call.

"I need you inside RIGHT NOW!!!"

With one more glance at the lake, I turn, sweep my flashlight several feet ahead, and sprint up the path I cleared for the wedding party. I mentally run through the chores I finished, trying to figure out what I might have messed up. I can't think of anything. Mom opens the door wide, letting me pass.

"What's all the racket?" Nana asks as I follow Mom into the kitchen.

"It's nothing, Ma," she says.

"It's not nothing if you're hollering like that. You could wake the dead."

"Everything's fine. I just need some computer help, that's all."

At the mention of computers, Nana frowns and heads toward her bedroom, but not before she murmurs her disapproval. I smile at her, letting her know I've got this. The last time Mom freaked out this much was when we received a negative review on TripAdvisor. It was from a woman who complained about a strand of hair she found on the suite's bathroom floor. *I* was the one who carried the cleaning supplies and a basket of complimentary goodies to the room at 10:45 p.m. *I* was the one who scrubbed the bathroom as the woman stood over me with her arms folded across her chest in her sheer nightgown. And that strand of long black hair on the floor? It was hers. But did I point that out? Of course not.

Mom closes the apartment door behind us. She sits at the reception desk and moves the mouse. The computer screen comes to life. Her voice comes out in a soft hiss. "How do you explain this, Cade?"

I shake my head as if that's not me, as if it's a big mistake. It is a mistake. I was supposed to have time!

LAKE TOWNS JOURNAL
Riviere High School Students Oppose Holocaust Debate Assignment
Posted at 7:45 p.m.

The article fills the screen. There's the picture of Logan and me at the library, sitting side by side, looking into the camera. The inn's logo is clearly visible on my shirt.

Mom's voice is filled with controlled fury. "I got a phone call from Mrs. Stoke. Imagine my surprise when she told me about this article."

There are already 82 shares and 41 comments!

I can't breathe.

Through clenched teeth Mom says, "She informed me that Joe and Mary Bartley are her neighbors and best friends and that she won't do business with someone who is out to destroy a great teacher's reputation."

Mom points to one of the last lines in the article.

"Cade and Logan do not want Bartley to lose his job. They believe the teacher and administration should apologize and acknowledge that the assignment was inappropriate and offensive."

"Mrs. Stoke said *you're* the ones who owe Mr. Bartley an apology. She canceled her daughter's bridal shower and said that the wedding guests will no longer stay at the inn. How could you have done this to us, Cade?" She sets her hand over her heart. Her lips tremble.

"I—"

"How is it that you didn't tell us about this assignment and your disagreement with Mr. Bartley and Principal McNeil? How is it that you spoke to Humanity for Peace and Justice *and* a reporter without talking to us first?"

Mom glances at our closed apartment door. "We're not going to have this discussion here. I don't want Nana to know about this." Her anger hits me like a battering ram. The printer spits out the article and the first three pages of comments. Mom shuts down the computer, and I follow her upstairs.

CHAPTER 28

Riviere High School Students Oppose Holocaust Debate Assignment

Comments: 41

Retired social studies teacher

I'm shocked that a teacher would give this assignment. These teens are heroes! Thank you for having the courage to speak out against hate.

6 Like   Reply

I Salute NZS

There's a furnace waiting for Cade and Logan. I'll light it myself!

0 Like   Reply

TripleK4Evr

@I Salute NZS

Or we can just sterilize them.

0 Like   Reply

Riviere resident

@I Salute NZS @TripleK4Evr

Serious question: What's happened in your life that you're filled with so much anger and hate?

14 Like   Reply

Bulldog

FIRE the teacher and principal!

3 Like   Reply

RHS senior

Cade and Logan never should have gone public with this. Mr.
Bartley is the best teacher and we're lucky to have him. Just
because you didn't get your way doesn't mean you can smear
his reputation like this. Did you think about his feelings? Do you
even care if he gets hurt? Also, just because I have to pretend
I'm a Nazi and explain my reasons why the Jewish people should
be exterminated, doesn't mean I personally believe it's okay
to kill anyone. God said, "Thou shalt not kill." I listen to God, not
Nazis.

1 Like   Reply

Bulldog
@RHS senior

If you'd lived in Nazi Germany, what would you have done?

3 Like   Reply

JUSSUK

Jews control every segment of society while the rest of us suffer
because we can't get jobs.

0 Like   Reply

HistoryBuff
@JUSSUK

Jews are 0.2 percent of the world's population. They've been
persecuted for thousands of years-FYI research pogroms,
Crusades, and the Spanish Inquisition. If you're suffering, it's
because you're lazy. Get up and get a job.

1 Like   Reply

BNice

The problem with this world is people blame and bully others as a means to gain power. They always find scapegoats. It's easy to blame Jews because it's been done for thousands of years. Hitler used them as political scapegoats, subscribing to faux science to declare that Jews are an inferior race. It was nonsense. He brainwashed German society with his charisma and lies. "Get rid of them and life will be great." Personally, I'm sick of people being cruel to one another. Enough of the racism, homophobia, misogyny, Islamophobia, and antisemitism.

1 Like   Reply

EinsteinFan

Google "Jewish contributions to society" and I bet people will be surprised by how much Jews have done to help this world for the better. If you hate them so much, don't be a hypocrite. Stop using your computer and cell phones immediately, because Jews developed a lot of that technology.

4 Like   Reply

TripleK4Evr
@HistoryBuff @EinsteinFan

We got a bullet for you, too. You can each hold hands with these teens.

0 Like   Reply

LegalEagle
@TripleK4Evr

Reporting you to site administration. Bye-bye.

10 Like   Reply

CHAPTER 29

LOGAN

Posted on my Twitter feed:

JUSSUK @jussuk
@loganmarchNY watch out. Hitler missed you, but I won't. I got
bullets, one for you and one for Cade.

And there is more:

A tweet saying we should put guns to our heads and kill ourselves.

A tweet saying we should never have children because we'll
contaminate the gene pool.

A tweet of a crematorium at a concentration camp and the
message: I'll light the match.

A tweet with a photo of a lynching and the message YOU'RE
NEXT.

They're anonymous. Faceless. Hateful people. My hands
tremble on the keyboard. I report each one.

I check the time. Dad went out to dinner with a colleague.

Should I call him to come home? I want to, but he rarely goes out. I know I come first, but he's due back within the hour. I can wait, right? I'll give it a few more minutes, then decide.

I return to Twitter. For the hundredth time, I tell myself to shut down my laptop. But I have this obsessive sick need to know.

Somewhere, there's a monster disguised as a human being who wants to put a bullet into our brains.

Dead. It reverberates in my head like a plucked wire. *Dead.*

Goose bumps rise on my arms. Gripped with fear, I stare out the breakfast nook bay window and scan the night, jumping at every shifting shadow. I close the curtains, grab my laptop off the table, and slide to the floor.

Who posted these comments? Someone wearing a white sheet and a hood? Or maybe the white supremacists I saw on TV, marching in Charlottesville, chanting, "Jews will not replace us." It's easier to believe it's a man or a woman far away, but it could be someone right here in Riviere.

I shudder. *What if these people know where we live?* I locked the doors, right? I set my laptop aside and crawl across the kitchen floor, making sure to stay way below the sightline of the bay window. Reaching up, I turn the stairwell doorknob and peek through the crack. I race down the stairs, yank on the door. Locked. Of course it's locked.

I dash from window to window, pulling down shades, drawing curtains. I run back to the kitchen, grab my phone, laptop, a quart of chocolate fudge brownie ice cream, and a spoon.

Safe in my room, I refresh the screen. There are now 132 comments. Lissa had said the article might garner attention. But

I never imagined this! I call Cade. It goes right to voicemail. *Arrgh! Why can't he ever leave his phone on?*

Should I call the inn? I doubt he even knows that the article was published. It wasn't supposed to post until tomorrow. Oh God. Did he tell his parents? I hope he told his parents.

My phone rings. But it's not Cade. My heartbeat kicks up a notch. It's my neighbor: Police Officer Shawn Sullivan.

After I tell him what's transpired, he says, "As a precaution, I'll have the department keep an eye on things. But I really don't think there's anything to worry about. Try and get some sleep."

Easier said than done.

CHAPTER 30

HEATHER JAMESON

Heather waits until her parents leave for the evening before shutting herself in the bathroom with the bag of supplies she'd hidden in her bedroom closet. She knows they'll be furious and deeply disappointed.

Heather is not the "disappointment" in the family. That title belongs to her older sister, Holly. Holly decided a long time ago to live up to her plant name, embracing the prickly and poisonous instead of the holiday cheer. After a stint in juvie for selling drugs, Holly dropped out of high school, stole from her family, shoplifted, and continued to use any drug she could get her hands on. A year ago Christmas, on her eighteenth birthday, Holly left with her twenty-four-year-old boyfriend, but not before she smashed every ornament on the tree, hauled off every present like the Grinch, and not only packed up her belongings but dinner as well.

Because of her sister, Heather's been the "good girl," and paying the price for Holly's actions. Her parents are super strict.

They pushed both daughters to excel and strive for perfection. Holly had enough.

No matter how hard Heather works to be their perfect daughter, she has never been able to live up to their expectations. "Only a ninety-three on your chemistry test? Clearly, you didn't study enough," her dad accused.

Isn't an A an A? Not in her father's book.

Heather would never do what her sister did. Where is her sister? Heather worries, but she's bone-tired of it, tired of being afraid, tired of not knowing who the real Heather is supposed to be.

She meant every word she said to Jesse, from liking him (past tense) to reporting him to Principal McNeil if he ever touches her again without her permission.

Standing in front of the vanity, Heather talks to the girl in the mirror. "You are not doing this because of Jesse." Although, she concedes, he did give her motivation. "You can do this." She laughs a little as she fights back tears that cloud her sky-blue eyes. She leans in close, whispers, "If you go through with this, people will see you. They'll notice you. You'll stand out. Do you really want to stand out?"

No, not really. But didn't Mr. Bartley do that to her by having her stand up in class? Remembering the smug look in Jesse's eyes, the way he laughed, fortifies her. She lifts her chin. "One day. That's all you need. That's all you'll get," she says, resigned, thinking of her father's wrath to come. If all goes according to plan, her parents won't know until tomorrow night. At dinner, she told them that she'll be leaving extra early tomorrow morning for an AP Lit and Composition study session. As long as they don't break their pattern, Heather will be out of the house long before they wake up. This one day will have to be enough. A full day to make her statement: Heather Jameson is no Aryan. Heather Jameson has a mind of her own.

Bracing herself against the sink, she says goodbye to the girl who always does what she's told. She runs her fingers through her long blond hair—her mother's pride and joy. No doubt Heather will be grounded—she's been grounded for a lot less, like leaving her clothes on the floor and for getting a B in Spanish freshman year.

This will be worth it.

Setting her phone on top of the toilet tank, she clicks on the playlist she created for this moment and hits shuffle. She opens her bag and empties the contents onto the vanity: conditioner, a plastic bowl, a croc clip, gloves, cobalt-blue semi-permanent hair dye, and the brush applicator. Thanks to several YouTube videos, she knows exactly what to do to get the best results.

After brushing out her long blond hair, she takes a before selfie, then strips off her shirt and puts on latex gloves. She mixes the conditioner and color and begins the transformation.

Forty-five minutes later, she spins around and sings along with Cindy Lauper's *True Colors*. The blue-haired Heather in the mirror looks badass-awesome. She takes an after selfie, posts both photos on Instagram. Within seconds, her friends respond:

"Gorgeous!!!"

"Omg I want!"

"Smokin' hot!"

"Damn, you're sexy, girl"

Emboldened from all the compliments, Heather emails Mr. Bartley, requesting the alternative assignment.

CHAPTER 31

CADE

I follow Mom to the farthest guest room from our apartment. The second I cross the threshold and she shuts the door, I blurt out, "I'm sorry!"

"You're sorry?" she huffs. "For what, Cade? Because from what I see, you didn't just happen to speak with a reporter. That was deliberate."

I slump against the wall. "I'm sorry we lost Mrs. Stoke's business." Tears glisten in Mom's eyes. I had told myself to stay calm, to explain, but the devastation on her face guts me. "Mom, you have to understand. Logan and I had to speak to the reporter. We did the right thing."

"The right thing? What was right about keeping this from us?"

"I tried to tell you. But you've been so stressed and busy—"

Mom cuts me off. "Not once did you say that you had an urgent matter to discuss about an assignment. Not once did you—"

I jump in. "I was going to tell you. If you think back, you'll remember I came to find you and Dad. You were in the basement freaking out over the busted furnace."

Mom grabs onto a bedpost. "There were plenty of other times you could have said something. You and Logan were working on an assignment, went to school early to discuss it with Mr. Bartley. You shared that much. Wouldn't that have been the time to tell us?"

For a brief moment, I close my eyes. I need to own this. "You're right. I could have, but I didn't. I chose not to tell you about the interview because I thought you wouldn't allow it."

Mom breaks her own rule and sits on the guest bed. "God Almighty. This is a disaster, Cade." She covers her face with her palms, moans into them. When she looks at me, her cheeks are covered with tears. "For one second, did you think about how this could impact this family? We needed Mrs. Stoke's business, Cade. You know that."

I slide to the floor, fighting back my own tears. Not once did it occur to me that we'd pay this kind of price. "I know. You're right. But we had to do this. *We had to.*"

"Start from the beginning. I want to hear every detail and later you'll explain to your dad."

It takes a half hour to tell the story and answer all of her questions. I watch her carefully. The hurt and betrayal I'm responsible for morphs to shock, frustration, and disgust aimed not at me, but at Mr. Bartley and Principal McNeil. Mom seems surprised and impressed by our actions, but it's hard to be certain because she doesn't say so. When I finally finish, I say, "That's it. I've told you everything."

I brace myself. Mom gets up and joins me on the floor. She picks up my hand and threads her fingers with mine. A tear trickles down her face, sending a spear of fear into my heart. She brushes the tear away with her free hand. "Losing her business hurts, Cade. But I'm proud of you and Logan."

I breathe a sigh of relief.

More and more tears stream down Mom's cheeks. I get up and grab the box of tissues from the bathroom and bring it over to her. She wipes her eyes, blows her nose, then says, "I'm sorry." I'm not sure why she's apologizing. She has nothing to apologize for.

"You're right. If you had told us earlier, I don't know how we would have advised you. That's the truth." She pauses. "I am fairly certain I wouldn't have had the courage to do what you and Logan did. I would have done the assignment and moved on, even if I didn't like it."

Mom's gaze is fierce, determined, stubborn. I've experienced this look enough times to know that whatever she says next is nonnegotiable. I brace myself.

"I have no idea where this is going to lead, Cade. I'm not sure what we'll do if—" More tears roll down her cheeks. "If we lose more business. Based on what I've already read, there will be more people saying hateful, disgusting, and vicious things about you and Logan. Sadly, it's just the way people are sometimes. When your dad and I got married so young, the things people said—" She cuts herself off, taps the spot above my heart, then my temple. "You're Granite. Steel. Titanium. You don't allow any of that hate to get through. You understand?"

I nod.

She continues. "What you said to the reporter showed tremendous dignity and respect. Let that be your guide. You and

Logan must be together on this, and if you need guidance, you can turn to us."

"What about Nana? What are we going to tell her?"

"Tell Nana what?"

Mom and I both startle.

Much to my relief, it's Dad. His gaze shifts from Mom's tearstained cheeks to me, then to the rumpled bed. "What's going on?"

CHAPTER 32

LOGAN

Jesse tags me in an Instagram post. It's a picture of the *Lake Towns Journal* article with the caption: CADE CRAWFORD AND @ LOGANMARCHNY ATTACK MR. BARTLEY. #RIVIEREHIGHSCHOOL

In the comments, I read:

> So not fair to Mr. Bartley. He's the best teacher.
> Logan thinks she's better than the rest of us. Obviously, she thinks she can do Mr. Bartley's job!
> Can they get suspended?
> Nah. Free speech. But they'll get what they deserve. I have no sympathy for them.

That one is from the private account RHSHockey4Evr.

There's more, lots more. I know every one of these people but RHSHockey4Evr. It could be anyone. No one, *not one person,* comes to our defense. Not one person says anything supportive. Lissa Chen had warned us not to respond to online comments, saying people have the right to express themselves. But it's so much easier to ignore when they come from strangers. I pick up my pillow, plant my face in the middle, and scream. I really had hoped we would get some support from people at school. *How could I have been so naive?*

My skin turns ice-cold. I burrow under my covers, struggling to come to terms with this reality. What is Mr. Bartley doing right now? What is he thinking? Does he hate us? Why do I want him to like us?

Blair's words come back to me. *A good teacher would never give that assignment.* But Mr. Bartley wasn't just a good teacher. He was my ideal teacher—challenging. Creative. Encouraging. Enthusiastic. Funny. Interesting. Supportive. I compared all my other teachers to *him*. He was my Zeus and now he's Ares. No, that's not right. A mere man I made into an icon, built a monument for. Not only has he come tumbling down, but I'm the one who threw the ropes and pulled. Why do I feel guilty? He's wrong, not us.

Who is the real Mr. Bartley? Trying to answer that question is like trying to grasp a cloud. Impossible.

My phone pings. I'm tagged in another comment on Jesse's Instagram post.

@LOGANMARCHNY HOW COULD YOU DO THIS TO MR. BARTLEY?

It's from an RHS junior.
I take a screenshot and text it to Blair.
Five minutes later, she responds.

BLAIR: Open his post.

I find this:

BlairinToGo So much respect for Cade and Logan. Did you read the article? Because if you did, you'll see that they did NOT attack Mr. Bartley. They spoke up for morality. I'm with them. Why not be courageous and join them?

ME: You are amazing.

BLAIR: YOU.

I refresh Instagram to see if anyone responds.

I scroll down.

And down.

And down.

It's gone. Blair's comment is *gone*.

ME: He deleted your comment!

BLAIR: (sends me a gif of Gal Gadot as Wonder Woman deflecting bullets, sparks flying everywhere) YOU!

ME: Ha! Right.

BLAIR: You're my hero. Tell Cade I think he's a hero, too. Keep your head up.

ME: (sends gif from *The Sound of Music* of Baron von Trapp ripping a Nazi flag in half)

BLAIR: Oh yeah. Go tear 'em down! Love you.

ME: ☺ Love you more.

Setting my phone aside, I stare at the ceiling. *I don't want to go to school tomorrow.* I bolt up. I have *always* wanted to go to school, and I resent Mr. Bartley and Principal McNeil for taking that away from me. How am I ever going to face all those haters? I reach for my phone and call Cade. Once again, it goes straight to voicemail.

I need a distraction, some entertainment. I Google "Movies where Nazis get their asses kicked." I spend the next hour on YouTube watching clips from *Captain America: The First Avenger, Inglourious Basterds, Raiders of the Lost Ark,* and *X-Men: First Class.* Watching history be rewritten temporarily improves my mood.

But reality kicks in, dragging me into a pit of despair. Replaying the Wonder Woman gif Blair texted me doesn't help.

Tuesday turned into Wednesday a few hours ago. In a few more, Cade and I are supposed to walk into school. I don't want to go.

"Stop, Logan," I say out loud, talking to myself like I'm another person. "You're not going to let Jesse and all the rest of those jerks get to you."

Cade and I won't be silenced. An idea comes to me, a way for Cade and me to speak to our haters without actually saying a word. I go online, find the perfect quote to contribute to Mr. Bartley's wall:

"I swore never to be silent whenever and wherever human beings endure suffering and humiliation. We must always take sides. Neutrality helps the oppressor, never the victim. Silence encourages the tormentor, never the tormented." —Elie Wiesel,

Holocaust survivor (Quote contributed by Logan March and Cade Crawford)

* * *

I turn the corner from Washington Avenue to Third Street and find Cade. He's bundled into his winter coat and the knit hat that Nana made him for Christmas last year. I'm wearing one just like his, but Nana added pompoms hanging from earflaps.

"Hi," he says, shifting his backpack on his shoulder. "What are you doing here? Are you okay?"

"Define okay." Dark circles ring Cade's eyes. "You look like you got as much sleep as I did. Two hours. You?"

"Maybe four. I fell asleep in Grandpa's workshop." He scoops up some snow, nails a fire hydrant. "We got a major cancellation at the inn because of the article."

"Oh, Cade. No!"

"I spent most of the night trying to figure out how I could help financially. I ended up in Grandpa's workshop. There are a few pieces of furniture he was building from reclaimed wood. I'm going to finish them. Sell them on eBay or Etsy."

I set my hand on his arm. "I'm so sorry."

"No regrets, okay?"

"And Nana? How is she?"

"She doesn't know. Mom doesn't want to tell her, and Dad thinks with pressure from outside sources, Mr. Bartley will cancel the assignment."

"That's what Lissa Chen said." When we reach the steps of our school, I stop. "I'm not ready for this."

He gives my pompoms a tug. "We got this."

"Maybe you do, but I don't."

Cade's lips quirk. "I know exactly what will help. Mom made me say this ten times this morning before she let me leave. 'I'm granite. I'm steel. I'm titanium. No one and nothing will get to me today.' Say it with me."

"No. I'm not going to."

He laughs. "Come on now. Say it. With conviction."

"*No!*" I stick out my tongue and Cade laughs harder. "You think it's funny, huh? Do you know how unfunny it is?"

He raps his knuckles on top of my head. "Oh yeah, solid rock."

"How about these, funny guy." I hold up my titanium fists and take a swing, but he manages to get his big paws around my wrists, turn me around in his arms so that mine cross in front of me. My back presses into his chest and I feel the vibration of his laughter. I wiggle and squirm. He takes several deep breaths and his laughter dies away. Other than that almost kiss, this is the closest we've been. If I turned around in his arms, I would be in the perfect position to kiss him. Before I can decide, he lets go and my hands fall to my sides. He steps back, but at least he's still smiling.

I catch my breath and watch the stream of students heading into school. No one says anything to us. They don't have to. Their looks say everything.

Cade's arm presses into mine. He whispers, "Ignore them." The first bell rings. He motions toward the door. "Ready?"

"Nope. Changed my mind."

"You want to skip?" He sounds so hopeful.

"Yes, but then they win."

He holds out his hand, palm up in invitation. "If we're doing this, let's do it together."

* * *

If only people were staring because we're holding hands. They whisper about the article, the assignment—crude and cruel murmurs and giggles—some juvenile name-calling like I saw on social media. I will myself to keep my eyes forward and follow Cade's stoic lead, but it's hard. Hoping it will help, I begin chanting to myself, *I'm granite. I'm steel. I'm titanium,* faster and faster until Cade stops walking. We stand in the middle of the hallway between our lockers. He steps in front of me, puts his hands on my shoulders. "Okay?" he whispers.

"Okay," I whisper back.

"We got this," he says. We split up to put away our coats and gather our books for the morning.

I enter my lock combination, open my locker, and . . .

OH MY GOD.

I recoil, and even though there's a lot of background noise, I swear I hear Cade gasp. I turn. For several seconds, our eyes meet. His are wide and dark and not Cade's. These are filled with shock, anger. People streaming by temporarily block my view, but I shift right and push up on my tiptoes. Cade grips his locker door and holds it open. Like mine, every inch is plastered with pictures and sticky notes filled with blood-red swastikas and hateful words.

A camera flash goes off. The hallway buzzes and crawls, closing me in. I face my locker. There's a small bag of dry dog food sitting on the bottom shelf and a note saying, "No dogs and Jew lovers allowed in the cafeteria."

I pull out my phone from my pocket and take a picture to show Mr. Bartley. I'd love for him to explain how the assignment promotes respect and tolerance.

More people stop, stare, whisper.

I spin around, meet them head-on with my glare. A few drop their gazes, shame-faced. Someone laughs behind me like this is a joke. My head snaps around whiplash-fast as I search for the comedian. Enraged, I call out, "Who did this?"

CHAPTER 33

CADE

I watch the scene as if I'm outside my body or in the middle of a bad dream and can't wake up. For a few heartbeats, my mind goes absolutely blank. Then the scene comes barreling at me. All the air leaves my lungs as if I've been sucker punched. A flash goes off. I inhale. Then another flash and another. I turn around and try to find Logan. I hear her, but can't see her.

"Who did this? *Who did this?*"

People stare, whisper, laugh, take pictures, and crane their necks to get a glimpse at the peep shows. I slam my locker door, but just my luck it bounces back and nearly clobbers me in the face. I reach in and grab a sticky note.

"Jew lover," it says. I stand there staring at it. But then, like someone hit a switch, it all comes full circle. I smile, deliberate and challenging. *Jew lover? Hell yeah.* I'd gladly side with Jews and my grandpa any day over these racist, hateful assholes. I stick the note on the front of my sweatshirt, and start to pick off the rest.

CHAPTER 34

MASON

A lioness. From ten feet away, that's what Logan looks like to Mason with her nose-flaring and wild-eyed "Who did this?" He admires her for it, but hell, does she really think someone's gonna confess?

He read the article and the pieces clicked into place—why Cade and Logan were in Principal McNeil's office with Mr. Bartley. Why Mr. Bartley's been . . . different—not exactly in a bad mood, but not his usual enthusiastic self, either. And why yesterday Mr. Bartley ignored Logan.

Last night, Mason's dad went on a tirade over the article. "How dare they embarrass our school like this! Mason, you call the team together for a meeting tomorrow morning in the locker room. I want them focused on hockey and not this nonsense. We cannot let this distract us from winning regionals." He used words to describe Cade and Logan that made Mason's stomach slither like a pit of snakes. His mom tried to calm his father and paid for it with a verbal lashing. Mason closed his bedroom door, stuck his earbuds in, and cranked up the tunes.

He spent the next hour reading through comments. The majority supported Logan and Cade. Some attacked Mr. Bartley. Those pissed him off. *These people don't know him, they don't know our school, and they don't know Cade and Logan,* he thought. Several times, he wrote a response, then deleted it. But finally, he couldn't help himself, and he posted his opinion under a pseudonym, of course, like everyone else. His comment was number 217.

> "I'm a student at RHS and I really like Mr. Bartley. He makes learning interesting, so for all those people who say he's a bad teacher and should be fired, you're wrong. But just because I like Mr. Bartley doesn't mean I support this assignment. Both the pro and con sides of the debate are morally wrong. On that, I'm with Logan and Cade. It's a fact there are some racist students at our school. They hate Jews and Blacks and gays and they've said it. Unfortunately, this assignment supports and promotes their beliefs. Right now, students have the option of doing an alternative. I've read several comments saying this should be sufficient. Personally, I disagree. Since the alternative meets class requirements, it's the best choice for everyone."

Mason would prefer to do the alternative assignment, but what if his dad found out? Ever since Mason struck back, the tyrant found a more effective way of controlling him. Threatening his mother. He swallows hard, and as he watches Logan struggling, he hears his father's firm directive to the team. "Anyone asks you about the assignment, you answer, 'No comment.' Your focus is hockey. STAY OUT OF IT!"

Towering over the crowd, Mason watches Logan. People are giving her a wide berth.

Reg laughs, and says, "They wanted the attention. They're definitely getting it now."

"The dog food was classic," Jesse says.

Mason ignores them, refocuses on Logan until a girl walks by with big blue eyes rimmed with dark eyeliner, deep red lips, and long kickass blue hair. She stops three lockers from his, catches Mason staring, and sends him a shy smile.

"Heather? Heather Jameson?"

She blushes and nods.

"So, what do you think?" Reg asks Mason, pulling his gaze away from Heather.

Mason blinks at Reg. "About what?"

"You haven't said anything about the article or Cade and Logan."

Mason shrugs. "Didn't read it."

Spencer makes his way over. Half the hockey team stands and watches like Cade and Logan are a part of a sitcom. Mason can't stand here anymore. He takes two steps away and stops. Dammit. He turns around and shoulders his way through the gawking crowd and into the crosshairs of Logan's fury.

"Did you do this?"

The insult hits him hard, but he ignores it, ignores her. He can't ignore the sticky notes.

He rips them off the door: Swastikas. "Burn baby burn." "Kikes and dykes not welcome here." He tears them in half, shoves them into his pockets, and begins to pick off the rest.

157

Logan joins him, clawing at the notes, littering the ground at their feet. "I'm sorry. I didn't mean that. I know you'd never—"

"Don't worry about it," he murmurs.

"Do you have any idea who could have done this?"

Mason's neck prickles. He glances back. Spencer, Reg, and Jesse watch him with disbelief and contempt. To hell with them. He's sick of them, sick of having to toe the line and keep the peace at home and in the locker room. But what makes Mason sick most of all is the painful gut feeling that several of his so-called teammates are probably—if not definitely—responsible for the disgusting messages in Cade and Logan's lockers.

"Who knows your combinations?" Mason asks.

Logan turns around. "Only Cade and me. Whoever did this must have somehow gotten their hands on the master list." Her eyes narrow. "Doesn't your girlfriend work in the office?" It's not a question.

Mason flinches. His brow furrows. "You think Kerrianne did this? Or me?"

"No."

His gray eyes turn into a thunderstorm. But there's more than frustration, there's hurt and defeat. He's tired of walking the tightrope that defines his life. He's too much, not enough, and pleases no one, especially the tyrant and least of all himself. Shaking his head, he walks away, mumbling, "What the hell's the point if no matter what I do, I can't win?"

"Mason!" Logan calls. "Mason, I'm sorry!"

Ignoring Logan, Mason kicks himself for caring. He reaches the stairs leading to the second-floor math and science wing and conquers them two at a time. The seed Logan planted in his head grows. Could Kerrianne get the master combination list? Hell yeah. She's worked in the school office for nearly four years. Miss Wather has given Kerrianne plenty of responsibility, and even though Kerrianne has her own login on the office computer, she's smart enough to figure out how to access the locker combination list.

He slips a hand into his pocket, removes one of the crumpled sticky notes, and smooths it out. "Burn with the rest of them," it says.

Mason knows Kerrianne's handwriting, and it's not hers. She may not have written the notes, but it doesn't erase logic.

Did Kerrianne give someone the locker combinations? It's highly probable, and he has a list of suspects. His conscience tugs at him. Should he confront her? Find out who she gave the combinations to? When she tells him, if she tells him, then what?

CHAPTER 35

DANIEL

Although there's commotion all around him, Daniel isn't a part of it. His mind takes him on a journey back to freshman year when it was his locker plastered with disgusting sticky notes and photos with anti-gay slurs and crude sexual comments and drawings.

Shaking, he closed the door, went right to the office, and asked Miss Wather if he could speak with Principal McNeil. And then he sobbed his eyes out. It was Miss Wather who brought him into the conference room, shut the door, and hugged him. It was Miss Wather who said she'd been there and understood. It was Miss Wather who handed him a box of tissues, two pieces of candy, and said, "Those jerks don't deserve your tears." It was Miss Wather who cleaned up his locker and gave him a new lock. And it was Miss Wather who checked up on him every day, even on weekends, for months to make sure he was doing okay.

Principal McNeil sent a letter to parents condemning bullying, telling them to talk to their kids about hate speech and to appreciate each other's differences.

For Daniel, not much has changed.

The same assholes strike out whenever they can—mostly rude comments about him being gay mumbled in passing or crude illustrations of certain body parts dropped through the slats of his locker.

He's lived with it; figured out that if he doesn't speak, doesn't respond to taunts and cruel jokes, and does his best to be invisible, he can endure school. If it weren't for his supportive parents, he would have shattered. He can't wait to go to one of the large universities he applied to that have LGBTQIAP+ student groups.

But seeing Cade and Logan's lockers, seeing their reactions and their strength, cracks a piece of his wall. He photographs Logan's locker and the pile of notes on the floor, getting close-ups of the swastikas and slurs.

In colorful language, Logan promises to shove the sticky notes into every crevice of whoever did this. She drags the big rubber garbage can from the girls' bathroom, scoops up a pile of hate, and drops it in. Mason picks up a handful of notes and tears them in half before throwing them out.

Daniel takes more photos while Cade stands a foot away, scanning his locker. There's a ghost of a smile on his face. Why is he smiling? When Cade shakes his head, it's not from disgust or annoyance. More like he's baffled by it. Daniel can't help but find Cade's reaction disconcerting. Why isn't he pissed? Hurt? Disgusted?

After a few more beats, Cade starts pulling the notes down. Daniel approaches and wordlessly asks permission to help. Cade nods.

Red splotches dot Logan's cheeks and neck as she watches Mason retreat. "Mason!" Logan calls. "Mason, I'm sorry!"

A Post-it note falls from Mason's pocket. Daniel rushes over and picks it up. He tears the swastika in half. Logan's sad smile hurts Daniel's heart. He looks at his feet. "I'm sorry," he murmurs.

"Why should you be sorry?" she asks, ducking her head so she can meet his eyes. "The ones who did this should be sorry. But some things are just too much to ask of pea-brain cowards."

"You need to report this. I took photos. I'll email them to you."

Logan explodes. "And what's Principal McNeil going to do? The last time we were in his office, he dismissed us. He shut us down and shut us up."

"But—"

"When this happened to you, did reporting it make any difference? Did McNeil's letter stop people from harassing you?"

Daniel rocks back on his heels. "Maybe this time it will?"

Logan laughs coldly. "You think someone's going to confess? You think someone will snitch? I don't think so. We're not going to be victims here. We've done nothing wrong, and we're not going to let a bunch of pricks intimidate us. Don't go to McNeil. He'll hear about it, but I expect nothing from him."

Daniel nods.

CHAPTER 36

LOGAN

Cade reaches across our lunch table and snatches a handful of fries off my plate. I scowl at him, then go back to glaring at the small pack of whispering, wide-eyed freshmen staring at us. I so want to walk over there and sit down at their table. Wouldn't that freak them out? From the corner of my eye, I catch Cade going for my burger. This time I whisk it away before his greedy fingers can get it.

"Switch places with me," he says.

"Why?"

"Because you always sit there and it's good to change things up." He walks around our table, nudges me with his knee. I refuse to budge, but then he takes my hand and tugs. "Come on."

"But I like sitting here." He bends down like he's going to pick me up and toss me over his shoulder. As amusing as that would be, I would prefer not to attract any more attention.

"Fine," I say, switching spots, but only because Cade refused to move until I got up. I stare at the cafeteria's baby-blue walls and a ridiculous poster with super-expensive luxury cars. The caption says, "Hard work pays off." I can think of ten reasons why it's absurd, but welcome to RHS. "Tired of this view, huh?" I point to the poster.

He shakes his head. "Logan. We should talk about this." His eyes dart over my shoulder and I know exactly what he's referring to. His leg brushes against mine. "Do you want to get out of here?"

I pick up a fry, but I have no appetite. Pushing my tray aside, I sigh. "I don't know . . . I thought today would be hard, especially after the crap people said about us on social media. But this?" I tilt my head, motioning to the audience behind me.

"I know." Cade's eyes remain on me, and it finally clicks why he wanted to switch places. He's much better at ingoring the unwanted attention. I really do have the best friend in the world. He smiles, but it's sad. "I'm not sure this is what my grandpa meant by being in the spot—"

I jerk. Something hit me in the back of my neck. I spin in my seat, look around, down. A paper airplane lies belly-up next to my chair. I grab it and set it on the table. Swastikas decorate the wings. Someone snickers.

I stand and scan the tables across from us. Any one of the dozens of people could have made this. I call out, "See my face? This is me laughing." I glare at anyone who dares to look at us. "Coward," I yell.

Cade unfolds the wings and smooths them out. That's when Mrs. Ingram, my AP Lit and Composition teacher, walks over.

"I'll take that," she says, reaching for the flattened airplane. "Do you know who made it?"

Cade snatches it away from Mrs. Ingram and hops onto his seat. He holds the swastikas high over his head for everyone to see, putting as much wrath into his expression as he can.

The room grows quiet. I slide my chair around Mrs. Ingram, and join Cade. Stretching my arm, I grasp the other edge of the paper. Every time my eyes meet someone else's, that person looks away.

Silence morphs to whispers, but no one laughs or taunts us like they did at our lockers before school. *This* is what I believe Cade's grandpa meant by being in the spotlight. Cade slips the paper from my fingers and slowly and deliberately tears it to pieces. He crushes them in his fist, hops down, and strolls over to the garbage. When he returns, I push my seat back into place and sit.

Mrs. Ingram hasn't moved. She removes two locks from her pants pocket. "I was in the office, and Miss Wather asked me to bring you these. Your new combinations are taped on the back. Just so you know, I checked. Only Miss Wather and Principal McNeil are able to access the file with everyone's combinations. They have their own logins. Miss Wather looked. The last time the master list was opened was the third week of school."

So maybe it wasn't Kerrianne? I think. *But then who? How?*

Heather walks over, book in one hand, her tray in another. Her blue hair cascades over her shoulders like a waterfall. "Can I sit with you?" she asks, loud enough for half the cafeteria to hear.

I pull out the chair next to me, and motion for her to join us. "Of course."

"Thanks." Her tray bobbles, and I reach up and take it from her. For several beats, she doesn't move, so I turn to see what she's staring at. Jesse. Though he's at a table filled with hockey players, including Mason, he has this odd expression on his face that gives me the impression that he's oblivious to everyone around him. At that moment, there seems to be only Heather in his world until Reg nudges his shoulder, breaking the spell. Heather sets her book down and joins us.

"I'd rather sit with you any day," she says without elaborating. I don't need specifics. I'm glad she's here.

And then Daniel comes over. "Is it okay?" He motions to the empty chair.

Cade smiles. "Heck yeah."

Mrs. Ingram straightens her yellow scarf, leans down. The four of us look at her. She whispers, "You should know quite a few teachers support you. A couple of us went to Principal Mc-Neil. Unfortunately, we walk a fine line, but I felt it was important for you to hear." Her eyes dart around the room, then back to us. "If there's anything I can do, come and see me and we can talk about it, okay?"

"We appreciate it, Mrs. Ingram." Cade picks up a fry, drags it through his ketchup, drawing a line down the middle of his plate. Then he wipes it out with his finger. He turns his defiant gaze on her. "We know about lines. You may walk a fine one, but we don't."

CHAPTER 37

PRINCIPAL MCNEIL

Principal McNeil's voice booms out of the loudspeaker. "Good afternoon, Riviere High School students. It's been called to my attention from multiple sources that some of our students were targeted and violated with hateful speech and vandalism. I ask for anyone with information about the perpetrators to come forward. Hate in any form will not be tolerated at Riviere High School. Your teacher will pass out a copy of our school's Hate Speech and Anti-Bullying Policy, which is also available on our website. Beginning today, it must be read and signed by every student. Teachers, please keep track and set aside a copy for any student absent today. These must be collected and turned in to the office before you leave this evening. Students of Riviere High School, this behavior is beneath you. I expect your actions will be exemplary and will reflect the spirit of friendship, hard work, and dedication proudly displayed by our Riviere Rockets varsity hockey team. Violating this policy, including any online posts, will result in immediate suspension with a review for possible expulsion. Given today's events, I expect teachers and students to be extra vigilant. It is imperative that you come forward and hold the person or people accountable. Our school must be a safe, welcoming environment for all students. That is all. Have a good rest of the afternoon."

CHAPTER 38

LOGAN

When the bell rings at the end of History of World Governments, Mr. Bartley comes over to me. "Logan, one moment please." He walks to his desk. I exchange a look with Cade that says, *Now what?* He sets his backpack on his desk and waits for me. Mr. Bartley picks up a piece of paper that's folded in half and stapled shut. My name is scrawled on the outside. "Mr. Lane dropped this off and asked me to give it to you."

He holds it out, and when I take it, Mr. Bartley walks to his coat closet without saying another word. To his back, I say, "Thanks."

Mr. Lane was my sociology seminar teacher and our National Honor Society advisor my sophomore and junior year.

The moment Cade and I enter the hallway, I open Mr. Lane's note. "Please come and see me after school today or sometime tomorrow. Mr. Lane"

"What do you think he wants?" Cade asks.

"No idea. The last time we spoke was a few weeks ago, when

he told me he nominated me for the Outstanding Senior College Scholarship Award. Maybe it has something to do with that?"

Cade nods. "You want me to go with you?"

"Aren't you supposed to help your dad repair the furnace?"

"I'm sure whatever Mr. Lane wants will only take a few minutes. I can wait."

"No. Don't keep your dad waiting. I'm sure it's nothing. He didn't make it sound urgent, so I doubt it's anything too important."

"Are you sure?"

"Yes." I give him a playful shove. "Go. I'll call you and fill you in."

When I open Mr. Lane's door, he gets up from his desk. "Logan. Good of you to stop by. Come with me." He motions for me to follow, which is odd. But there are several students I don't recognize working on what looks like a test, so maybe he doesn't want to disturb them?

I trail Mr. Lane into the alcove a short distance from his classroom. When he reaches the farthest corner from the hallway, he spins around, startling me with his anger.

He takes a step back, putting several feet between us. "Logan, it breaks my heart to say that I expected so much better from you."

I flinch as if he struck me across the face. "W-what?"

"You heard me," Mr. Lane whispers with a hiss. "I'm shocked. Not in a million years would I have ever thought you were capable of being unkind and thoughtless. It's a shame I can't retract my recommendation for you to receive the RHS Outstanding Senior College Scholarship Award. You don't deserve it."

His words knock the wind out of me and I have trouble catching my breath. My legs turn to jelly. I brace a hand on the wall as Mr. Lane continues his verbal assault. "What you and Cade did, going to the press, harassing Mr. Bartley, is deplorable."

"Harassing him?" Black dots dance in front of my eyes.

"Were you so desperate for attention? Was that it?"

"N-no!"

"There are people calling for his resignation! You've not only damaged his impeccable reputation but our school's. You've damaged this community, a community a lot of us care about."

"I care!"

Mr. Lane shakes his head in disgust. "There were so many other ways you could have handled this. Like treat him with normal human decency. You should have talked to him, resolved the matter privately."

"W-we tried."

"Clearly not enough."

"We talked with Principal McNeil and—"

"And that's the problem. People are way too sensitive about every little thing these days. There's no respect for authority, even after Mr. Bartley did everything he could to accommodate you."

I press myself against the wall. I can't think. I can't speak. My mind is blank.

"I want you to really think about what you've done, especially the ramifications your actions have had on other students, this school, and our community. Then come back and we can discuss—"

Suddenly, Daniel is at my side. He glares at Mr. Lane. Did

he hear everything? "Let's go, Logan. Mr. Lane has nothing more to say."

* * *

I want to *scrreeam*!

The second Daniel and I round the small alcove, I hold on to my backpack and run. Pissed. Furious. I can't think of one word that properly describes the mixture of rage, embarrassment, hurt, and shock that came from Mr. Lane's lecture. If only I could go back and say the thousands of things that now pop into my head. I'm so relieved I don't have a class with him this semester. There's no way I could have endured being in his room.

When I reach the stairway, I grab the railing and hurtle down two stairs at a time, accidentally bumping a petite girl. She stumbles into a guy wearing a hockey jersey.

"Hey! Watch it!" he yells, not to me but to the girl. I call out, "Sorry," and keep going, passing students and even a teacher, who shouts at me to slow down. I don't.

Daniel keeps up, offering platitudes like: "You have every right to be upset. What he said was so wrong."

I power through the crowded hallway so furious that I no longer take notice of anyone or anything. How many other teachers agree with Mr. Lane? Do they really believe we've ruined the school's reputation? The community's?

It's so messed up.

Mrs. Ingram said there are other teachers supporting our position, but where are they? Are they afraid if they do, they'll lose their jobs?

I need to talk to Dad, except he's in class right now. Would he find validity in what Mr. Lane said? No. No. He supports us. He said we're doing the right thing. How can I doubt that?

"Logan, wait!"

I forgot about Daniel. But I can't wait. I have to get out of here.

Breathing hard, he catches up with me, matching my foot-falls. "Let me help you figure this out."

"What's to figure out? You heard Mr. Lane."

"He was way out of line."

I spin around so fast that Daniel almost stumbles over his own feet. "You think?" My frustration pours out in a long exhale. "I'm sorry. I didn't mean to snap. I'm not angry with you."

"I know."

"It's all Mr. Lane." But then I wonder . . . did Mr. Bartley know what Mr. Lane was going to speak to me about? He was fine in class. He called on me, and though he wasn't his usual upbeat self, he wasn't upset or angry, not even when I put up the Elie Wiesel quote.

I start walking again, but this time at normal speed. My gaze meets Kerrianne's and she freezes as if I've hit her with a stun gun. She lowers her head, scurries by like a mouse running back to its hole. Did Mason tell her what I said about her having access to our locker combinations?

My brain hurts. I need a break from it all—the comments online, the sneers, whispers, swastikas, Mr. Lane. It's too much. "I need to get out of here. I'm sorry, but I can't deal with this now." I start moving again, this time at a less punishing pace.

"You don't have anything to be sorry about."

"Right now, I am."

At my locker, I spin the dial on the new lock Miss Wather gave me. *Dammit!* I kick the bottom. *What was the combination?* I try to remember, but I draw a blank, nothing but zeros. Somewhere in my backpack there's that tiny piece of tape with the numbers. I start digging through my stuff, but . . . "To hell with it."

Leaving my coat behind, I take off, hobbling a bit. I stick my hand into my pocket, grateful one thing has gone my way. At least I have my car's key fob.

CHAPTER 39

CADE

I take one step into the kitchen and I'm instantly chilled. Not because the furnace isn't working but because something must be drastically wrong. I've never come home to this scene before. Mom, Dad, and Nana are sitting around the table. Nana's skin is as white as flour.

"Cade, come sit down. How was school?" Nana asks, wrapping her fingers around a mug that rests on a folded copy of the *New York Journal*. I heard Nana, but Dad's grim expression might as well be a sock that's been shoved down my throat. I try to suck in oxygen, but I can barely wheeze in a breath. A thousand nightmarish thoughts run through my mind—the assignment, Nana's health, the finances of the inn.

"Family meeting," Mom says. Dad hooks his work boot on the leg of my chair and pulls it out for me. At my place, there's a mug of hot chocolate and a plate of gingersnap cookies. Nana's doing.

Nana slides her mug off the newspaper almost as if it's too heavy for her to lift. She flips over the paper and pushes it across

175

the table. Under "State News," there's a picture of Logan and me below the headline: UPSTATE TEENS FIGHT MURDEROUS ASSIGNMENT.

How? We didn't give them an interview.

"I'd like to hear the details," Nana says, her accent thick. "Tell me about this assignment."

I glance at Mom, and she motions with her hand for me to go ahead.

Stalling, I bite into a gingersnap. Where am I supposed to start? Finally, I say, "Mr. Bartley gave my History of World Governments class an assignment to re-create the Wannsee Conference."

"What is this conference?" she asks.

"Are you familiar with Hitler's Final Solution for the Jews?"

She nods. I give an abridged version of what transpired, and when I mention that Mr. Bartley wanted us to examine the Final Solution from the Nazi perspective, she reaches for Mom's hand and grips it tightly. I explain what we said to Mr. Bartley, Principal McNeil, and the reporter, highlighting why we have wanted the debate canceled from the beginning. I don't mention Grandpa or his stories.

Nana listens. Her free hand trembles against the table. She doesn't ask any questions. I filter out the cruel comments online, the swastikas and hateful words plastered in our lockers. When I finish, she stares into her mug.

Mom tries to loosen Nana's grip. "Ma, are you all right?"

Nana lets go of Mom's hand, raises her head. Her eyelids are heavy. "You need to stop the debate. This assignment is evil, Cade. You have to stop it."

I look helplessly at Mom.

"Ma. He's working on it. It'll be okay," Dad says, trying to calm her down.

"No, it's not okay. It's never been okay." Nana's hand flutters to her heart, and it sends panic into mine. A tear trails down her cheek.

"Nana. I didn't want to upset you."

She shakes her head. "You have been nothing but a blessing to me and your grandpa." Another tear tracks down her check. "Grandpa told me that he told you. Have you told them? Have you shared your grandpa's stories?"

Hot chocolate spills onto the table as I set my mug down.

"What stories?" Mom says. Confusion flashes across her face.

"Your pa wanted to tell you, Mikayla, but I wasn't ready. I couldn't. You have to understand I only wanted to keep you safe, to keep us *all* safe. But Pa didn't want to leave this world without someone besides me knowing his history. And when Cade asked . . ." She trails off.

Mom whispers, "But I asked."

Nana pushes away from the table, braces herself as she stands. "I need to lie down."

Mom wraps her arm around Nana's shoulders.

"I'm fine. Don't fuss. Come. We'll talk in my room."

Dad and I follow. As Nana gets into bed, my mind races through scenes from Grandpa's stories. How much am I supposed to share?

Drawing her quilt over her lap, Nana says, "Mikayla, if you're going to be upset with anyone, you should be upset with me.

This is my fault." She turns to me, pats a spot next to her, so I sit. "Cade, do you remember the story about the Jewish boy your grandpa saved?" I nod. "His name was Yankel." Nana takes my hand, gives it a squeeze, urging me to continue.

"Yankel was one of Grandpa's best friends. Grandpa told me that Yankel lived in the town closest to his family's farm and that Yankel's parents owned a bakery."

Nana nods, then picks up the story. "One day, truckloads of Nazis showed up at his family's farm. They checked their ID papers, raided the house for food and valuables, then left, heading toward town. Your pa asked his parents what the Nazis were going to do. They refused to say and forbade him to follow.

"Waclaw didn't listen. As soon as he had a chance, he went into town. The Nazis had gathered up all the Jews. Every single one and forced them to stand in the square. Over a thousand people. An SS officer announced that if anyone spoke, they would be shot. There was a crying baby. The mother tried to get her to stop, rocking her, pressing her to her breast, but nothing got her to stop. What that Nazi did to that precious baby, that angel." Nana gestures like she's tossing a ball into the air. "The mother *screamed*! Her husband tried to console her, but he couldn't. They both received bullets to their heads. Such cruelty." Tears stream down Nana's cheeks.

"Grandpa didn't tell me about the baby," I whisper.

"Ma, we don't need to hear this now. You're upset—"

"Mikayla, I have lived with this burden almost my entire life. It's time."

Mom sits at the bottom of Nana's bed, one arm across her

178

stomach and her other hand covering her mouth like she's trying to suppress a cry. Dad stands near Nana's dresser, motionless.

"These Nazis were beyond vicious; they were pure evil. Six of Grandpa's friends were hung on gallows—the oldest was fifteen and the youngest was twelve." Nana closes her eyes. "He was so small—like a marionette." Her voice chokes. "It took him the longest time to die."

"Oh Ma, that's awful."

Mom brings over a box of tissues. Nana motions for me to continue, and I fill them in on how Grandpa found Yankel hiding in the barn and how Grandpa's mom said Yankel couldn't stay. "They bleached Yankel's hair, gave him a cross and a Bible, and told him which Catholic prayers to memorize."

Nana fixes her gaze on Mom. "Yankel was given Waclaw's identification card. Waclaw, your pa. Yankel became Waclaw." Her eyes narrow, as if she's saying, *Are you listening? Have you heard every word?*

"So Yankel became Waclaw," Mom confirms.

Nana nods. "There's something important you need to know." She clings to my hand, motions for Mom to come close. She sits next to me.

"What you don't know is what happened to that boy, Yankel. He barely survived. For over three years he slept in farm fields or in the forest or in barns—any place he could find a little shelter. He lived in constant fear that the Nazis would find him. Through rain, through the heat of summer, and worst of all, the bitter cold of winter. He ran, hid, and somehow managed to survive. He clung to life, even as death chased him. During his third winter, he was sick and exhausted, but most frightening of all was what happened to his hands. His fingers were so frostbitten that he was certain they'd snap off at the slightest touch. He prayed for a miracle.

"The next day, he spotted a woman washing clothes in a stream. His first instinct was to stay hidden. If she turned him in to the Nazi authorities, there would be a good chance they'd closely examine his ID and wonder why he was so far from home. Even if he said that he was an orphan, the Nazis could easily check, and then they'd know he was an impostor. Waclaw was terrified. He didn't know what to do. He looked down at his hands and his blackened fingers. And that's when he heard a small voice. 'You can trust her,' the voice said. 'She'll help you.' Reluctantly, he walked over to her. He held up his hands, not in surrender, but to show her what had happened to them.

"Waclaw saw sympathy in her eyes. Carefully, she examined his fingers. And then she asked him if he was Jewish. For three years Yankel had been Waclaw. For three years he had hidden his true name, his true identity.

"That small voice said, 'It's okay. You can tell her.' He said, 'I'm Jewish.'

"The woman's expression changed from pity to sorrow to compassion. She said, 'I will help you. We'll say that you're my nephew. But you have to promise me you will never speak of this to anyone. You can never tell anyone you're Jewish. It's not safe. Do I have your promise?' And he did."

Tears track down Nana's cheeks and I wipe them away.

"It was too dangerous to bring Waclaw home then, but she

promised to return after dark and instructed him to wait for her in the shelter of trees near a cornfield. He waited and worried. Hours and hours passed, and then the cold day became a bitter night. Nearly every minute he questioned his decision to wait. His thoughts would teeter between hope and fear. What if she brought Nazi soldiers? But that small voice came to him again, reassured him, comforted him, promised him that the woman would help."

She pauses, lowers her eyes, and loosens her grip on my hand.

A minute passes, two. Then Nana lifts her eyes, breathes deeply, and continues.

"The woman returned, reminded Waclaw that he couldn't tell anyone that he was Jewish. She brought him to her house, fed him, gave him a bed, bartered home-churned butter for salve, and nursed Waclaw and his hands back to health. During those weeks, she shared a few things about herself. She was a widow and her sons had been taken from her, forced upon pain of death to fight for the Nazis. For six weeks he stayed with her. Her hospitality was second to none. She was kind and generous and nurturing. A guardian angel. Just like the boy who had given Yankel his name. For six weeks, Waclaw had a safe home. . . ."

Nana holds out her hands, stares, and flexes her fingers like Grandpa used to do. She takes my hand, turns it palm up, then folds her fingers over mine. She then scoots back, asks Mom to sit on her other side, and folds her other hand into Mom's. Desperation fills Nana's eyes, like she's pleading for us to understand.

Nana sniffles. Her accent is thick and heavy with emotion.

"Grandpa was the Jewish boy. He was Yankel. He's the one who took Waclaw's name, survived in the wilderness, was helped by the widow, and was eventually found by Jewish partisans who took him in. They fought against the Nazis. Sometime after that, Grandpa lost the Bible."

Mom and Dad are speechless. My mouth drops open.

Nana continues. "I, too, am Jewish like Yankel. I, too, lived in that town. I survived Gross-Rosen concentration camp, and that twelve-year-old boy, the last to die on the gallows? That was my youngest brother, Michoel. Michoel is Hebrew for Michael." It sounds like she's clearing her throat when she pronounces the middle part of her brother's name.

Nana take a deep breath, looks at Dad. "Adam, would you please go into my top dresser drawer? You'll find the cross that Grandpa received from his kind friend."

Dad shifts and opens the drawer. When he turns around, he holds up a cross dangling from a silver chain.

Nana looks from me to Dad to Mom. "Mikayla, I was afraid. I didn't want anyone to know we were Jewish. Your pa would have chosen differently. He stayed true to himself, silently. He was proud we had survived and grateful Hitler had lost the war. He lived every day seeing the bright side of life. I appreciated that. If it weren't for him, I don't know what I would have done. He loved me so much he agreed to keep our secret. You have to understand. We lost everyone—our parents, grandparents, brothers and sisters, and aunts, uncles, and cousins. We lost our friends and neighbors. *Everyone.* It was too much for me."

Nana's sobbing.

Mom's sobbing.

I'm sobbing.

Tears stream down Dad's cheeks.

After several minutes, Nana regains her composure. "When we first came to America, we lived in Brooklyn. We thought it was a safe, wonderful community with lots of other survivors. But one day, I witnessed thugs spitting at an old Jewish man. They knocked him down. They kicked him and called him awful names. They said Hitler should have turned him and his filthy family to ash. I couldn't believe this was happening.

"I've seen those ashes." Nana lets out a soft moan, then says, "I couldn't eat. I couldn't sleep. I was so scared. I begged your pa to take me away. I thought we would be safe in Riviere, where no one would ever know, a place without Jewish families to abuse. I thought we could have a fresh start. We wanted a family, but as you know, I miscarried so many times. Then you came along. Our miracle. I couldn't bear any more loss, Mikayla. I needed to keep you safe! When we were invited to attend church, I thought that would be one more layer of protection. I believed it was the right thing to do."

My lips tremble and tears pour down my cheeks. I shove a knuckle into my mouth, bite hard to keep myself from crying out.

Mom sucks in the biggest breath. "Oh, Ma," she sobs, and buries her head in her hands.

CHAPTER 40

LOGAN

Not until I drive out of Riviere and onto the one-lane highway do I fully realize exactly where I'm heading. I need Dad.

The moment I enter his lecture hall, he turns away from the whiteboard and looks up. I know he's surprised because he does a double take. He sets his marker down and addresses his students. "I have an important appointment, so today you're dismissed early."

Immediately, the room sparks into action—notebooks and laptops close, seats spring up, backpacks unzip and zip, phones ping. I move to the side. When there's a break in the stream, I head down. Dad meets me halfway. "What is it, Logan? What's wrong?"

The floodgates open. He pulls me in and runs his hand over my hair, murmuring that it's okay. I'm not sure exactly what's okay, but it's the tenderness that gets through and helps me breathe again.

Letting go, I sit on one of the auditorium seats. Dad shuffles into the row below me and sits on the edge of the upholstered chair behind him. I tell him everything that happened from the moment Cade and I walked into school this morning until I left without my coat.

"I'm not naive, Dad. But I didn't expect us to find swastikas plastered all over our lockers or have Mr. Lane deliver a nasty lecture." *Was Mr. Lane right? Did we destroy our school's reputation? Was there something else we should have done?* These are the questions swimming around in my head.

He hasn't said anything and I really, really need him to respond. I look up at him. He seems lost in thought. I mumble, "Well, that's it."

Dad loosens his tie, unbuttons the top button of his oxford. "Mr. Lane said he expected better from you?"

I nod.

"Well, I expect better, too." He sees my shock, then quickly adds, "From him. *Not* you. I'm so proud of you! Don't ever doubt that. You can't let Mr. Lane knock you down or cloud your judgment. Who does he think he is? You've done everything you could to be reasonable and respectful, and when you needed guidance, you sought out expert advice and followed it to a tee. Right now, the only thing that could disappoint me would be if you backed away from this challenge. Don't let this other nonsense distract you and Cade from the task at hand."

As agonizing as this experience has been, it feels so good to have my dad. I smile.

"How come you're smiling?"

"'Cause you're right. And because you're my dad."

"Whew. That's a relief." He mock-wipes his brow. "This parenting gig isn't so easy, you know."

My smile turns into a laugh. "You've done good."

"Thanks. Do you want me to call Mr. Lane? Because I will. I'd love to give him a big piece of my mind and tell him where to shove his self-righteous expectations."

I shake my head. "Probably not a good idea."

"Probably not. I doubt he has any sense to listen to me anyway. You need to get in touch with the woman at HPJ. Tell her what happened today. You need her professional advice."

"Thanks, Dad. What I really need is pizza. White sauce, garlic, and cheese. And Cajun fries. This day needs fries, too."

"You make the call to HPJ. I'll order the food and we'll eat it at home."

CHAPTER 41

CADE

Grandpa and Nana—Jewish. Mom's Jewish? *I'm* Jewish? How can we be Jewish?

Dad isn't Jewish, but I am. What does that even mean?

Looking around, I suddenly feel like I don't belong—my bed, my clothes, *everything* feels like it belongs to someone else.

I walk over to my dresser and pick up the photo of Grandpa and me. I loved him, respected him, but did I really know him? All these years, how did Nana and Grandpa endure keeping their true identities a secret? I close my eyes and imagine Grandpa as a starving, terrified boy wandering alone in the wilderness. And Nana forced to watch her brother hang from the gallows. To stifle my cry, I bite my bottom lip hard. I lay the photo facedown, sit on the edge of my bed, and stare out my window. I had my whole life mapped out, proud to carry on my grandparents' legacy. But what is that? How could they have hidden something so BIG and important?

I need to get out! This room. This apartment. This inn!

Nana is in her room and the TV is on. I go in search of my

parents and find Mom sitting at the reception desk. Gross-Rosen concentration camp is on the screen. Mom gets up and hugs me. "I didn't know or even suspect," Mom says. Her eyes flick to the screen. "My entire life—lies."

"Where's Dad?"

"He needed some air. He'll be back soon. I think." She clasps the locket dangling from its thin gold chain—the one Dad gave her when I was born.

"Can I borrow your car? Logan needs my help with the assignment." She doesn't, but I couldn't come up with another excuse that would guarantee my freedom from this cage.

She glances at the time. "Nana wants to bake tomorrow and needs a few things from the grocery store. I was planning on going in a few minutes."

"I'll go," I say. "I'll stop before I head over to the Marches'."

"That's fine. Are you okay?"

"Are *you*?"

She shakes her head. For several long beats neither of us says anything. What's there to say? She holds my hand, then gives me the list. It takes every ounce of self-control not to run out the door.

I'm adding bags of flour to my cart when I hear someone say my name. I look over my shoulder. At the end of the aisle, two women are standing with full shopping carts. They're not talking to me. They're talking *about* Logan and me, the assignment, and the article in the *Lake Towns Journal*. I don't recognize them.

Blue Coat has her back to me. The other is angled away. Her bracelets clang together as she talks with her hands.

"Those kids humiliated this town," Bracelet Lady says.

"Personally, I agree with them," Blue Coat says. "That assignment is ridiculous."

"It doesn't matter if you agree with them or not," Bracelet Lady says. "The publicity has ruined our community's reputation. How are we going to sell real estate if outsiders see us as racists and antisemites? Imagine the type of people who will want to move into Riviere. This could destroy our town. I could strangle those teens."

"It isn't their fault. That's not how I want my kids educated. Put the blame where it belongs—on Mr. Bartley. That teacher should be fired."

"Why? The damage is done." Bracelet Lady looks over, and in a blink her expression changes. Does she recognize me? Blue Coat turns around. I sprint in the opposite direction, dodge people and carts, and dash through the exit.

Within a half block I realize I'm in no condition to drive. I'm trembling so badly that I can barely keep my hands on the steering wheel. I put on my blinker, turn onto a side street, and pull over.

What did we do? What if she's right? Have we destroyed our town?

I slam my fist against the dashboard, angry with myself for running away, angry for not defending us, angry with Bracelet Lady for blaming us, and angry with Mr. Bartley and Principal McNeil. This is *all* their fault!

189

How is it that doing the right thing can be so devastatingly wrong?

My cart is where I left it. I push it aisle to aisle, looking for the women, but they're nowhere in the store. I check out, disappointed, frustrated that I didn't have the opportunity to speak with Bracelet Lady.

If it had been Logan—*Logan!* I completely forgot her meeting with Mr. Lane. I check my phone. No text. I pay for the groceries, put them in the trunk, and call her. It goes straight to voicemail. I text and get no response.

* * *

Twenty minutes have passed since I parked across the street from Logan's house, waiting for her and Professor March to come home. I sit with my regrets, drumming my fingers on the door armrest, staring out the window at the Marches' Victorian. It's dark, but the streetlamp and bright white snow cast enough light to outline the house.

Logan, where are you?

And just as I'm about to call Logan again, someone raps on the passenger window. I drop my phone and nearly leap out of my skin. A burly man rests his forearms against my roof, leans down, and peers at me. I start the engine and crack the window.

"You've been sitting in this car for a long time. You need help with something?"

"No. Just waiting for my friend."

"And who might that be?"

"Logan March?"

"You don't sound so sure."

"Logan. I'm sure. She lives right over there." I point across the street.

"Your family owns the Lake Ontario Inn. Your dad is Adam Crawford—one speeding ticket—and your mom is Mikayla Crawford—no traffic violations. You're Cade. How are you holding up? No troubles from those online trolls?"

"You're Officer Sullivan."

He laughs, clearly enjoying this exchange. "That I am. It's nice to finally meet you. How was Friday night? Did you get the information you needed from the Safe Haven Museum?"

I nod, wondering if Logan told him or—

"My wife, Wendy, is on the board. She made the arrangements. You do know that in exchange for the keys and full access, Logan promised to volunteer at the museum's fundraiser, right? It would be nice if you'd join her. Wendy could use the help."

To my relief, Professor March's SUV turns into their driveway. Logan is right behind him in her own car. Officer Sullivan straightens. I drop my sweaty hands from the steering wheel. Officer Sullivan heads toward Professor March. I roll up the window, shut off the engine, and get out.

"You know this guy?" Officer Sullivan asks Logan. There's humor in his voice. "He's been waiting for you for a while."

"Really? Everything okay?" she asks, scanning me from head to toe.

"Yeah, everything is fine."

191

She swings her backpack over her shoulder and fills her hands with an extra-large pizza box and a greasy white bag balanced on top.

I take off my jacket and drape it across her shoulders. "Where's your coat?"

"I left it at school."

While Professor March talks with Officer Sullivan, I follow Logan to their side door. She hands me the pizza box, pulls her keys from her pocket, and lets us inside.

I want to tell Logan about Nana, but the thread I'm holding on to is so thin, I'm afraid it'll break. So I ask, "What did Mr. Lane want?"

"That's why you came over?"

My throat tightens. Logan scrutinizes my face and it's obvious she knows something's up. When it comes to guests, I'm great at putting on a cheerful mask, but with Logan it's harder. I set the pizza on the kitchen counter and shrug. "I was worried."

"Sorry. I know I promised to text you." She sits at the table and fills me in on her nightmare confrontation with Mr. Lane. "He expected *so much* better from me. Now I'm certain I have no chance of getting the Outstanding Senior College Scholarship Award."

Swear words explode from my mouth. I pace the kitchen, calling Mr. Bartley, Principal McNeil, and Mr. Lane every name I can think of, cursing them all.

"Wow," Logan says. "Feel better?"

"No. Not really. Okay, maybe a little." My lips quirk up, but my smile fades fast as I fill her in on the grocery store conversation.

192

"Ah, that explains so much."

Not even close, I say to myself.

She stands. "C'mere. I think we both could use a hug." Setting her head on my shoulder, Logan asks, "Are you sorry we talked to the reporter?"

"Not at all. You?"

She pulls back, drops her arms. "Definitely not."

"Good."

"I spoke with Lissa Chen. She thinks Principal McNeil should know about what happened with Mr. Lane. I don't want to tell him. It'll just make him hate me even more."

"But—"

"Are you hungry? Dad and I kind of went overboard. Comfort food."

"Yeah. I could use some of that."

CHAPTER 42

BLAIR, LOGAN, CADE

Video chat:

> **BLAIR:** (on her phone at Glenslope High School, onstage in the auditorium for *Grease* rehearsal) How are you holding up?
>
> **LOGAN:** (on her laptop, in her bedroom, sitting with Cade propped up on her bed) We've had better days.
>
> **BLAIR:** (a face fills the screen) This is Liam. He's playing Danny.
>
> **LIAM:** (waves) Hi. Blair's told half the school about Mr. Barfley and that messed-up assignment. Just wanted to say that I have so much respect for you.
>
> **LOGAN AND CADE:** Thanks.
>
> **BLAIR:** (her face joins Liam's) We're really sorry the two of you had such a horrible day.
>
> **CADE:** (shrugs)
>
> **LOGAN:** Nothing we can do about it, so . . . (trails off)

BLAIR: We'll be right back, okay?

LOGAN AND CADE: Okay.

BLAIR: (the camera sweeps all over the place, giving Cade and Logan a floor-to-ceiling view of the auditorium, including a couple dozen feet, rows of empty seats, and bright lights above. Blair's face reappears) Hi, sorry about that. I'm giving you to Mrs. Rajurkar.

LOGAN AND CADE: (glance at one another, confused)

MRS. RAJURKAR: (on Blair's phone, smiling, eyes on the stage, she nods) Ready! (she flips the camera, the entire stage is filled with GHS theater students holding white pieces of paper) One. Two. Three.

GHS THEATER STUDENTS: (they flip the papers, reveal handwritten #WeSupportU signs, and shout) WE SUPPORT YOU, LOGAN AND CADE! (whoops and shouts, fists pump the air)

BLAIR: (grins, skips forward to her phone, takes it from Mrs. Rajurkar, turns camera to face her) Love you.

LOGAN: (leans into Cade, misty-eyed) That was . . . amazing.

BLAIR: *Aww.* I'll text you a photo so you two can look at it anytime.

CADE: (smiles) Thank you.

LOGAN: (brushes away a tear) Thank you. Love you.

CHAPTER 43

LOGAN

"He said *what*?" Cade's expression mirrors my shock. He sinks onto the edge of my bed as I slip into my desk chair, setting my laptop onto my desk.

Through my phone's speaker, Bethany Beshett says, "The New York education commissioner said that the assignment, and I quote, 'seems to be a topic worthy of analysis. Looking at both sides of the debate fosters critical thinking skills. Students can gain a lot from different perspectives. Of course, a teacher has a responsibility to give grade-appropriate background information and material when presenting any new topic.'"

"Critical thinking? He said looking at both sides fosters critical thinking skills?" I type the words into a blank note, then add a header: Education Commissioner's Comments.

"That's what he said. I have a recording of it."

"When did this happen?" Cade asks.

"He was speaking at the New York Teachers Convention this

afternoon. I caught him on the way out and was able to ask him about it."

"Wow." Cade gets up and moves to my side. I scoot over, pat the chair for him to sit with me. Even the top educator in New York is against us.

"My boss would like to post my article within the hour. I already have a strong response from the deputy director of Humanity for Peace and Justice, Nathan Goldstein, but I would also like to include your thoughts."

"What about Lissa Chen?" I ask.

"Nathan is her boss."

Cade and I share a look. "Can you tell us what Mr. Goldstein said?" I ask.

"He contacted Commissioner Munro's office and asked him to review the assignment closely, stating that the assignment is not only an affront to the Jewish people, but all humanity. It's his strongest recommendation that the commissioner ask the school to apologize to the students for requiring them to defend the Nazis' points of view and to rescind the debate. He said, and I quote, 'Cade and Logan are brave teens who deserve not only our support, but our deepest respect and gratitude.'"

I'm so surprised I temporarily lose my ability to speak. Cade stops rolling a pencil back and forth on my desk.

"Can I get a quote from you two?"

I let out a shaky breath. "Sure. Would it be okay if we email you a statement?"

"Absolutely, and I appreciate it," Bethany says. "Take your time, but not too much time."

I get up and pace in front of my desk. "Why would he comment without fully reviewing the assignment?"

"Who knows? It defies logic. This *entire* situation defies logic." Cade opens a new email on my laptop. "You fed me pizza and fries and made me feel a thousand times better about bailing at the grocery store, so I'll type."

It takes us a half hour to finish our response. I trade places with Cade, read our statement out loud, and tweak a few words.

"This is good," Cade says.

"Ready?" I ask.

He nods and I hit Send.

Forty-eight minutes later, the *Lake Towns Journal* article "NY Education Commissioner Munro Defends Final Solution Assignment" goes live.

COMMENTS:

NYRes4ever

I'm outraged! Not only should this teacher be fired, but it's time to show Munro the door.

8 Like   Reply

Instructor1

@NYRes4ever

That's extreme and unfair. Because it's the Holocaust? Sounds like a super-sensitive response. The Holocaust was deplorable, but I support this teacher and Munro—we need our students to learn how to analyze and think for themselves. No one is going to take this assignment and conclude that what the Nazis did was right.

1 Like   Reply

NYRes4ever

@Instructor1

Extreme? Unfair? Sensitive? I have a family member with cognitive disabilities. In Nazi Germany, he would have been murdered under their practice of eugenics. For the millions of people in this world who fall into any of the "categories" Nazi Germany found unworthy of life, I find this assignment grossly offensive.

4 Like   Reply

CHAPTER 44

HEATHER JAMESON AND JESSE ELTON

JESSE: (texting on his phone, sitting on the couch in the basement) Why did you dye your hair?

HEATHER: (texting on her phone, in her bedroom, curled up in her hanging bubble chair, a book lying open on top of the crocheted blanket draped on her lap) Because I wanted to.

JESSE: Is it because of what I said?

Heather hesitates. The hesitation seems like an affirmative answer and that annoys her. But she's not sure what to say to Jesse. Does she owe him an explanation? Why is she texting with him?

Jesse keeps his eyes on his screen, waiting for those three dots to show that she's responding. He's blown his chances with her twice. The first time was at a Fourth of July party last year at Kerrianne's house on Lake Ontario. He'd spent more time talking with Heather at that party than in the twelve years they'd gone to school together. Kissing her was one of the best moments of his life, and that says a lot, considering the successes he's had playing hockey. They had fun on the beach—volleyball, roasting hot dogs at the bonfire, collecting rocks, walking in the surf. When it was time for the fireworks, they shared a blanket. He couldn't believe how perfectly she'd molded to his body, cradled between his legs, leaning back against his chest, where a different set of fireworks was going off. He moved too fast, too far, and should have asked. He knows that now.

He can't figure out how he messed up the second time. He wasn't joking about forming the Aryans. Why was she offended? She should be proud. He's proud to be a part of a superior race—good stock, as his father would say.

His younger brother calls from upstairs. "Hey Jesse, when you coming up to watch the Rangers? Dad wants to rewind and show you Hendrik Lundqvist's amazing save."

"Be right up," he calls, but then those three dots appear.

> **HEATHER:** Added incentive. I don't believe in that
> superior bs. It's wrong. But I've also wanted to dye my
> hair for a long time. I like it this way."
> **JESSE:** Your dad grounded you?
> **HEATHER:** Who told you?

Heather knows the answer, but since she was honest, she's curious to find out if he'll be honest back.

> **JESSE:** Kerrianne told Mason. Mason told me. For
> how long?

HEATHER: Until I dye it back or leave for college. So college.

JESSE: That long?

HEATHER: Yup. But you knew that.

She'd expected her dad to be angry, to ground her, but his reaction was way over the top. He yelled, called her horrible names. And even when she explained about the assignment and her reasons for dyeing her hair, he wouldn't listen. She didn't expect him to.

JESSE: I was hoping it wasn't true. It's just hair dye. It doesn't change who you are. Maybe I could explain that to your dad?

Will he ever get it? Heather wonders.

HEATHER: I don't think so.

JESSE: What can I do?

HEATHER: I don't understand the question.

JESSE: You used to like me. I like you too.

HEATHER: And you show it by being an asshole?

JESSE: I was drunk. It was a party. Parties are supposed to be fun.

HEATHER: Being groped by you was not fun. Having Mason pull you off me was not fun.

JESSE: That was last summer. I thought you'd forgive me by now.

HEATHER: Proof you're an asshole.

JESSE: I really am sorry.

HEATHER: Why are you texting me, Jesse?

JESSE: I don't want you to be angry with me.

HEATHER: I'm not angry anymore. I just don't want to be with you. That's final.

Heather blocks him on her phone, then tosses it onto her unmade bed. Restless, she gets up, walks around her room that's both her safe place and her prison. Standing in front of her mirror, she takes a good look at herself. Changing the color of her hair no longer feels like enough. She needs more, but what's more?

Jesse sits back on the couch. Anger rises, not toward Heather but toward Cade and Logan. He smashes his fist into a pillow, then picks it up and whips it at the wall. It's their fault Heather won't give him a second chance. Their fault for planting ideas in her head, and how dare they challenge Mr. Bartley. Traitors.

The memory of kissing Heather on the moonlit beach frustrates him. He wipes his mouth, disgusted with himself, disgusted with her. He stands, rubs his shoes on the carpet. Heather and her blue hair aren't worth the dirt under his feet.

Heather opens her top desk drawer, takes out scissors, grabs a chunk of hair, and—

A knock on her door startles her just as the blades *snap*. She drops the scissors. Several blue strands fall to the floor. Her hands fly up, combing through her locks. What did she do? She checks the mirror, closes her eyes, and sinks to her knees, grateful she missed.

Another knock.

"Can I come in?" It's her dad.

Heather opens her door, stands in the threshold, blocking him from entering her room. If her dad has something to say, he can do it from the hallway.

He rests his hand on her doorjamb. "I want to talk with you."

Heather doesn't move. She catches a glimpse of her mom listening at the top of the stairs.

"When I'm wrong, I say I'm wrong, and I was wrong," her dad says.

She answers with a blank stare. How can she respond when she doesn't have any idea what he's talking about?

"Your mom and I looked into that assignment. You're right. It goes against our family's values." He stops talking. His eyes appraise Heather's hair, appraise her. "As I said, when I'm wrong, I say I'm wrong. You're not grounded anymore."

It's not an apology, but close enough. Heather bites back a smile and nods.

Her dad answers with his own nod, then turns around and goes back downstairs. Her mom follows, but only after she grins at Heather and blows her a kiss.

CHAPTER 45

LOGAN

I check my phone. It's been forty-two minutes since I last went online. After reading the same paragraph in *The Glass Menagerie* three times, I consider getting up and giving Dad my laptop. It keeps calling to me like the shiny poisonous red apple that tempted Snow White. I really have to finish this play for AP Lit and Composition, but it's so . . . mundane.

Don't bite. Ugh. I'm as weak as Snow. I sit at my desk and refresh Bethany Beshett's first article. This can't be right. I refresh the page again. And blink.

There are over 10,000 shares and 824 comments! It links to Bethany's other article on Commissioner Munro's response, and those numbers are close behind.

"Dad?" I push my chair away from my desk and open my bedroom door. "DAD!"

We nearly collide outside his bedroom. "What is it?"

"It's gone viral. We've gone viral. The assignment. The article. You gotta come see this." I motion for him to follow me into my room.

"Is that right?" he asks, pointing to the numbers.

"Seems that way." I Google our names. There is a long list of articles. The articles have gone viral! It's stunning, terrifying, and thrilling. I begin at the top, bringing up a new window for each. Many are a version of Bethany's article, linking back to hers. No wonder her numbers are so high!

A few articles are frustrating, not because of the content, but because the reporters refer to me, Logan, as "him" or "he." Is it too much to expect reporters to use correct pronouns? Apparently.

I click on another headline: "Offensive Holocaust Assignment Protested by New York High School Seniors."

Dad hovers and reads the article over my shoulder. I point to the first comment. It has a link to a letter written by members of our state government. "Wow. Look at this. Five state senators and three aldermen call for Munro's resignation."

"I don't even know what to say. This is a stunning development, Logan."

Opening up Google Docs, I set up a list of articles and op-eds with their links, then send an email to Cade, Dad, and Blair so that they can view and edit. I also set up Google alerts. Almost immediately, I get a notification that the *Huffington Post* and the *Washington Post* wrote about the debate. I receive notices from political blogs, Jewish online papers and magazines.

Blair texts: "Got your email. OMG! AMAZING! Mr. Buttley should be crapping in his pants. At work now, will read more articles later."

"This will change things," Dad says. "I'll be right back. I'm going to get my tablet."

I begin reading an article titled "Assignment Requires Upstate New York High School Students to Debate How to Exterminate Jews." When I reach the third paragraph, I suck in a breath, then exhale. The reporter calls the assignment "child abuse and a sly way to indoctrinate Nazi beliefs on impressionable minds." *Abuse. Sly. Indoctrinate. Impressionable.* Strong words. *Abuse?* This person doesn't know Mr. Bartley, has never taken a class from him, and it bothers me that he wants him fired. So many people want Mr. Bartley fired.

In our interview with Bethany she quoted us. "Our purpose is only to have the debate canceled and for it to never be a part of the curriculum again."

What baffles me is Mr. Bartley's silence. He hasn't made one statement to the press. But maybe with this kind of global response, he will finally understand?

Dad returns to my room. I give him my chair and bring my laptop to my bed.

Not every article supports our position. One website declares "Politician Conspires to Fire Teacher over History Lesson." It says that Cade and I are pawns to bolster New York Senator Andrew Kelly's reelection campaign and his platform to increase spending for public education. It's so absurd, I laugh. Cade and I have never met Andrew Kelly, but obviously people will say anything to promote their agenda.

Are we supposed to do something about it? It's a question I'll ask Lissa Chen.

"Teacher's Creative WWII Lesson Deserves High Praise" calls the assignment ingenious. Valuable. Honorable. The site is run by a white supremacist.

And "High School Teacher Dares to Teach Truth."

207

It starts out like many of the other articles, talking about the assignment and the debate. But then it takes a massive turn, explaining how the assignment reinforces an authentic portrayal of Jews. Accompanying the article, the writer posts caricatures of Cade and me with large hooked noses, menacing grins, and horns coming out of our heads. We clutch a wad of money in one hand and a lizardlike tail in the other. Flames surround us. The caption reads: "The devil's children spread evil lies about good Christians."

The devil's children? Now we're being called the devil's children? Painful chills spread from the top of my head to my toes.

Could Mr. Bartley be affiliated with a hate group? Even thinking it feels like a betrayal, and it doesn't make sense, not when he talked about genocides still going on today, the concentration camps in China. Yet, his strongest support comes from individuals connected to white supremacist groups.

Is he a wolf in sheep's clothing like someone suggested? A monster? One of those guys everyone is *shocked* when they discover his true character—like the police officer who was a pedophile or the talk show host who sexually assaulted women in his office? I don't want Mr. Bartley to be despicable. A voice in my head whispers, *But hasn't he been acting that way?*

"Logan, you have to see this!" Dad says, bringing his tablet over to me. The article is titled, "Non-Jewish Students Protest Assignment Advocating for the Annihilation of Jews." He points to a line toward the end of the article. "I want to frame it," he says.

"Oh wow. I have to call Cade."

"Do that," he says, walking to my door. "I better get back

to work. Tons of papers to grade. If you need me, I'll be in my office."

Feeling a bit giddy, I pick up my phone, flop onto my bed, and call Cade. When he answers, I give him my best imitation of Mr. Lane. "Cade, I expected *sooooo* much better from you!" And then I burst out laughing.

"Oh yeah?" I hear the humor in his question.

I stay in character. "Oh, definitely."

"So, Mr. Lane, what did I do *this* time?"

"Well, Cade Crawford . . ." I return to my normal voice. ". . . Bethany Beshett's articles have gone VIRAL!! We've gone viral, Cade. Can you believe it?"

"Wow. I—I don't know what to say."

"Listen to this. According to *Today's Teens for Teens* magazine, 'Cade Crawford and Logan March are what America needs— brave young adults who recognize injustice and are not afraid to take action. They possess more sensibility, sensitivity, respect, and compassion than the adults who were supposed to be our role models and mentors.'"

"It's—"

"Incredible?"

"Humbling," he says.

"Yeah." I sigh. Another Google alert pops up. "There's more. Do you want to hear?" Before he answers, I say, "Wait! Oh no."

"What? Is it bad?"

"Hold on a sec." I scroll down, reading fast. "The *Lake Towns Journal* published a letter to the editor written by Reg!"

CHAPTER 46

Lake Towns Journal

Student Supports Teacher and Final Solution Holocaust Assignment

Shares 9

To the Editor,

    I'm writing to offer support for Mr. Bartley, my History of World Governments teacher at Riviere High School. He has been unfairly accused of being a racist, an antisemite, and a bigot. He is the absolute opposite of those things. Anyone who knows Mr. Bartley would describe him as respectful, open-minded, accommodating, and an outstanding educator. He only wants what's best for his students, providing opportunities for us to expand perspectives and to learn about the realities that history can teach us.

    What's most frustrating is how our Wannsee Conference assignment has been misinterpreted.

The media has blown the Nazi debate way out of proportion. Mr. Bartley has done everything he can to accommodate those who are overly sensitive about the Final Solution, allowing them to research and present an alternative assignment. The vast majority of students, however, chose to participate in the Wannsee Conference debate, proof only a tiny minority found the assignment offensive. It's their problem!

Like our teacher, Hitler dared to think outside the box. Exposing our mind to ideas that may be contrary to our own, especially valid beliefs, isn't evil. This assignment has allowed us to keep our minds open and nonjudgmental to all sides, to humanize what happened during World War II and to broaden our perspectives. It's been a great experience, allowing us to think critically and form opinions based on facts.

The people spewing hate toward our teacher? They're the ones who are closed-minded, judgmental, and evil.

Sincerely,

Reginald (Reg) Ashford, senior,

Riviere High School

Comments: 3

Student1

Way to go Reginald! It's obvious you're a thoughtful, considerate person. The lesson asked you to think critically and to broaden your perspective. You did just that and should be commended.

0 Like   Reply

WarVet

This letter is appalling. I don't want my tax money going to a school that allows students to support ideas spouted by white supremacist groups.

2 Like   Reply

StudentLife

Why would a student feel the need to defend his teacher? Where is this teacher? He hides behind students instead of coming out himself and explaining his actions. Pitiful.

21 Like   Reply

CHAPTER 47

ELIAS DYGOLA

From: Elias Dygola Wednesday, 10:52 p.m.
To: LoganMarch@riviereschools.org,
CadeCrawford@riviereschools.org
Re: Thank you

Dear Logan and Cade,

I am the son of Holocaust survivors. If they were alive today, I have no doubt my parents, of blessed memory, would have written and thanked you for your courage for speaking out against the Nazi Final Solution debate. So, in their stead, I felt it was important to contact you.

Both my parents were protected and hidden by heroic non-Jews who risked their lives for the sole purpose of doing what is morally right. Here you are, decades and decades later, doing the same.

There is absolutely no justification for this assignment, but please know that it pains me to read how your teacher's misguided attempt to teach history has resulted in him being demonized. Life, I have learned, isn't always so simple. I will be reaching out to him in the hope that I can be of assistance.

Stay brave. Stay strong.

Thank you,
Elias Dygola
Community Relations Director,
Voices of WWII Vets and Holocaust Survivors

CHAPTER 48

MASON and KERRIANNE

Furious, livid, pissed. Nope. None of those words come close to Mason's father's controlled fury before this morning's hockey practice. Reg flinched as Coach Hayes told him to remove everything from his team locker as the rest of the team stood by and watched in awed fear—fear that Coach Hayes would bench the Riviere Rockets' top defender for regionals.

Nope. Mason knew better.

He also should have known better that his father wasn't upset about the embarrassing antisemitic content of Reg's letter to the *Lake Towns Journal* editor, only that Reg had defied his order. "You're going to act outside the rules of this team," Coach Hayes said in Reg's face, "then you don't belong here. Go get dressed in the public locker room. On the ice, I expect you'll remember you're a part of a team."

A small slap on the wrist and a free pass to use words of hate.

Disgusted, Mason parks his SUV and heads into school. The letter to the editor made things a little clearer, and Kerrianne had a part in it. At least, that's Mason's theory. He strolls into the office, surprising her. "I need to talk with you."

This is it. He's breaking up with me. She's sensed it coming for weeks. The signs have been there. Not returning her Snapchats, turning her down when she invited him to her bedroom, forgetting to pick her up after her choir practice. He's never done any of those things before. She sets a hand on the stack of papers she's going through. "I can't. I have to finish entering attendance before Miss Wather gets back."

Mason leans over the counter. "This can't wait."

She grips the arms of her chair, bracing herself. "Then say it."

He drops his voice to a whisper. "You gave Reg the master locker combination list."

Kerrianne almost wishes Mason were breaking up with her. This is a hundred times worse. "H-he told you?"

"No. You just did."

She can't move. The expression of betrayal on Mason's face destroys her. What did Reg do *this* time? After Cade's and Logan's lockers were vandalized and Principal McNeil had everyone sign the school's Hate Speech and Anti-Bullying Policy, Reg promised he was done.

Mason watches Kerrianne carefully and reads the guilt on her face, tearing him apart. He doesn't know what to do about this. He stalks to the door, then stalks back, coming around to Kerrianne's side. He crouches in front of her. His voice is low and angry. "Why? Just tell me why you would do that?"

She lifts her palms in a plea, begging him to calm down, as she glances toward Principal McNeil's office.

"You're that jealous of Logan?"

"No! I'll explain. I *promise*! But not here, okay?"

Mason has no patience for this. "Here and now or we're done."

"Everything all right, dear?" Miss Wather shuts the office door and steps over to the counter. Kerrianne nods, tries to smile, pretty certain she looks like a demonic clown. She motions toward the hallway. "Could I—would it be okay if we—I need to speak with Mason."

Miss Wather transforms from protective granny to a ferocious mother bear. She wags her finger at Mason. Mason would be amused if he wasn't so pissed. "Whatever's going on that has you all revved up, dial it down ten notches or you can go have a seat right over there." She points to the chair next to Principal McNeil's office. "Understood?"

"Yes, ma'am."

Hands on hips, she doesn't let him off the hook so quickly, and Mason admires her scrutiny. She nods. "One moment, please." She grabs her pen and the pad of late passes, rips off two, and writes Mason's name on one and Kerrianne's on the other. "You have a half hour."

Kerrianne reaches out for her pass, but Miss Wather jerks it away, narrows her eyes like a cat set to jump on its prey. "Before you head into class, I expect you'll stop in for a piece of chocolate fudge. I ordered them online and I'll need to know if I should buy them again. That's nonnegotiable." She looks at Mason. "That goes for both of you."

Mason nods. Message received.

Mason drives out of the school parking lot with no destination in mind. He can't look at Kerrianne, and he refuses to be the first one to speak. He wants an explanation, and no amount of sniffling will soften his now stone-cold heart.

Where should she begin? One of the reasons Kerrianne fell in love with Mason years ago was how well he listened. He'd surprise her months later with a playlist of various songs they'd talked about. He was patient and fair, and even though she knew he didn't love her, she could count on his loyalty. Could she count on it now? She hoped so.

Two miles pass before Kerrianne finally speaks. "I gave the combinations to Reg freshman year when I was helping out during orientation."

"When the two of you hooked up?"

"It was the worst three weeks of my life." Kerrianne trembles, stares out the passenger window, the past haunting her again.

"I still don't understand. Why would you give him the list?" When she doesn't answer, his eyes flicker from the road to Kerrianne. She's doing some serious landscape gazing. Mason knows Reg is clever, a manipulator, a gambler. He plays to win. He tests, pushes the limits, just like he did with that letter to the editor. Something clicks in Mason's mind. "What does he have on you?"

Mason turns into the Riviere Marquee parking lot, chooses a semi-secluded spot next to a fir tree, and shifts into Park. He unzips his jacket, then faces her. She still won't face him.

Impatient, Mason pushes Kerrianne over the edge. "Maybe we need to talk with Principal McNeil?"

The floodgates open. Sobbing, her words come out in fragments. In between, she gulps in air. "A few photos. Of me in my bra. And underwear. That I texted him."

Mason reaches into his glove box and hands Kerrianne a stack of fast-food napkins.

He has never seen Kerrianne this vulnerable and filled with despair. For a half second, he wonders if it's an act, but in the same half second he dismisses it. Kerrianne definitely knows how to pour on the drama, but this would be an Academy Award–winning performance and she's not that good of an actress. She wipes her eyes, smearing her already drippy makeup.

Mason understands what it's like to be powerless with his dad, the asshole of assholes, and he's done tolerating it from anyone else.

He reaches over and gently sets his hand on Kerrianne's shoulder. Through the thick layer of her coat, it's barely a touch, but it's enough. She unbuckles her seat belt and buries her head in his chest. Grasping the lapels of his letter jacket, she sobs as he holds her.

Now what? Mason wonders. There are other questions, but he's not sure this is the time to ask. Their half hour is ticking away, and he has no doubt Miss Wather is also watching the clock. He loosens his grip and finally Kerrianne loosens hers.

Mason finds it hard to calibrate his mind to this Kerrianne. She must notice because she says, "You believe me, right?"

"Yeah, I believe you."

"But?"

"But I also don't understand how you could stay friends with Reg."

She snorts in disgust. "Have you ever heard of keeping your friends close and your enemies closer?"

He gets it. "Sure." How many times has he given his teammates a pass because they're supposed to be friends? He's walked that tightrope so many times and he's still on it. Can't blame Kerrianne for doing the same. He's stood on the fringe with these guys for a long time. Too long. *What a mess,* he thinks. He's determined to fix it.

His gaze slides over to her. "I understand Reg has the pictures, but if you explain this to Principal McNeil—"

Kerrianne lets out a derisive laugh. "You don't get it."

"Then explain it to me."

"I gave Reg the list. When he vandalized Daniel's locker, he told me he did it. He's stolen from people's lockers and gotten away with it. It's a game for him. He promised that if I turn him in or if he gets caught, he'll make sure I go down in flames with him. He said he'll tell Principal McNeil that I've been in on it from the beginning. It's his word against mine."

"I'll back you. We'll tell him that he's threatened you. Reg can't get away with this."

She shakes her head. "Please, Mason." The tears return. "Reg has the power to destroy my reputation, my *life*. You've kept me safe. There's only three more months until graduation and this nightmare will be over."

Mason doesn't have a clue how to respond. Rage seeps into him like black smoke from a smoldering fire. As much as he feels sorry for Kerrianne, it's not enough. He shakes his head. "No. There has to be some way I can make Reg pay for everything he's done."

"Please, *please,* Mason. I'll get expelled. I won't be able to go to college. My life will be *over.*"

Mason starts the engine and doesn't respond to Kerrianne. On way too many occasions, Reg *and* Jesse *and* Spencer have gone too far. How many times for the sake of the team did Mason do nothing?

He's done with doing nothing.

With unshakable resolve, Mason says, "I'll handle it and I'll keep you out of it. I'll keep you safe."

"How?"

"When I know, you'll know."

CHAPTER 49

CADE

Thwack.

I spin around and there's Logan standing ten feet away on the sidewalk, grinning at me like a fool. Seeing her again after a day being treated like an infectious disease makes everything better. I wipe the snow dripping down the back of my neck. "You serious? You're challenging *me* to a snowball fight?"

She answers by scooping up more snow, then runs by and smacks me in the chest. She takes cover under a pitiful young maple tree at the end of Washington Avenue, dodging left, then right, laughing the entire time.

"Aren't you supposed to be heading to work?" I call as I amble toward her. I reach down, grab a softball's worth of snow, packing and shaping it and trying to decide what part of Logan I'm going to aim for.

"Not for another hour. I thought I'd walk you home and come back for my car after."

I still haven't mentioned anything to her about Nana and our

Jewish heritage. This morning, when I was ready to go to school, Nana was still sleeping. She's always the first one up. I found Mom exactly where I left her last night—sitting at the reception desk. This time she had an empty pot of coffee and a mug on the desk. A website on Judaism filled the computer screen. Her eyes were red with dark shadows underneath, and she was wearing the same clothes from the day before. Dad walked over and tried to be supportive. He told Mom and me that he's never been big on religion but believes in God. "Do whatever you need to do," he said.

"I don't know what that is," Mom said. "How do I process this?" She stood and slumped into Dad's arms. He led her into our apartment.

Alone, I walked into the parlor. The inn, which has always been a place of comfort and warmth even when we have no guests, felt cold and haunted, even with the fire blazing in the fireplace. For the first time ever, I couldn't wait to leave for school.

Logan lobs another snowball at me and misses by a mile. I nail her right shoulder, spraying snow into her face. She squeals and takes off running toward Sunrise Park. "Catch me if you can," she calls.

I chase after her and purposefully let her stay ahead as I plan my next move. She's just about to enter the park when I pitch a loosely packed snowball high above her. It showers down onto her hair.

She turns, rubs her gloved hands together, and makes a cackling sound like she's the Wicked Witch of the West. "You're in for it now, my pretty." This time she scoops up snow using her hands and forearms as a shovel. She braces the wet, fresh snow against her chest and stalks forward with her snow bowl. I can't help it, I laugh.

With three snowballs in hand, I plant my feet and start juggling, planning to use one to wash her face the moment she's within arm's length. Five, four, three . . . Ready, aim—

Logan comes in low like a linebacker, knocking me flat into a snowbank with a loud grunt. She heaves her arms up and covers my face in snow and the rest of me with her body. "I win. I win!!!" She pants like a puppy.

I grab her around the waist and roll us over, shaking melting snow all over her like a wet Saint Bernard. She covers her face with her gloves. "Who won?" I ask.

"I won!" I take her wrists and hold them above her head. She grins, a mega-watt smile. Her clumped dark lashes accentuate the gold flecks lighting her eyes. Her grin slides off her face into something intense and serious. We're both breathing hard. I should let her up, but I find myself drawn closer, so close that I'm barely a breath away.

"Remember our bet?" I whisper.

"Yes," she whispers back.

"I'm cashing in. What's going on in that mind of yours?"

"This." She kisses me and I'm kissing her and it's not enough. Her arms come around my back. I press into her, pouring every ounce of myself into this one kiss. One kiss and it's not enough, it will never be enough. How is it that we've spent so many seconds, minutes, hours, days, inches from each other and deprived ourselves of *this*?

A car honks and startles us apart. We laugh. Logan lifts an

arm and waves at the passing car. I roll off her, stand, and reach down, offering her a hand. Her cheeks are pink from the cold and from our PDA.

"Not bad," Logan says, brushing off some snow from her jeans.

"Not *bad*?" I fake insult.

"There might be room for improvement."

"Maybe not interested."

She fists my coat, yanks me forward. "Maybe I'm not, either."

We're kissing again, and it's everything, *everything*, and yet not enough. I want more. Her. Me. Us. Together.

"There's an inn down the street if you need a room," a girl calls from the open passenger window of a pickup truck. The guy in the driver's seat gives me a thumbs-up, then drives away.

Laughing, eyes sparkling, Logan starts walking backward toward the inn. "C'mon, Mr. Room-for-Improvement, I'm starving. Let's go see what Nana baked for you today."

My kiss-crazed high tanks as I take my time joining Logan.

* * *

When we enter the inn's parking lot, Mom is dragging a large plastic garbage bag toward our fenced-off dumpster. Oh no. I forgot to take out the trash? On warp speed, I recheck my daily a.m. to-do list, but for the life of me, I don't remember.

I jog over to Mom and head off the lecture. "Sorry. I got it," I say, taking the bag out of her hands and hoisting it off the ground. Spying the unfamiliar car, I ask, "We have guests?"

She nods. "Walk-ins. Mr. and Dr. Schaefer will be here through the weekend."

I know what she's thinking 'cause I'm thinking it, too. Dollar signs.

Mom turns to Logan. "What happened? You're soaking wet. You're *both* soaking wet."

Logan laughs. "Snowball fight. I won," she adds, smiling at me as I dump the garbage. I send her a pointed look. *We both won.*

"Did things go all right at school today? Any problems?"

"Nothing more than we expected," Logan answers.

Mom glances over to me for an explanation, but before I can say more, Nana, dressed in a housedress and a flour-covered apron, comes around the corner with the recycling bin in her hands. I rush to take it from her.

"You brought us Logan!"

"Hi, Nana." Beaming, Logan strides over and kisses her cheek.

"Ma, I told you I'd get that. Go inside before you catch a chill."

"I'm perfectly capable of carrying a little trash. Stop treating me like I'm fragile, Mikayla. I'm fit as a fiddle."

"Ma—"

Nana lifts her chin. "I'm going, not because you've ordered me to but because these young ones need some hot chocolate." She takes Logan's hand. "Come with me, sweet girl. Let's get you warm and dry. We have a nice fire blazing in the parlor."

As they go ahead, I hang back with Mom, and just as I open my mouth to say something, Nana's strangled scream stops me cold.

We run, Mom at my heels.

Nana's hand shoots up, shaking, pointing. It takes my mind a second to comprehend. On the stone above our apartment entrance, someone's written in blood-red spray paint, "Death to Jews!" Next to *Jews* is a swastika.

"Oh my God!" Mom cries.

With more force than I could have ever imagined, Nana shakes off Logan, making her stumble. "Not again!" Panic rises in her thick-accented voice.

CHAPTER 50

LOGAN

I pull my phone out of my pocket and dial 911. As I talk to the dispatcher, Mikayla tries to get Nana inside, but she won't budge. Nana's face is sheet white.

Cade clings to Nana's hand, telling her, "We're all right. . . ."

With blaring sirens and flashing lights, a squad car pulls into the inn's parking lot.

Tears crystallize on Cade's lashes. Mikayla shivers and huddles in her coat.

My neighbor Shawn and another officer stride over. The swastika and "Death to Jews" looms above us. Shawn's eyes flicker to the vandalism, and then he says, "This is Officer Tisdale. We've been patrolling the area as promised and pulled in here not more than forty minutes ago." He slips a hand into his coat and removes a small notebook from his breast pocket. "Why don't we go inside and we can get your statements," he says.

Cade opens the apartment door and holds on to Nana, leading her inside. She says, "I need to lie down." She slips her arm out of Cade's, shuffles to her room as Cade stares helplessly after her.

"Who did this to us?" Mikayla asks, once we're sitting around the kitchen table. "Who could do something so hateful?"

"We'll do our best to find out. Do you have surveillance cameras?"

Cade shakes his head. "No."

"We never thought we would need them," Mikayla adds, looking shattered. "This is a good community." The words hang in the air, hollow.

Cade updates them on the additional articles and the letter to the editor by Reg Ashford.

Shawn frowns. "This isn't the only incident that's occurred within the last twenty-four hours. The *Lake Towns Journal* reporter's car had swastikas keyed into the paint and—"

"Bethany Beshett?" I ask.

Shawn nods. "And headstones were toppled and smashed in a Jewish cemetery forty-five minutes from here."

"Because we spoke out against the assignment?" Cade asks.

"Because people hate," Shawn says.

Officer Tisdale asks us to email a list of every student who taunted us, threatened us, called us names. I ask, "What about teachers?"

"Everyone," Shawn responds. "We'll check around the premises, canvas the area, and speak to some of the other business owners nearby."

"Are we safe?" Mikayla asks in a whisper. She reaches for Cade's hand.

"If it will make you feel better, we can make arrangements to have someone keep an eye on the inn 24/7."

Nana shuffles into the kitchen. "We'll never be safe," she says. Then she turns to Mikayla. "Where are your manners? These officers need some coffee and cookies."

CHAPTER 51

CADE

After the police officers leave to speak with the neighboring business owners and Logan heads off to work at the library, Mom goes into Nana's room to "talk." The fear gripping Nana leaves me cold and scared and confused. Nana's words replay in my mind. *We'll never be safe.* No one but Mom and I understood what she meant, and when she served coffee and cookies, we talked about the community's reaction and the lack of support. Officer Sullivan's expression was grim. Officer Tisdale listened but showed no response. I had always thought of Riviere as a warm, welcoming town, but when Logan talked about the homes flying Confederate flags, the last remnants of our idyllic life crumbled into a pile of rubble. How did I not see it? What else have I ignored or missed?

As I sweep the kitchen floor, Mom walks in. "Nana's resting."

"This scares me, Mom," I say. "What are we going to do?" My statement and question are so much bigger than the vandalism. It's Nana. It's her past. Our history. Our identity. The look on Mom's face tells me she's struggling just as much as I am.

"I don't know," she says. And I realize that I had hoped she had an answer. I had hoped somehow she could help put our lives back together again. We're drifting on an ocean in a boat without any oars.

The reception desk bell rings, bringing us back to reality. "Can you take care of that?" Mom asks. "I need to call your dad."

An older couple waits for me at the front desk. "Hello," I say as cheerfully as I can. Two suitcases are next to them. "Checking in?"

The man sets a key on the counter. "Actually, we're checking out."

"You're Mr. and Dr. Schaefer." I can't hide the disappointment in my voice. "Was everything okay with your room? Is there something we can do for you to make your stay more comfortable?"

"The room is lovely." Dr. Schaefer shifts on her feet and exchanges a look with her husband. "As you know, we spoke with those kind police officers. We're sorry for your trouble. Truth be told, I just don't feel comfortable staying here anymore. We hope you understand."

Mr. Schaefer adds, "Please charge us for a night's stay."

I swallow. "No, sir." The little extra cash would have helped, but I can't take their money. "If you ever come back this way, we hope you'll visit us again and stay. May I help you with your bags?"

"Thank you, no." Mr. Schaefer takes a suitcase handle in

each hand as Dr. Schaefer digs through her purse. She pulls out a twenty-dollar bill and sets it on the counter. "We took a nap," she says, then walks with her husband out the inn's front door.

I drop into the reception desk chair, rest my arm on the desk, and lay my head down. I can't cry. I can't scream. All I can do is breathe. For one more minute, I just want to breathe.

CHAPTER 52

MASON

To protect Kerrianne, Mason will carry her secret. But he's done with her, and he told her so. Three more months until graduation and they'll also be done with Riviere High School.

But that doesn't mean Mason is going to sit back and not have Reg pay.

Mason's plan is simple. Reg will hammer the nails into his own coffin.

Sure enough, with Reg's return to the team's locker room, all Mason has to do is light the fuse. "So, Reg. About that letter to the editor. Did you read the comments?"

Reg explodes—a full-on antisemitic, racist, anti-gay rant.

So predictable, Mason thinks, and smirks to himself.

Reg grabs his junk, proudly bragging that he's the only one who had the balls to speak out in Mr. Bartley's defense. "I'm a hero," he says. "We should take those Jew lovers and shoot them like rabid dogs. We'll be doing Mr. Bartley a favor."

"Shut up," Mason says, and as predicted, Reg continues on.

The threats that Reg makes against Logan and Cade send shivers down Mason's spine. He forces his fingers to stay open at his side even though they want to curl into a fist to pound Reg's face. Mason stands there and listens to every. Single. Word.

CHAPTER 53

NEW YORK COMMISSIONER OF EDUCATION,
FRANK MUNRO,
ANNOUNCES RIVIERE HIGH SCHOOL ASSIGNMENT
WILL NEVER BE GIVEN AGAIN

CHAPTER 54

LOGAN

CADE: Can I come over?

ME: Of course.

CADE: I'm outside your side door.

I drop my phone on my bed, run down our back stairs into the kitchen, then into the entryway, and fling open the door. The motion sensor light shines on Cade. He lifts his head, and I get the biggest shock of my life. He looks absolutely wrecked.

"What happened?"

He takes one step, reaches for me, and buries his face in my neck. "Nana," he chokes out. His hands come around my back and clasp onto my shoulders. He's shaking. I brace us against the doorframe to hold us both up. Something unthinkable has happened to Nana. Tears pool in my eyes. I can't form words to ask the question that might lead to the answer I fear the most.

I tighten my grip around Cade's waist. His warm tears drip into my Georgetown sleep shirt. My skin cools in the bitter cold wind. Goose bumps rise over my arms and legs, and the freezing cement numbs the bottom of my feet. But I hold on, hold on and try to imagine how we'll live without Nana.

He takes several deep breaths and pulls away. "I'm sorry."

"W-what happened to Nana?"

"She's okay. Or as okay as she can be under the circumstances." He pauses. "I'm sorry. I shouldn't have scared you like that. I just—I had to get away."

I nod as if I understand, but I don't. In the kitchen, Cade takes off his coat and drapes it over a chair.

"I'm confused. Did something else happen?"

Cade leans against the kitchen counter. He struggles to speak. "Where's your laptop?"

"Upstairs."

He motions with his head to the stairwell, and I lead the way to my bedroom.

Kicking off his shoes, he flops onto the pillows I have propped up against my bed's headboard. "Look up Gross-Rosen concentration camp," he says, then closes his eyes. "Read about it, then tell me when you're done."

Sitting at my desk, I open my laptop. Wikipedia's site pops up first. I click on it, read about the tens of thousands of people the Nazis tortured as slave laborers to mine the granite quarries and to build 102 prisoner sub-camps. From the summer of 1940 until the Red Army liberated them on February 14, 1945, some 125,000 people passed through Gross-Rosen and the other camps—40,000 were murdered. I go to the official Gross-Rosen Concentration Camp Museum website. It's located in

Rogoźnica, Poland. On the left side, there are tabs. One of them is labeled "Database of the Dead." I've seen enough. I need to know what this is about.

"Okay?" My voice is barely a whisper.

"Nana was there."

"What?"

"And that story I told you about my grandpa saving a Jewish boy?"

I nod. "Uh-huh?"

"My grandpa didn't save the Jewish boy. He *was* the Jewish boy."

"Oh my God!" My hands fly up to my mouth.

Cade struggles not to cry again.

"Oh, Cade." I get to my feet, but he stops me by holding up his hand. I sit back down at my desk and wait.

Several minutes pass before Cade is able to speak again. Then he tells me the rest of his grandpa's story, the parts he didn't know until Nana told him. "Every single member of my grandparents' families was murdered," he says. "They're Jewish." He rakes his fingers through his hair, then scrubs his face. "We're—" He cuts himself off. "I don't know what we are."

He stares down at his palms, flexes his fingers. "I don't know who I am."

My heart breaks for him and it takes all my willpower not to cry. He doesn't need my tears. "You're Cade. This doesn't have to change anything. You always knew there was something about your grandparents' past, right? Now you know."

His eyes darken, fill with misery. "There is so much I *don't* know! And it could have been me! *Me,* Logan." He slaps his palm against his chest. "They would have killed *me.* Those evil, filthy excuses for human beings killed my family! Murdered for what? Do I look any different than I did yesterday or the day before or a month before?"

"Not at all."

He covers his eyes with his arm. "I'm Jewish, Logan. What makes me Jewish?"

I get up, sit at the bottom of the bed. "There's a rabbi at SUNY-Lakeside my dad knows. We could get in touch with him?"

He pushes himself up onto his elbows. "I don't want to talk to a rabbi. I—I can't. Maybe someday." He scoots off my bed, checks his phone. "I gotta go. My parents and Nana were sleeping when I left. But if they wake up—I took the car and didn't leave a note."

"Call me when you get home."

"Sure."

I walk him to the car, then watch him drive away.

I climb into bed and finally allow myself to cry for Cade, for his family, for me. I replay what's transpired over the past week, the misery and pain this assignment has caused. I want to put it all on Mr. Bartley. It belongs on Mr. Bartley, but as I stare up at my ceiling, Mr. Lane's words haunt me. *There were so many other ways you could have handled this.*

Were there?

I seriously consider it. The answer is no.

So many nights I've lain awake, worrying about Mr. Bartley, how this has impacted *him.* Enough! On the surface, I raged

240

that Mr. Lane blamed Cade and me, but inside? I bought into his blame and piled it onto my back like a packhorse. He's the one who behaved outrageously. I'm done making excuses for him.

My phone buzzes. Cade doesn't call. He texts: "Home."

CHAPTER 55

MIKAYLA CRAWFORD

Long after Cade and Adam are asleep, Mikayla gets out of bed and walks to her mom's bedroom door. Mikayla had left it cracked open in case her mom woke up and called for her. Like the thousands of times her mom had checked on her in the middle of the night when Mikayla was a child, she feels compelled to look in on her mom.

But from the dim glow of the nightlight, she can't tell if her mom is breathing, so she tiptoes into the room, peers down on her. She seems at peace, but there's a vulnerability to her mom that Mikayla's never seen before. Her mom has never been fragile or weak. Not even when Mikayla's dad died. She can't remember her mom crying. But . . . *maybe* when she was a little girl?

As she watches the rise and fall of her mom's chest, snippets of Mikayla's childhood come back to her.

Her mom had wanted a big family. After four miscarriages, Mikayla became her mom's miracle at age thirty-nine. Sometimes Mikayla thought that all the people her parents welcomed at the inn became extended family. Growing up without grandparents, aunts, uncles, and cousins, her parents surrounded themselves with strangers who were always made to feel at home. Her parents doted on them, listened to them, and most of all, fed them. God forbid anyone should ever be hungry.

It makes sense now.

Her parents rarely slept, but when they did, the TV was always on. Now Mikayla wonders if the screams or crying she heard in the middle of the night came from her mom and not some actress on the screen as they'd said? Were the nightmares brought on by memories of Gross-Rosen concentration camp?

Mikayla has so many questions.

When she was a child, she attended catechism. Her mom rarely missed Sunday Mass, but her dad *never* went to church, using the responsibilities at the inn as his excuse not to go. He always said that his contribution was making toys for Santa to bring to children in hospitals and shelters. Every year they went all out, decorating and celebrating Christmas and Easter at the inn.

Through the years, none of it made her feel particularly religious.

Maybe because her parents didn't talk about God or Jesus? But they did talk about kindness. If anything, they placed their faith in kindness. She wonders about the *real* Waclaw, the one who gave her dad his identification, the cross, and the Bible. What happened to him?

Now Mikayla understands her parents better. When she was a child, there were moments when her father went out of his way to help guests, from making bag lunches for their picnics, to buying their favorite snacks and putting them in their rooms, to picking up items at a pharmacy. Mikayla felt that some guests took advantage of him, and it enraged her. But her father insisted that a small kindness could transform a person's life, even save it. If only she had understood then.

Mikayla's gaze drops to her mom's exposed arm. Her gnarly finger rests on her stomach, and Mikayla wants to reach out and hold her hand, but she doesn't dare in fear of waking her. Did her father ever hold her mom's hand? She can't remember. They weren't ones to show affection, at least not that way.

More memories flood back. The time Mikayla left for school without letting Mom know. Hearing her frantically call for Mikayla as she ran after her, barefoot in the snow. She grabbed Mikayla, shook her, pulled her into her, screaming, "Don't ever, ever, *ever* leave the house without saying goodbye!"

She always needed to know where Mikayla was, what she was doing, whom she was with, and when she would return. If Mikayla came home a minute late, there was hell to pay. Mikayla learned. If a movie ended at nine, she said nine-thirty. She padded time and arrived home early. Mom always waited up for her, staying busy by knitting, sewing, polishing, baking, or cleaning.

"Hi Ma. I'm back," she'd say. Her mom would nod. Mikayla would say goodnight, and only then would her mom go to sleep, though she never slept for long. Mikayla would wake to her mom covered in flour and the smells of freshly baking breads and breakfast treats.

Her mom's quirks and habits were Mikayla's normal.

Mikayla could never have imagined, not in her wildest dreams, that her mom had spent some of her childhood in a concentration camp. It explains so much, yet she can't help but feel that her mom is a stranger. And just as she thinks it, her mom stirs.

"Mikayla?"

"Yeah, it's me."

"What are you doing here? Is everything all right?"

"I didn't mean to wake you."

"What's the matter, darling? Sit. Talk to me."

Several long beats pass before Mikayla is able to speak. "I know you said you're not ready for questions, but . . . I don't understand." She meets her mom's gaze. "Why did you keep this from me for so long? Why didn't Pa—" She chokes. "W-we're Jewish?"

"Oh, Mikayla. I thought it would be better if we blended in. I am not ashamed of being Jewish. I was afraid. I live with the terror every day, Mikayla, especially in nightmares. And now, even here in beautiful Riviere, such *hate*! Decades and decades past World War Two, and evil is alive and well." She takes Mikayla's hand in hers. "I regret not honoring my family in Poland, but it's hard for me to regret wanting to protect you. You understand?"

"I think so. Did you name me for your youngest brother? The one who the Nazis hanged?"

Her mom stares up at the ceiling. Mikayla has to lean in close to hear her. "It's our Jewish tradition to name a child after someone who passed away. Michoel was special. He was the sweetest, happiest boy, gentle and kind and so smart, like you. He had thick brown curls, like you, and hazel eyes that sparkled with mischief. He and your pa used to play pranks on one another." Her lips curve into the tiniest of smiles as a tear rolls down her cheek. "Michoel was your pa's dearest friend. They were two peas in a pod."

There is so much more Mikayla wants to know, but even this has caused her mom too much pain. She leans down, kisses her cheek, and whispers, "I love you, Ma."

CHAPTER 56

CADE

I planned to stay home today to spend some time with Nana, but if that wasn't reason enough to skip school and have a long weekend, Officer Shawn Sullivan gave me one. Knowing we're early risers, he called at six a.m. and spoke with Mom. Still no leads, but he told her that members of the Riviere Police Department as well as several Riviere storeowners will gather at nine a.m. to remove the hateful graffiti from our inn. Officer Sullivan is arranging everything.

It's only 6:20, but I call Logan.

"Hi. What's going on?" she asks, sounding wide-awake.

"I'm staying home." I fill her in on Mom's conversation with Shawn. "After everything that's happened and all the negative publicity, we need to show the good side of our community."

"I'll be there," Logan says.

Of course, I knew she would. Still . . . "And ruin your perfect high school attendance record?"

"You think that matters?"

"Just a little," I say honestly.

"More proof you know me so well. But I wouldn't miss this for the world. We'll spend the day together."

"Come over as soon as you can. I'm working on something."

"Oh yeah? Can I have a preview?"

"Nope. I'll show you when you get here."

* * *

Through Nana's window, we see that the inn's parking lot is full—not full, *packed*! This isn't a few people, it's a rally!

"Nana, come outside," I plead. "All these people are here to support us."

"I don't like crowds and I don't like a fuss," she says.

"They'll be asking for you."

"Then they can come into the inn for coffee, tea, and cake after. Now go."

"All right. I'm going, but if you change your mind—"

"I won't."

With a sigh, I head outside and join Logan in handing out the posters I designed and had printed on heavy cardstock. At Logan's insistence, I made one hundred, thinking it would be too much. I was so wrong. Logan's dad will be bringing two hundred more.

People gather underneath our apartment entrance and fan out across the parking lot. Many stand together in small groups, talking and drinking coffee in to-go cups that Dad and Mom provided. Some point at the vandalism. To its right, a wooden ladder leans against the stone wall.

It's a warm day for late February—forty-six degrees—and I unzip my coat and scan the crowd for Logan. I finally spot her with Mom, standing off to the side surrounded by several women I recognize from the Junior Women's League. When Logan spies me, she waves.

"No luck getting Nana to come outside?" Mom asks when I reach her side.

"Nope."

"I'm not surprised," Dad says, joining us with Professor March. "She hates crowds."

"Exactly what she said."

Dad sets a hand on my shoulder. "Cade, we want you to speak to the crowd."

"What? No. I can't."

Mom cuts in. "You and Logan," she says, like it's an opportunity we can't refuse.

"But I hate giving speeches," I say.

"It would mean a lot to everyone if you did it," Dad says.

Resigned, I ask, "What should we say?"

"Whatever's in your heart," he answers.

Professor March gives Dad some more posters and says, "We're going to finish passing these out. You did a great job with these, Cade. I have no doubt after today we'll see these in the windows of every business and many Riviere homes. It's exactly what our community needs."

Mom leads Logan and me through the crowd, stopping to greet people and to give and receive hugs. Logan and I are stopped, too. Over and over people tell us that we're brave, that they are proud of us. I can't help but smile and thank them for their support.

When we get to the front, I glance around. Nerves dance in my stomach.

Officer Sullivan, wearing his uniform, steps onto the ladder. As he climbs a few rungs, Dad grips the side, holds it steady. Officer Sullivan raises his palm and the crowd quickly grows silent.

"Hello, everyone. Thank you so much for coming on such short notice. I know I'm overwhelmed, so I can only imagine how the Crawfords must be feeling right now." He smiles warmly at Mom, then lifts his gaze. "This is *our* community. We're here to show unity, to let the Crawford family know they're valued members of Riviere. Their presence and generosity make us better. We are privileged to speak out against hate and intolerance."

Shawn climbs down the ladder, nods to Logan and me.

There's not much room, but we're able to balance on the same rung, cling to the ladder, and mostly face the crowd.

With my free hand, I give a small wave. "Hi. I'm Cade Crawford."

"And I'm Logan March."

We get a few chuckles from the crowd. Of course they know who we are. I spot Officer Tisdale and, to my big surprise, Miss Wather. She waves to us.

Taking Dad's advice to speak from the heart, I begin. "On behalf of my family, thank you for the overwhelming support." I pause, look over at the swastika, then refocus on the people gathered around us. "Today, your presence is a positive statement about who we are as a community. We're saying that bigotry, racism, and antisemitism, and everything else this symbol of hate represents, are not welcome here."

The crowd breaks into applause.

"History teaches us that being silent and not speaking against injustice allows injustice to thrive. Let's show the world who we are. Please hold up your signs!"

Three hundred people hold up HUMANKIND WELCOME HERE! Many others are empty-handed. We needed more signs.

"Humankind welcome here!" The crowd chants it over and over again, louder and louder. I spot Bethany Beshett with her phone out. Standing next to her, there's a woman taking pictures with a professional-looking camera.

When the chanting dies down to a murmur, I lift my chin, motioning for Logan to continue. She shifts her grip and pivots, facing more people. "As you may have heard, the New York education commissioner announced that the assignment will never be given again. We're relieved and grateful that there will be no debate. But it's not enough." She points to the vandalism. "We're getting rid of this symbol of hate today, but we need to continue to work hard to ensure it never happens again. Today is only one day. Every day we need to be vigilant against all forms of hate. We hope you'll join us and display these signs in the windows of your homes and businesses."

Logan takes the HUMANKIND WELCOME HERE! sign, holds it high. A chant starts up again. Logan ends with, "Thank you for adding your voices to ours. Thank you for your support."

Her dad nods, beams at her, then me.

As we step down to more applause, Officer Sullivan takes our place. "We have a special guest with us today. Representing our district, State Senator Laura Luddy!" She gives a heartfelt statement on unity and community, then asks George Zentner, owner of Armageddon, the tattoo parlor that's within a short walking distance from here, to come forward. Nana's always had a soft spot for George. She calls him up and has him stop over whenever she makes his favorite blueberry crumb pie. George announces that funds are being collected to help us through this difficult time and gives the details on how people can contribute. Mom dabs at her damp eyes.

George holds a bucket and a scrub brush in his rubber-glove-covered hands. He dips the brush into the bucket and runs it over the spray paint. Almost immediately the paint begins to drip like bloody tears. Officer Sullivan brings over our garden hose. During the winter, we have it stored in the basement, but Dad must have hooked it up. People in front take a few steps back. George sprays the stone, washing away the paint.

A cheer goes up.

Some of the crowd begins to disperse, but many surround Mom, Dad, Logan, and me, sharing their opinions on the assignment. Several people tell us that they wrote Principal McNeil to express their disapproval. I thank each and every one. Standing among supporters with Logan is one of the most incredible feelings I've ever experienced.

From the corner of my eye, I notice Logan's dad trying to get her attention. I nudge her and point to her dad. He holds up his keys, motions that he has to leave, and gives us a thumbs-up. I answer with one of my own.

Miss Wather comes over to us. "You did an amazing job speaking," she says, clutching one of our HUMANKIND WELCOME HERE! signs. Before we can thank her, she adds, "You mentioned the commissioner's announcement, but as far as I know the debate is still scheduled. In the future, the assignment will never be given again. Mr. Bartley is still holding the debate on Monday."

CHAPTER 57

MASON

Fury radiates off Coach Hayes as he stands next to Principal McNeil in the team's locker room. Mason plasters a puzzled expression on his face, hoping he looks innocent among his teammates. With a clenched jaw, Reg stands near Mason's dad, glaring at everyone.

"Late last night, I received an anonymous email with an audio recording of one of our players spouting racial, anti-gay, and antisemitic slurs. I take this very seriously. This is a grave of-fense, one that would require expulsion under our school's Hate Speech and Anti-Bullying Policy."

Protests sweep through the locker room. Several teammates stay silent as they shoot glances at Reg, Jesse, and Spencer. Jesse and Spencer stand in the back. Both look nervous.

Principal McNeil calls out, "Quiet down!" He waits. "Thank you. Now, after speaking with Coach Hayes and the player al-legedly using such filth, I have determined that this anonymous audio is fake, a manipulation of technology by someone determined to destroy one of our top players in order for us to lose at regionals tomorrow afternoon."

Many players nod and vocalize their agreement.

Mason swallows hard, forces his eyes to remain steady on Principal McNeil until his father's gaze burns so hot that Mason can't ignore it. He meets it measure for measure. *He knows I sent the audio,* Mason thinks, and when his father flexes his fists, Mason also knows his father not only wants to use them on him but *will* use them on him. Refusing to be intimidated, Mason folds his arms over his chest.

Principal McNeil adds, "Obviously, I am concerned. I ask each and every one of you to be careful. You represent the integrity and respect of Riviere High School, and I expect you will uphold our high standards as outlined in the Athletic Code of Conduct you signed. Unless the person who sent this audio comes forward, I'm putting this completely behind us. Now go out there and win big for Riviere!"

CHAPTER 58

LOGAN

It's Saturday morning. Cade and I stand outside the Bartleys' Victorian home. We're here for one reason: to speak with Mr. Bartley and get Monday's debate canceled. Somehow—maybe it was wishful thinking—I assumed that the commissioner's announcement also applied to our class's debate. Miss Wather made it clear that I was wrong.

"Ready?" I ask Cade.

He nods.

A light dusting of snow covers the wraparound porch steps and railing. Our footprints are the only ones leading to their front door. On its left, there's a small glass coffee table with an empty flowerpot on top. On the right, two wicker chairs sit under a window. And in that window is Cade's sign! HUMANKIND WELCOME HERE!

How did the Bartleys get one?

"Cade, you see this?" I ask. He stares at the sign, his expression neutral. Right after the rally, the signs started popping up in storefronts and homes around Riviere. My Instagram post with

Cade holding the sign, and the picture of the crowd with the signs in Bethany Beshett's follow-up article, has led to hundreds of requests for copies. With everything that's been going on, we haven't had time to respond.

Cade whispers, "Maybe we should wait until Daniel and Heather can join us tomorrow?"

"With the debate less than two days away, I don't think we should risk it." I tuck the folder with the information we collected under my arm.

Cade grips the banister, then says, "You're right. We need to do this. For Nana."

"For Nana," I repeat. I peer through the beveled glass door into a small entryway closed off by a second door of solid wood. In the left corner, there's an ornate wrought-iron coatrack that looks more for show than to hang wet winter gear.

I lift my fist to knock, then lower it. Woodpeckers have invaded my gut and I have to breathe through the pain. I glance over at Cade.

He leans in and rings the doorbell.

A curtain flutters behind the window with the wicker chairs. A woman calls out, "I got it."

Mrs. Bartley opens the inner door, then closes it behind her as she steps into the entryway. Her frown deepens. It seems to take her forever to unlock the next door.

"Yes?" Her tone is sharp, temporarily paralyzing my ability to speak.

Cade shoves his hands into his pockets. His friendly customer smile and his friendly customer voice come out so smoothly, I'm in awe. "Hi, Mrs. Bartley. We were wondering, is Mr. Bartley available?"

She hesitates, then calls, "Joe? You have visitors." She motions for us to step inside. "Wait here."

She opens the interior door, then shuts it behind her. I track the *tap, tap, tap* of Mrs. Bartley's shoes against the wood floors. A sports broadcast pouring out of some room in the distance clicks off.

"Are you sure?" Mrs. Bartley says.

"I'm not sure of anything, but I want to hear them out."

Mrs. Bartley says something else, but I can't make it out.

"They're my students, Mary. You're here. I'm not worried. I need a minute, then I'll bring them in."

Cade's hand brushes against mine at my side, and stays.

Footsteps, this time heavier, have us both turning to the door. It swings wide open.

"Logan. Cade. Come on in. Feel free to hang up your jackets." Mr. Bartley motions to the coatrack in the foyer, but we leave them on. He glances at the folder under my arm. "We can talk in the dining room."

As Mr. Bartley leads us through a small parlor and an arched doorway, I take in the antiques. Framed old posters for presidential races sit on the fireplace mantel, a worn oriental rug covers most of the floor, and chairs and a couch look like they've been in this house since the late 1800s.

The dining room has a floor-to-ceiling built-in china cabinet and a magnificent wood table with clawfoot legs. Mr. Bartley sits at the head. Cade and I flank his sides. Mr. Bartley laces his fingers together and rests his forearms on the table.

He doesn't say anything, but his expression holds the question *Why are you here?*

Cade gives me an almost unperceivable nod.

Shifting in my seat, I focus on Mr. Bartley. "These are all the hateful and antisemitic acts we're aware of that have taken place as a direct result of this assignment."

I slide the folder over to Mr. Bartley. He flips it open.

I tap the first line. "It starts from the beginning when our classmates gave the Nazi salute. This is the latest incident." I slide my finger to the photo of the hateful spray-painted message on Cade's family's inn. "With the online attacks, they're extensive.

"And yes, Mr. Bartley, we've read some of the terrible things people have said about you online and we're sorry you've had to endure that." I dig my fingernails into my palm to keep the tears at bay. "We also know many have come to your defense."

"As they have for you," he says.

Mrs. Bartley comes into the room with bottles of water, sets them on the table, and pulls up a chair next to her husband. Mr. Bartley reaches for her hand. He says, "We, too, have been deeply distressed by the hateful actions you've endured.

"I realize I'm the one who should be apologizing to you. It's not the other way around. I'm sorry for the way I treated you in class. It was unfair and unprofessional. This is not your fault and I accept full responsibility. I'm the teacher. You're the students. And I *am* sorry. I should have put an end to the assignment immediately. It's not enough, though. I give you my word; I will resolve this on Monday."

Cade's surprise and relief mirror mine. He says, "So, does this mean you're canceling the debate?"

CHAPTER 59

JOE BARTLEY

Joe needs to explain, but this is new territory and it's way out in the stratosphere. He starts to speak, fumbling his way through, hoping he doesn't add to this disaster, trying instead to clean it up. "It was and still is my intention for my students to personally understand how easy it is to normalize hate, to misplace blame, to use marginalized people as scapegoats for anything and everything. The Final Solution allowed almost the entire civilized world to turn their backs on the Jewish people."

"And that's your justification?" Logan takes a water bottle, uncaps it, and drinks half of it down.

"I was wrong."

"You were wrong." Cade shakes his head in disgust like it's too little too late. Cade's right.

"I was wrong on many different levels and I'd like to explain." Mr. Bartley pauses because he needs a moment to collect his thoughts. Mary squeezes his knee, being his rock, as always.

"At first, I was offended that you questioned the validity of my assignment. That's on me. I was focused on my perspective and I was frustrated that you didn't understand. Then you went to Principal McNeil, infuriating me even more. I'm ashamed I wasn't open to any criticism."

Logan straightens in her seat. "You didn't say one word, and even worse, you ignored us."

"I was told by administration not to speak to you or to the press."

Cade and Logan have no response to that.

"My treatment toward you was way out of line. I did ignore you. I was defensive and angry. I had to work through it. I'm not proud of it, and I *am* sorry. It's not an excuse; it's fact."

Cade sits with his hands clasped together. He's angry, and Mr. Bartley deserves it. Logan's expression seems to give Joe more benefit of the doubt.

"I've come to the realization that my biggest mistake was creating the assignment and believing I had valid reasons. Re-creating the Wannsee Conference was my way of not justifying the Nazis' actions, but my way of enlightening my students on a very personal level. In the history of world governments, the Wannsee Conference was a pivotal point of no return. There have been many other despicable moments, but the Final Solution . . ." His voice trails off. "I could argue that it was the coldest, most heartless, most brutal, most callous, most despicable debate in the history of humankind. My goal was to have my students come to that conclusion. I was absolutely clear that I didn't want anyone to sympathize with the Nazi perspective. Over and over again, I said their actions were abhorrent. That seemed obvious to me. But I was wrong."

Spencer Davis, Jesse Elton, and Reg Ashford come to mind.

"Now you realize some students used this assignment to justify their prejudice and hate?" Cade asks.

Joe rubs his temple. "Yes."

"I'm still struggling to understand how you came up with this assignment in the first place. Where did the idea come from?" Logan asks.

"I had been watching the movie *Conspiracy*. With the actors around the table discussing the Final Solution, I thought re-creating that event would be a powerful, creative, and interesting way to learn that history. I was fascinated by the Nazis' debate, how that one meeting changed history."

"But it was *never* a real debate," Logan says. "The sole purpose of the Wannsee Conference was to create a systematic way of annihilating the Jewish people."

"I made a mistake."

"Then cancel the debate," Cade says.

"Cancel the debate," Logan echoes. "It's not enough that the assignment will never be given again."

"I understand, but I'm asking you to trust me. I altered my lesson right after you first spoke with Principal McNeil. He approved the changes. And because of everything that's transpired since, I've made more alterations. When I spoke with the commissioner of education, he, too, was satisfied that this will bring a positive resolution. I know you two weren't going to attend the debate, but I'd like you to come to class. Give me a chance to make this right."

Once again, Cade and Logan share a look. Logan's expression gives Joe hope. It says he's earned her trust in the past and has a good chance to earn it back. Unfortunately, Cade appears skeptical.

"What are your concerns, Cade?"

"I get that you're going to try to fix this—"

Joe cuts him off. "I *will* fix this. I have a lesson planned for the debate, and it will put an end to this."

Cade's knee bounces. His eyes flicker to the folder. "Logan and I—" His composure cracks. His hands shake against the table. Guilt washes over Joe as he watches Cade struggle to bring his emotions in check. Mary, visibly shaken, opens a water bottle and slides it across the table to Cade. He picks it up, takes a sip, then another. After several deep breaths, he sets the bottle down. "Why should we trust you?"

"Because I care. Not only about what has transpired, but because I recognize how my actions have negatively impacted you, our school, and our community. At the very least, I want to have the opportunity to express this to the class. I promise, I will give my absolute best."

CHAPTER 60

CADE

The moment I reach the bottom of the Bartleys' porch steps, I bolt. I want to punch, smash *something,* anything to release the emotions I've felt since we sat at their dining room table.

Mr. Bartley wants our trust. He promised to do his best. But the debate is still on. I'd *promised* Nana I'd do everything I could to stop the debate.

It wasn't enough.

One block, then two. Logan catches up. I don't stop. I run and run and continue running along the tree-lined path through snow-covered Sunrise Park. I reach the center fountain and stop. I leap onto the wide marble lip, tilt my head back, and scream, *"Ahhhhhh!"*

Logan's right beside me, and just like the other night, she opens her arms wide.

This time, Logan's the one crying.

She says, "I want to be done with this! I want to be done with *him*! Mr. Bartley said he was concerned for us? How did he show it? By ignoring us? Humiliating us? Not once over the past week has he expressed any kind of compassion or sympathy for the personal attacks we've endured, at least not until I said it to him first! He used Principal McNeil as an excuse, saying he wasn't allowed to talk to us? What about decent human courtesy? It's inexcusable. I don't trust him. He doesn't deserve our trust! He wants us to come to class. What are we going to do?"

I take Logan's hand, brush the pad of my thumb over her knuckles. The question lingers in her conflicted eyes. I give her the only answer I have. "I wish I knew. Let's just wait and see how we feel about all of this on Monday. Last minute. That's when we'll decide."

CHAPTER 61

DANIEL

Appalled and disgusted by the debate, Daniel took action immediately. He did the research on the Nazis' Final Solution of the Jewish Question, wrote his paper expressing his disapproval and horror, and turned it in last Monday along with a personal note explaining why he could not, would not, attend the debate.

Dear Mr. Bartley,

As you will see in this report, I did extensive research on the Wannsee Conference to understand the Nazis' positions. I did not, however, do it from their points of view, but as myself—Daniel. Everything I learned about the Nuremberg Laws and Nazi Germany's political ideas and military was based on false science, a quest for power, and oppression and discrimination. The Nazi mentality of hate is not something I can relate to nor do I ever want to.

How was it that a society was brainwashed to believe such lies? Where is human decency?

This assignment specifically targeted the Jewish people. But under Hitler's Germany, people with disabilities were murdered, homosexual men were murdered, people of color were murdered, the Roma were murdered, and so many more. If I had lived in Germany under Hitler, I would have been arrested. I would have been put in a concentration camp, humiliated and forced to wear a pink inverted triangle, experimented on, tortured and tormented, murdered. My uncle, who became a quadriplegic after a horrible car accident, would have been euthanized under Hitler's leadership. He would have been perceived not as a person, but as a thing adding no value to society.

You've opened my eyes, Mr. Bartley. I've had nightmares from the gruesome descriptions of the torture, bolted awake because I saw myself in a concentration camp wearing that pink inverted triangle.

This knowledge, however, has also fortified me.

People are not born to hate, they're taught to hate, and I won't be a part of that. I cannot, I will not, I choose not to argue in favor of hurting or murdering the Jewish people. Therefore, I will not attend or participate in the debate. Whatever you need from me, including a note from my parents to excuse my absence, I will make sure you receive it.

Daniel

Daniel sat on the sidelines and watched as Cade and Logan fought to get the debate canceled. Now, according to Logan, Mr. Bartley has asked them to trust him and attend tomorrow's class? No. There is no way Daniel will ever listen to that debate.

CHAPTER 62

MASON

Monday, 7:08 a.m.

Mason sits across from Principal McNeil, waiting for him to respond. His cell phone rests on Principal McNeil's desk. He itches to pick it up and tuck it back into his pocket. Mason has already played the audio recording of Reg's rant three times and sworn that it's authentic.

Folding his hands over his stomach, Principal McNeil leans back in his chair, sighs deeply. "Why now?" he asks. "Why come forward when your team is going to play in the state semifinals next week?"

There's so much more to that question and Mason knows it. Reg had his best game in regionals—two assists and three goals. The Riviere Rockets won because of Reg. Even though Mason has thought of little else since the team meeting this past Friday, he struggles. He's walked the tightrope for so long, trying to balance between living up to his father's expectations and his own moral code.

Mason glances out Principal McNeil's window. He's fully exposed.

"Reg was the one who vandalized the lockers," Mason finally says. "And though I could have withheld this information until after the state championship tournament, I realized hockey can't outweigh integrity. Reg has done and said despicable things." Mason sits up a little straighter. "You said the recording was fake. I sent it anonymously because I was afraid. I'm still afraid of the consequences, but I'm willing to live with them."

"Coach Hayes will not be pleased."

Mason gives Principal McNeil a firm, succinct nod. His chest feels tight. "If you want to tell my dad your source, that's up to you. I've given you the proof. Now you get to decide what to do about it. You want to wait until after the tournament, that's up to you, too. I've done what I needed to and I can live with my conscience."

CHAPTER 63

CADE

I push open the door of the boys' locker room, step into the hallway, and find Logan waiting to walk with me to History of World Governments. Her face lights up, sunshine in a forest of gloom. We decided to give Mr. Bartley a chance and attend class today. Does he deserve our trust? We'll find out.

"Hi." The smile slips from her face. "Blair sent us a text wishing us luck." Logan rubs the silver bracelet her cousin gave her for her last birthday like it's a good-luck charm.

"We're going to need it," I mutter. I glance around. Practically every wall has signs congratulating the Riviere Rockets hockey team on winning regionals and cheering them on for the state tournament.

Forget hockey. All I can think about is the disappointment on Nana's face when I told her the debate was still on. Logan's voice is quiet. "We don't have to go to this."

I stop, take her wrist, and move to the side of the hallway. I drop her hand and return mine to the safety of my pockets. Right now, I'm really tempted to smash the trophy case. Unfortunately, that won't stop the debate. "I don't want to do this, but I'm going to. Not for you, but for me and for us. We're finishing this. But I reserve the right to walk out at any time."

"You walk. I walk. And vice versa." Her fierce, steady gaze is the reassurance I only now realize I've needed.

"Okay." I give her a grim smile and offer my hand. She takes it. "Let's do this."

Dread slows me down. Logan pulls me forward. When we finally reach the top of the stairs and turn toward Mr. Bartley's classroom, the hallway is bottlenecked with students. I push up on my toes and get a glimpse of signs being raised above our heads. Someone calls out, "Stop the debate!"

Logan's fingers slip from mine, and we weave our way until we reach the center. Right in the middle of it all are Daniel, Mason, Heather, and three other students not in our class. They loop around in front of Mr. Bartley's closed door, chanting, "Stop the debate!" They hold up signs:

NAZIS NOT WELCOME HERE OR ANYWHERE!

NO JUSTIFICATION FOR GENOCIDE!

ADVOCATE FOR LOVE, NOT HATE!

HUMANKIND NOT HUMANHATE!

OUR SCHOOL SHOULD BE A SAFE ZONE NOT A HATE ZONE!

NO DEBATE!

When Daniel spots me, he steps away from the circle. His face is bright with excitement. "Hey Cade," he calls. "We have extra signs, if you want to join us." He points to a stack leaning up against lockers near Mr. Bartley's door. HUMANKIND WELCOME HERE! is on top.

"I'll join you." Kerrianne takes the "NO Debate!" sign out of Daniel's hand and holds it high. She moves in front of Mason, and even though it's a circle, she has this way about her that makes it look like she's leading everyone. She turns the chant from "Stop the debate!" to "No debate!"

Logan darts around Heather and comes over to us. In the short time since we got here, the crowd has doubled. Almost everyone has their phones out, snapping pictures or taking videos. An electric current runs along my skin.

Heather motions to Allie Fitzpatrick—the other girl Jesse had dubbed his Aryan sister—to join them, but she backs away. People shift around Allie like sand, then fill the space as if she'd never been there. Heather looks at me and smiles, and from her expression I'm fairly certain she expects us to join in.

"You organized this?" Logan asks Daniel.

"Yeah. Got everyone together over lunch."

"Why didn't you tell us?"

"I did. I texted you both. You didn't respond."

No surprise, since I left my phone in my locker. But Logan? Blair texted her during lunch and we video-chatted with her. Logan takes her phone out of her pocket. "That's weird," she says, flashing it at me. There's a text from Daniel. It came through at 11:21 a.m.

"Grab a sign. We're going to stop this debate."

Logan opens her mouth to respond, but a burst of laughter cuts her off.

Jesse Elton mocks Mason's movements, high-stepping like a soldier marching in a parade. He pretends to hold a sign in one hand. He lifts the other to his temple and salutes the crowd.

Spencer pairs with Kerrianne and mimics Jesse's moves. But what shocks me the most is Spencer's belt buckle. It's a Confederate flag. Way to own your hate.

Daniel grabs a sign, rejoins the protest, and shouts, "No debate! No debate!"

Spencer starts chanting, "Save the debate! Save the debate!" Like an orchestra conductor, he motions to the crowd, encouraging others to join him. Several people do, like this is some joke.

"Stop!" I shout, but the chanting smothers my voice. This has to end now. I try again, moving between Spencer and Kerrianne as they battle from opposite sides.

Where the hell is Mr. Bartley?

Someone pushes me from behind, and I have a split second to raise my arms as I fall into a locker. Heather pitches forward. Her sign drops from her hands, barely missing Daniel's head as it crashes to the floor. She grabs my shirt. Her nails dig into my shoulders, and I slam into the locker again with her on top of me.

More and more people pick sides, and it's nearly impossible for me to tell who's yelling "Save the debate!" or "No debate!"

I scan the chaos and spot Mrs. Ingram, waving her arm and pointing her index finger like she's ordering students to leave. I look for Logan's purple Converse. And just as I spot her next to Kerrianne, arms spread wide, Jesse pins Mason against Mr. Bartley's closed door. They're both grasping the sign handle, pushing one another. Jesse yells at Mason, something about ruining their team. I don't think. I don't wait. I jump in, straight-arm both of them, and shout at the top of my lungs, "STOOOOOOP!"

CHAPTER 64

LOGAN

Pandemonium. The word flashes in my head as I spread my arms wide, trying to protect Kerrianne after Spencer shoves her. "You bitch," he says, to her, to me, to both of us. I brace myself; prepare to take him down with a swift knee to his family jewels, a defensive move that Blair and I learned from a YouTube video. Spencer raises his hands. His nostrils flair like a bull's, but he backs off.

I turn to Kerrianne. "Are you all right?" Those are the most words I've spoken to her since she cornered me in the bathroom at the beginning of the school year, staking her claim on Mason.

"Yeah, thanks." At least that's what I think she says. It's growing louder by the second and there's more pushing and shoving. Suddenly, a piercing voice overpowers all others. "STOOOOOOP!"

Cade.

And to my surprise, people quiet down like Cade hit a mute button.

But what's even more surprising is what happens next.

Heather grabs my hand, raises it up. She begins to sing "Hallelujah," a song she sang with the RHS choir during the holiday concert that Cade and I attended. I take Daniel's hand and lift it high, and suddenly, in a chain reaction, people join in.

Only a minute ago, the hallway reverberated with shouts—and now it reverberates with song. More and more people clasp hands, add their voices. Chills shoot down my spine as I join in on the one-word chorus. For a brief moment, my eyes connect with Heather's. A soft smile curves on her lips as she pours her soul into the lyrics. I'm in awe of her and the power of music.

When we finish, Heather breaks the silence by calling out, "Hey, everyone, that song was written by Leonard Cohen, and in case you didn't know it, he was Jewish!"

Mr. Bartley makes his way through the crowd, pushing an elderly man in a wheelchair. The man wears a baseball cap that says "World War II Vet." It's decorated with pins. Mr. Bartley opens his classroom door and ushers everyone in.

I move to the side and wait for Cade.

Now that the chaos has calmed down, it occurs to me that Mr. Bartley has let us down again. Why wasn't he here waiting for us? He knew how contentious things have been, and with the debate scheduled today, wouldn't it have been logical for him to greet students and usher us into his classroom? Couldn't he have had someone else, like Miss Wather or a student, escort the veteran? This entire scene never would have happened if he had been here. Logic and common sense is exactly what's been missing from this entire assignment.

He betrayed us, eroded my respect for him day after day, and even though I'm willing to hear him out, all the excuses, all the platitudes, and all the apologies in the world won't change this fact: Although the assignment will soon be a part of my past and eventually I hope to forgive Mr. Bartley, nothing, *nothing* will ever be the same. I will never forget this. I will never, ever be able to step into his classroom or any classroom without being on guard. It's a bitter pill, and Mr. Bartley shoved it down my throat.

Cade comes over. We take two steps into the classroom when Cade freezes. I follow his gaze. There's a Nazi flag on the Smart Board. I look over at Cade. A small vein bulges along his neck. I wave my pointer finger between us and mouth, *You walk. I walk. I walk. You walk.*

He nods, his expression grim.

Our desks are arranged in a circle facing each other. Cade and I take the two closest to the door. Toward the front of the room, there's a one-chair gap, and that's where Mr. Bartley locks the wheelchair in place.

I look closely at Mr. Bartley. It's hard for me to believe that I used to hang on every one of this man's words.

Mason and Jesse huddle together a few feet away from Cade and me, their voices low, angry. Mason looks ready to explode, but then Mr. Bartley steps in. "Mason, Jesse. Take a seat. I want the two of you sitting next to each other."

"Why?" Jesse asks, furious.

Mr. Bartley holds up his hands, palms an inch from each other. "Because I'm this close to sending both of you to Principal

McNeil's office and having you expelled for fighting. Prove to me you can behave like gentlemen and I'll give you a stay of execution."

Mason glances over at me and takes a seat. We haven't said a word to each other since the day he helped me remove the hateful Post-it notes. I need to talk with him. Even though I apologized, it doesn't seem like enough. Rumor has it that he broke up with Kerrianne, but since she sits next to him, I'm not sure that's true. Jesse grudgingly fills the chair on Mason's other side, but scoots as far over as he possibly can.

The veteran has a penetrating gaze. He seems to be sizing up our class. He probably was a drill sergeant, and I get the sense that he's not impressed. I'm not impressed, either. My faith in Mr. Bartley slips to below zero. From the way Cade's angled toward the door, I'm pretty sure he's set to bolt and that the only thing keeping him chained to his seat is me.

Notably, Daniel is absent. I'm not sure where he disappeared to after the protest.

There are two empty desks, and—no surprise—they are on either side of Spencer. One should have been for Reg, but rumor has it he's been suspended or expelled. No one knows why or if they do, they're not talking.

Mr. Bartley stands to the right of Spencer, resting his hands on the back of that empty chair. He looks at each of us, exuding authority like an army commander. Earlier, I thought he was furious. But that doesn't come close to the controlled anger he radiates now.

When the silence is nearly unbearable, Mr. Bartley says, "I

made a grave error in judgment. I'm canceling the Wannsee Conference debate. Please get out your papers and pass them to me."

I close my eyes for a brief moment. After all this time, he finally, finally gets what we've been saying all along. It's not a victory. It's sad and pathetically long overdue.

CHAPTER 65

CADE

I wish I could pick up the phone and call Nana to tell her the debate is canceled. This morning, before I left for school, she said, "It's not too late. It could still happen." Even though the protest was complete mayhem, at least it was the answer.

Under our desks, I reach for Logan's hand and lace our fingers together. She slides her desk closer, pressing her leg against mine. Our contact helps ease the mixed emotions stirred up during the protest—the fights and the incredible performance of "Hallelujah." From shouting, my throat is raw, matching my emotions. The combination makes it hard to swallow.

Mr. Bartley pushes one of the empty desks against the wall. It takes me a few seconds to realize that Daniel and Reg are missing. It never occurred to me to ask Daniel why he wasn't going to be in class today. As for Reg, I heard he was suspended. How is it that no one knows why?

Secrets.

My mind keeps wandering. I've spent the past few days pretty much thinking only about Nana and Grandpa's secrets and came to the conclusion that what they endured is not something I'll ever fully comprehend. No matter how much I try to grasp their painful past, there's slim to no chance I'll ever know what it's like to starve, to be a slave, to be beaten, to watch the people I love murdered. As much as I struggle to figure out what it all means for me, to come to terms with our Jewish identity, I don't blame Nana. My entire life my grandparents showered me only with love. I don't fault Nana for trying to protect us, for doing what she felt she needed to do in order to feel safe. I've thought about Grandpa and wonder how much he suffered by keeping his Jewish identity a secret.

On Sunday, no one in my family went to church. Instead, Nana baked, and Dad, Mom, and I walked down to the inn's beach and talked. Dad told us that being Jewish doesn't change the fact that we're a family, that wherever this journey takes us, we'll do it together. Mom cried a little. A few minutes later, she asked me, "If we'd known my parents' history all along, would you have told us about the assignment right away?"

I picked up the largest rock I could palm and hurled it into Lake Ontario. I thought about what I said in Principal McNeil's office, the irony. *If there were Jewish students in our school, would you have us look them in the eye and deliver reasons to kill them?* "Yeah," I said, nodding. "I would have."

Mom reached for me, pulled me into her arms. She said, "You spoke out because it was the right thing to do. That fills us with so much pride, Cade." She shifted away, then added, "Dad and I talked about how much we admire your conviction and integrity.

If you want, you could leave here. Go anywhere. We know you love the inn, but it doesn't have to be your life. We want you to pursue your own dreams."

Leave here. Go anywhere.

The idea is both exciting and terrifying. Leave Riviere. My family. The inn. Its walls, its history, our family's legacy have always felt solid and safe. Even with financial struggles, we've survived. But this assignment, Nana, the spray-painted message of hate—they've taught me that safety is a facade, one that can fall in a second.

Do I want to stay in Riviere?

I don't have an answer.

Looking around Mr. Bartley's classroom, I see Mason inch his desk as close to Kerrianne without touching her. He stares straight ahead and so does Jesse. The largest gap between chairs is between those two.

Sliding into the empty seat next to Spencer, Mr. Bartley completes our circle. "I have some important things to say and I need all of you not only to listen, but to understand."

I brace myself. *This is it,* I think. *Do or die.* Mr. Bartley said he's going to fix this mess he made. I'm not at all confident he can. But hope is a strange partner. It keeps you holding on to a thread, even as you watch it unravel.

Mr. Bartley looks around to make sure he has everybody's attention. Sixteen pairs of eyes, including the World War II veteran's, are fixed on him.

"The Nazi debate at the Wannsee Conference was morally reprehensible. I now see that the assignment was misguided, insensitive, and grossly inappropriate. I accept full responsibility for what has transpired since I gave it to you. I take full responsibility for my failure as a teacher. I owe each of you an apology and I ask for your forgiveness."

Wow. Didn't expect that.

Mr. Bartley looks at Logan and me.

A murmur goes through the room.

I'm grateful he doesn't hold our gaze for long. It feels like he's asking too much. At this point, to say I forgive him would be a lie.

CHAPTER 66

LIEUTENANT PETER FRANKLIN

Lieutenant Peter Franklin is now ready to speak. He scrutinizes Mr. Bartley's class, and it pains him to see how the assignment has torn these youngsters apart. The girl with the blue hair impressed him with her powerful voice, so it gives him hope that he can make a difference. He motions to Mr. Bartley. "I'm going to need each student to have a piece of paper and a pen," he says.

Mr. Bartley says, "I'll take care of it."

He goes to his desk, picks up a stack of printer paper, and asks a young man with a Confederate flag on his belt buckle to hand each student a sheet. Peter's gaze locks on that belt buckle, then on the boy's face. Defiance is written all over it, but Peter isn't intimidated and he easily wins that round. A young woman passes out pens.

When both students take their seats, Mr. Bartley says, "Raise your hand if you know of anyone who's served in the US military."

Every hand but two goes up. This, the lieutenant thinks, is a good sign. He's found that when he speaks at schools where students know military personnel, there's a deeper level of understanding about what it means to serve the country.

Motioning to the Nazi flag, Mr. Bartley says, "This is a symbol of hate and it represents the most heinous crimes against humanity." He advances to the next screen. The photo of Peter in his army uniform fills half the screen. On the other, he's wearing shabby pants that hang on him along with a threadbare long-sleeved shirt. It still gives Peter a start.

"It is a great honor for us to have with us today a speaker from Voices of World War Two Vets and the Holocaust Survivors. Lieutenant Peter Franklin is a decorated World War Two veteran and was the leader of a secret sabotage initiative behind enemy lines. You're looking at an American hero."

The word "hero" makes Peter flinch.

Gingerly, Lieutenant Franklin gets to his feet and walks over to the girl sitting in the seat next to Mr. Bartley. He's going to address the boy with the Confederate flag belt buckle last. He asks the girl her name, shakes her hand, and moves on to the next. When he gets to the girl with the blue hair, he says, "That song is one of my favorites. I hope you'll record it someday. I've never heard a better rendition."

She blushes and says thank you.

From the photographs in the newspapers, he recognizes Cade and Logan. Unlike the other students, they stand and introduce themselves. "I'm honored to meet you," Lieutenant Franklin says. His grip is gentle but firm. His voice is quietly respectful. "I admire your bravery and am proud of you both for not backing down. Thank you for coming today." Humbled, Cade and Logan murmur, "Thank you."

Jesse salutes the lieutenant. The lieutenant does not salute back. He comments on Jesse's varsity hockey jersey, asks him about his future plans, encourages him to consider the military. "It's a good place to channel your energy, young man," he says, eyeing Jesse as if he knows his inner secrets.

When Mason rises to his feet, he introduces himself and offers his hand. The lieutenant's grip is strong, decisive. The wrinkles around the lieutenant's eyes crinkle. Mason is surprised when he says, "I'm impressed. Thank you."

Stammering, Mason answers, "I don't understand, sir."

The lieutenant leans in, whispers, "Courage comes in many forms, and so does speaking up for what is right."

Lieutenant Franklin releases Mason's hand and exchanges greetings with students around the circle. At last, he stands in front of the boy with the belt buckle.

The boy doesn't get up, but sticks his hand out to greet the lieutenant. Calmly and quietly so only the boy can hear, the lieutenant says, "Stand up, young man."

He does.

"Name?"

"Spencer, sir."

The lieutenant nods, looks down at the buckle, then directly into Spencer's eyes. "Spencer." He offers Spencer his hand, then shakes it firmly, not once dropping his gaze, holding it like he's seeing the depths of Spencer's soul. At that moment, it's as if no one else in the room exists but them. Finally, the lieutenant nods again, but this time like they have some kind of understanding. Spencer sits and rests his clasped hands on his lap, covering his Confederate flag belt buckle.

Lieutenant Franklin returns to his seat.

"I am honored to be here to share my story," he begins. "In 1945, I was a twenty-four-year-old who'd already served our country for five years. I spoke German, Italian, and Russian fluently. I had a very special job working with the OSS, the Office of Strategic Services, which is similar to today's CIA. My job involved espionage, coordinating clandestine operations and bringing in military supplies behind enemy lines to assist Austrian partisans who despised the Nazis. My spy name was Hans Mueller." He taps his shoulder. "A good strong German name.

"Because of circumstances beyond my control, the Gestapo became highly suspicious of me. Without a doubt, someone discovered my cover. I was in grave danger. I didn't run away from that. For months I avoided capture, but during a botched parachute mission into Austria, the Gestapo was waiting."

He pushes up a sleeve. "I have these scars and many more to show for it." His arms have white lines like hashtags from his wrist to his elbow.

"I could tell you about my experiences with the interrogation, the brutal beatings in the Vienna prison, but I want to focus on what took place after the Gestapo transferred me to one of their worst extermination camps in Germany: Mauthausen."

He pauses, looks around the room, making eye contact with every student.

"It's a miracle I lived, and what I and others in the slave labor camp endured is still vivid in my mind." He taps his temple. "One of the first things I noticed was what you youngsters call zombies. They were people so thin I couldn't comprehend how they were still standing. It terrified me.

"We were pushed, slapped, and beaten almost around the clock. We were told that if we attempted to escape, we would be shot dead on sight. If we missed roll call, we would be found and shot. If we sat down, we would be shot. The list of infractions went on and on. To show they meant it, an SS officer walked over to a British POW and, for no reason at all, shot him in the head.

"They took all my clothes, my boots. I was naked as the day I was born. They shaved my head. This is what they did to all new prisoners. Instead of going to the gas chambers as many did after selection, the rest of us were forced to stand under a cold shower, then forced to stand barefoot in the cold for several hours. The rags they gave me to wear had a number and an inverted red triangle, the symbol used for political prisoners. We were then marched to our barracks. Three of us shared a wooden plank bunk. The other two were prisoners of war, airmen from France and Britain. We had to sleep together curled on our sides in order to fit. Take a moment to think about your beds. Comfortable, I hope.

"Two days after I arrived, I had my first bite of food. It was watery soup with a tiny piece of potato skin." He holds up a hand, tucks his pointer finger into his thumb and narrows the gap until it's barely visible.

"The Nazis tried to strip us of our humanity and our identities, and in the weeks that followed, I found out how hard it was to keep them."

Lieutenant Franklin looks at Mr. Bartley, then shifts his gaze to Spencer.

"I was assigned to work on building a new crematorium with a small group of prisoners. There were so many corpses piled up that the SS officers were desperate to burn the evidence of their brutality and hate efficiently and quickly. We had to haul water, sand, and cement. We did everything we possibly could to slow down the process, moving at a snail's pace in order not to complete the crematorium. We knew that once it was done, they would murder more people. Everyone was beaten. I received blows from a club and a rifle butt was slammed into the side of my head. We were told that if we didn't finish the crematorium on time, we would be the first to be consumed by its flames. Inevitably, we finished by the deadline. The next day, three hundred twenty-seven men and forty women were gassed, then burned in the ovens I helped build."

He pauses again, struggling for composure. "My British bunkmate was shot in the head for trying to escape. My other bunkmate, the French airman, was caught trying to steal the sawdust mixture they called bread. The Nazis punished him along with some Polish and Russian prisoners of war by stripping them naked, dousing them with water, and forcing them to stand in the snow for forty-eight hours. They all froze to death. Dutch Jews were pushed off a hundred-foot cliff. Dogs tore others apart. I tell you this because it's important to understand how hate can be twisted to the point where men feel no shame for their actions." This time, Lieutenant Franklin looks at Jesse.

"One of my most difficult moments was when a prisoner I had become friendly with informed me that my name was on a list for execution. He worked in an office that kept the records, and he said I was to be gassed the next day. I didn't ask and I don't know how, but he said he could exchange my name for another. Not for a second did I consider allowing that. I couldn't be responsible for another person's death."

Mr. Bartley has his eyes closed and his brow is pinched.

"Then a miracle happened. The next day, May 6, 1945, a platoon of men from the Eleventh Armored Division of the US Third Army liberated us. To this day, I celebrate on May sixth like it's my birthday."

Lieutenant Franklin nods to Mr. Bartley. He picks up the clicker and all eyes turn to the Smart Board. Mr. Bartley says, "This is a short documentary of Mauthausen after liberation. It shows the results of hate, bigotry, antisemitism, and the apathy from a world that did next to nothing to stop this from happening until eleven million had been murdered. Six million were Jews from across Europe."

As the students watch the short film, Lieutenant Franklin notices that Cade is staring down at his upturned palms, flexing his fingers.

Other than a few sniffles and an occasional creaking chair, the room is silent.

When the film is done, he lets a minute pass. Then two. Then three.

Lieutenant Franklin breaks the silence. "My testimony given during the American Military Tribunal at Dachau helped convict over sixty SS officers. Many received a sentence of death by hanging. After the war, however, it's known that plenty of Nazis who committed heinous crimes against humanity walked away with no punishment. Because of that, Nazi hunters tracked down notorious murderers and helped get justice. One of their targets was Adolf Eichmann. You might recall that he participated in the Wannsee Conference and was a key player in the Final Solution. He was executed in Israel in 1962."

He pauses, takes a deep breath.

"I got through the hell of Mauthausen by living minute by minute. There were some days I prayed every waking second, begging God to give me the strength to survive. There were days I wanted to kill those Nazi bastards and free every prisoner. Holding on to hope wasn't easy. It slipped away like water through my fingers. But I was lucky. Some drops stuck and got me through.

"Mr. Bartley called me a hero, but I don't see it that way. Survival doesn't make me a hero. Doing the right, moral, responsible thing doesn't make me a hero. It makes me a decent human being."

He gets to his feet. "Each of you has a piece of paper and a pen. Write down your answers, please.

"If you could have the best, most unforgettable day with someone you love or someone important to you, who would it be and what would you do? Write it down."

He waits.

"Now imagine the worst, most terrible thing that could happen to the person you love. Write it down."

He waits.

"Now imagine that worst, most terrible thing happens to you."

He waits.

"Imagine that you have the power to stop it. You can prevent that worst, most terrible thing from happening to the person you love and to you."

He waits.

"Now imagine that you have *no* power to stop it. No matter what you do, what you say, or how hard you try, it happens."

He waits.

"This, my friends, is what happened to every victim of the Holocaust. This is what happens to every victim of hate."

CHAPTER 67

JOE BARTLEY

Last day of school:

Principal McNeil motions to Joe to take a seat across from his desk. Rocking back in his chair, Arthur says, "I'll get right to it, Joe. I'm sorry, but this is your last day teaching at RHS."

Joe chokes on the piece of candy that Miss Wather had given him. He coughs and coughs and struggles to get his breath. His eyes water, raining down like tears. Arthur takes a water bottle from his office mini-fridge, twists the cap open, and hands it to Joe.

"I'm fired? Why?"

"Come on, Joe. The assignment. All the negative publicity. That fight during the protest hit way over a quarter million views and comments, and even though the students were praised for their peaceful resolution, it never should have gotten out of hand in the first place."

"But I apologized. Lieutenant Franklin's presentation was highly impactful. You saw the students' evaluations. The assignment will never be given again. Isn't there anything we can do?"

"You were fortunate to finish out the year. The commissioner wanted me to fire you on the spot. But I advocated for you, did everything I could to save your job. You're a year shy of tenure, so there's nothing we can do. This assignment put us in a horrible situation. I'm still getting calls about it."

The office closes in on Joe and spots dance before his eyes. He picks up the water bottle and drains it dry. Fired. Terminated. His stomach lurches and he fights getting sick by closing his eyes, but it only makes the room spin faster.

Opening his eyes, he says, "I'm a good teacher."

"I know."

"But—"

"I'm sorry. The decision is final."

Joe loses his ability to speak. Thinking back, he'd expected to be fired after the protest went viral. One more black eye for the school, but things settled down. His apology leaked onto the internet, not his exact words because they weren't recorded, but close enough. Sure, people said it was too little, too late, but his students supported him. Arthur had supported him, or at least he thought so. A reporter had asked Cade and Logan if they wanted him fired. Logan had said, "This was a learning experience for all of us."

Realizing he's been lost in his thoughts for quite some time, Joe looks up. There's concern on Arthur's face, but Joe knows him well enough that arguing will be futile.

Reality hits its mark. Fired. How did this happen? It's still a shock to him. The light in the room shifts as everything Joe worked hard for unravels and floats away in a black void of nothingness. Who is he if he doesn't teach? He loves it, loves the kids.

Color leaches from Joe's face. His breath is short and shallow, and beads of sweat form on his forehead. Arthur takes out another water bottle and pushes it across his desk. He leans as far forward as he can, taps his fingers to get Joe's attention.

"Joe?" He doesn't respond. Arthur gets up, comes around his desk, and sits on the edge. He rests a hand on Joe's shoulder. "Do you want me to call Mary? She could come in, help you clean out your room?"

Joe slowly meets Arthur's gaze. "No. That's all right." He gets to his feet.

"You'll bounce back from this. I know you will." Arthur sticks his hand out.

For several heartbeats, Joe stares at Arthur's peace offering. Then he turns around and walks out.

* * *

At the urging of many of his loyal students, Mr. Bartley attends their graduation. For about five minutes, it feels amazing to have them flock around him, offer their support. He has a few awkward moments of meaningless small talk with his former colleagues. One even turns his back to him.

Keeping his head up, he takes a seat closest to a side exit.

Joe sits through the usual speeches. And then, in celebration of Miss Wather's retirement, the graduating class honors her with a video, chronicling her years at Riviere High School. There isn't one photo with Joe in it.

The choir surrounds her and sings "True Colors" by Cyndi Lauper. They escort Miss Wather onto a platform, and then each member gives her a flower until there are so many she can't hold them all in her arms. Heather, with her hair dyed pink, is the last one. She goes to the podium and announces that an outdoor garden with picnic benches will be dedicated in Miss Wather's name. Mason, winner of the Outstanding Senior College Scholarship Award, stands and presents her with a beautiful plaque and a gift certificate for travel. Principal McNeil tells her to "come back and visit anytime, especially with bags of candy." The crowd laughs and so does Miss Wather through her tears.

Logan, as valedictorian, gives her speech and concludes with: "We all know what it's like to be intimidated, embarrassed, harassed, humiliated, or hated. We have witnessed others experiencing the same. The only way to counteract hate and illuminate the darkness is by lighting our lamps of kindness. We all possess a lamp within us. We just need to strike the match and outshine the darkness. How do you do that? Do not stay silent. I urge all of you to go out into this world and speak out against injustice. Wherever you end up, be ambassadors for change. Don't close your eyes, don't turn your backs, don't turn away from the past. Learn from it. Use it. Make a positive difference!"

The bleachers erupt with applause. Mr. Bartley joins in. He's so damn proud of her, but at the same time his heart is shattered. There will never be a retirement celebration for him. And if he is remembered, what will these kids say?

As the students receive their diplomas, Joe cringes when he recognizes that one student is noticeably absent: Reginald Ashford. An audio recording of Reg making racist, anti-gay, anti-semitic remarks was turned in to Principal McNeil, providing evidence that eventually led Reg to confess to vandalizing Cade's and Logan's lockers. With two months left of high school, he was expelled. Fearing retaliation for the student who came forward with the recording, Principal McNeil never named the individual. Reg's college hockey scholarship was revoked. Thanks to Mason's outstanding save, the Riviere Rockets hockey team went on to win the state semifinals, but lost in the finals. Joe had been there to cheer on the team.

Sadness coats him like a layer of ice on the rink. This graduation might be the last time he'll cheer for a Riviere High School student.

The moment the ceremony ends, Mr. Bartley leaves.

He applies for every teaching position within a sixty-mile radius. He doesn't get one callback. He searches the internet for new job ideas, takes a personality test, and looks at various PhD programs in the SUNY network. Everything points him to teaching, and it plummets him into despair.

Mary wraps him in her arms. She doesn't know what to do or how to help him. He doesn't know, either. One trip to the liquor store for a bottle of scotch led to a rumor that he's turning into an alcoholic. He drops his club baseball team, stops going to his favorite coffee shop, refuses to go out to eat, He wears the same sweats for days as he binge-watches shows on TV.

Then one day, Joe receives a letter in the mail. It's addressed to Mr. Bartley. No return address. No signature. Just a typed note:

Dear Mr. Bartley,

I've done a lot of things I'm ashamed of, things that hurt others, and I got away with them. The truth is, I was real proud of that.

It's been nearly five months since the assignment and I think about what happened every day. Your courage to say you made a mistake made a difference for me.

I feel pretty crappy about how my actions back then impacted innocent people.

I'm not ready to come forward and admit what I did. I don't know if I ever will. But I've changed. I wanted you to know that.

There's been a lot of talk. Were you forced to quit? Did you quit to write a novel? Most people believe you were fired. Whatever happened, I hope you'll teach again.

Sincerely,

A former student

The letter gets Joe thinking.

With their savings and Mary's income keeping them afloat, he decides to seek a different way to work with children. He gets in touch with a family shelter to volunteer and tutor kids. It's a new start, one he hopes will rekindle the joy and passion he lost.

CHAPTER 68

CADE AND *LOGAN*

Five days before Logan leaves for Georgetown University:

A cemetery. Only Logan would consider Oswego's historic Riverside Cemetery a great place to hang out. Cade stands back, shakes his head, and laughs to himself as Logan examines headstone after headstone as if she's taking in artifacts at the Metropolitan Museum of Art in New York City.

Glancing over at Cade, she says, "Isn't this place inspiring?" Obviously, it's a rhetorical question, so he doesn't respond. Though the temperature is in the mid-eighties, goose bumps rise on Cade's arms. With only a few days left to spend together, Cade can think of a thousand things he'd *much* rather do with Logan in a thousand less creepy places. But she'd said there was something important she wanted to show him before she left for college. It so happens to be in this graveyard. Logan turns to Cade, lifts an eyebrow. "Well?" Apparently, the question wasn't rhetorical.

"Inspiring, no. Depressing, sad, morbid, haunting. Any of those will do."

Logan scoffs and playfully shoves Cade. "But there's so much history. It's even on the National Register of Historic Places," she says. "Famous people are buried here." She lists a bunch of names that Cade has never heard of and their political accomplishments.

Boring under normal circumstances. But this is Logan. Like the first time she walked into the inn, Cade's drawn to her, drawn to her passion, the way it lights her face. He's going to miss her, miss moments like this.

As Logan goes on talking about the cemetery's history, Cade's mind wanders. So much has changed since Mr. Bartley gave them the assignment.

The HUMANKIND WELCOME HERE signs are all over Riviere—a reminder and a promise. People from across the globe, displaying the sign, have sent them photos. Folding to community pressure, all but one Confederate flag came down in Riviere. Although it's become less frequent, Cade and Logan continue to be recognized around town. Someone will whisper, *Those are the kids who* . . . Cade and Logan pretend they didn't hear.

"Look around," Logan says, sweeping her arms wide. "One hundred and forty acres of beauty."

She's the only beauty he wants to see. But, of course, he doesn't say it. Scanning the horizon, Cade tries to see the acres of rolling hills, old oaks, sugar maples, and manicured lawn through Logan's eyes. He inhales freshly cut grass and turned soil.

Nope. He can't do it.

Still a cemetery with so many dead people underfoot.

Logan seems to read his mind. She lifts an imaginary sword. "I promise, if anything grabs you, I'll fight it off."

Cade laughs.

"Come on. I have something important to show you." Logan starts jogging down the middle of the packed dirt road. Several long beats pass before she turns around, walks backward, and waves at Cade. "Hurry up," she calls.

On a small rise of land, Logan opens a gate to a fenced-off area. There's a Star of David above it. Just as Cade wonders why they are there, Logan points to a row of eight headstones. "This is why we're here."

"Died at Fort Ontario" is inscribed on many of them. "They were all refugees who didn't live long enough to experience freedom," Logan says, leading Cade to the shade of a maple tree. She kneels, rubs the dirt off a flat stone sunk into the ground.

The marker reads, "Rachel Montiljo. Born in Bari, Italy. Jan. 11, 1944. Died on the ship to America. Aug. 2, 1944."

"Her mom gave birth to her in a concentration camp," Logan says. "Somehow, her parents escaped and brought her to Naples, Italy. They, too, were refugees on the *Henry Gibbins*."

Logan moves next to Cade and, despite her grimy palm, twines her fingers with his. She rests her head on his shoulder. They stare at the tiny grave, lost in their own thoughts. Cade focuses on the Hebrew words on the marker. He'd like to know what they say, even to read them someday. His mind drifts to his grandparents' families. The desire to learn more about them, about Judaism, tugs on him like an invisible rope tautly tied between his past and present. Maybe after he starts classes in a few weeks, he'll talk to the rabbi at SUNY-Lakeside?

Perhaps. When he's ready.

Logan tightens her grip. "What are you thinking?" she asks.

Cade remembers the last time he asked her that question. It brought their first kiss. A shiver runs through him as he remembers the snow. He sighs. "I'm thinking about how much has changed since we got the assignment. Do you think five, ten, twenty years from now, what we did will matter? Will people forget?"

"That's why I wanted to bring you here." Logan raises their clasped hands, points to Rachel's marker. "It will matter to us. We won't forget, Cade. For baby Rachel. For your grandpa, your nana, and your family. For every victim of hate. No matter where we are or what we're doing, we'll remember."

* * *

Rochester International Airport, two hours before Logan leaves for Georgetown:

Outside security, Logan wraps her arms around Cade's waist, holding on tightly. Last night, she and her dad had a farewell dinner at the inn. It was the first time in several weeks she'd been with Cade and his family. As a graduation present, Dad gave her a trip to Milwaukee and for ten days, she and Blair hiked, hung out, and ate gallons of Culver's custard until Blair left for freshman orientation at UW-Madison. Instead of returning to Riviere, Logan and her dad explored New York City. He understood when Logan said she wanted Cade to drive her to the airport. They needed last-minute goodbye time.

Taking a deep breath, she inhales the smells of the inn—the rosemary-mint shampoo, firewood, cleaners, and Nana's cooking. If only she could bottle it, bottle *home*. Or better yet, take

Cade with her. But, for now, it's impossible. CadeandLogan/LoganandCade will be Cade and Logan/Logan and Cade, best friends, always.

They'd talked about it. Georgetown and Washington, DC, and SUNY-Lakeside and Riviere. A seven-hour drive. Four long years. Her new goal: getting a degree in culture and politics. For now, Cade has decided to study business and marketing and make a difference for his family's inn. But the inn isn't the only reason Cade needs to stay. He has no idea how many more days, weeks, years he'll have with Nana. Lately, she's been sharing more stories about their family in Poland. That history means everything to Cade, and he wants to be there to record every piece of it. She is also teaching him to bake, and since all her recipes are stored in her head, Cade is in the process of writing every one down.

"Miss you already," Cade says, pulling back.

"Miss you more." Logan hesitates, then adds, "What we went through with Mr. Bartley . . . I'm so glad we had each other. No one else will ever understand exactly what we went through, you know?"

"I know. Can't say I want to do battle with a teacher again."

Logan laughs. "For sure." Her face grows serious. "But if we have to—"

"—we will. And we'll do whatever we can speak up for others facing injustice," Cade finishes.

"Exactly."

They smile at each other, holding on to that moment until Cade drops his arms to his side and takes a step back. The rectangular outline in his cargo pocket catches Logan's attention. "What is that? Is it for me?" His expression tells her it is. She practically pounces, but Cade manages to trap her hand before she can extract the present.

"I had planned to give it to you right before you enter the security line. I don't want you to open it in front of me."

"We're at the security line and if I hate it, I'll regift it to my new roommate."

"You're not going to hate it."

"Of course not. It's from *you!*"

Reluctantly, Cade draws out the gift. Logan grabs it, tears off the paper, and then says gleefully, "Oh, Cade!" She looks at him with so much love, it knocks him back another step. "This is the best gift ever."

She flips through the pages of the inn's copy of *The Tenant of Wildfell Hall* by Anne Brontë, the same one that had been sitting on Cade's nightstand since the first week she waltzed into his life. "You annotated it for me?"

He nods.

She slips it into her carry-on pocket and throws her arms around his neck, giving him a quick peck before pulling away. She hands him her car's key fob. "Take good care of it," she says, moving into the security line.

They watch each other. When she turns a corner in the queue, she calls out, "Eighty-six."

Puzzled, Cade calls back, "Eight-six *what?*"

Logan smiles. "Check your pocket."

Each of his cargo side pockets is empty. But in his back

pocket, Cade discovers a folded piece of paper from one of the inn's notepads. He opens it just as Logan disappears from his view.

"Eighty-six days until Thanksgiving break. Can't wait to see you! Love, Logan"

Cade squeezes the note in his fist the way her words squeeze his heart. He'd had his future figured out. That is, until the assignment and those ten days turned his life upside down.

If you want, you could leave here. Go anywhere, his parents had said.

Cade smooths out Logan's note on his palm. He reads it again, folds it up, and returns it to his back pocket. Eighty-six days. He imagines sitting at the inn's reception desk, crossing off each day on a calendar. He imagines baking with and without Nana. Someday. He imagines what the inn might be like when his parents are Nana's age. He stops, looks up at the departure board—a long list of possibilities. He misses Logan already, but there's a whole world of possibilities. Who knows where they'll be, *who* they'll be, in eighty-six days?

A NOTE FROM THE AUTHOR

Dear Reader,

A question that has been important to me is this: Can you be proud of your heritage, your faith, your identity, yet also have a strong need to protect or hide yourself from the "outside" world? That duality was something I, as someone Jewish, often lived with, struggled with, ashamedly agonized over.

After I met Archer Shurtliff and Jordan April, two brave teens who refused to do an antisemitic assignment very much like the one depicted in this novel, I realized how much this duality had permeated my being. I felt compelled to confront the issue. This is one of the reasons I wrote *The Assignment*.

I recall once, as an eight-year-old, being asked by a woman I did not know: "What are you?"

"A girl?" I answered.

"No," she said. "Are you Italian? Greek? Spanish?" At the time, I couldn't quite grasp the full extent of the bias and racism behind her question. The olive skin, big brown eyes, and nose bump I inherited from the men on my father's side periodically had strangers asking something similar.

"I'm American."

That woman shook her head. "What is your name?" she asked.

"Liza Goldberg."

"Ah. You're Jewish." Her voice held disdain. I saw disgust as the woman pulled her daughter away. I loved my family but wished for a different last name. That moment left its mark. It also was the dawn of my recognition of the immense complexities, hostility, and hatred people of color and other marginalized groups face every day.

I grew up in a Milwaukee suburb where Jewish people were a small minority. In elementary school, swastikas were carved into my desk. I was asked to show my tail and horns, and comments like "dirty Jew" and "Jew them down" were commonplace.

Antisemitism was not exclusive to my youth. In recent years, my family and I have endured violent antisemitic actions. Writing this novel has brought those horrific moments to the forefront of my mind, providing opportunities to reflect.

Two teens, Archer and Jordan, made a choice—a courageous and life-changing choice. Given an antisemitic assignment, they thought about the message it sent. They refused to blindly accept that it was okay because a teacher gave it to them. They held fast to their moral compasses and never faltered: It was wrong. Something had to be done. Their courage was the catalyst and, after meeting them, I went on to interview other activists and read about other immoral assignments and hateful incidents in our schools. All of the following actually happened, justified by educators as being done in the interest of bringing history alive for their students: In Wisconsin, students were asked to write "three good reasons for slavery and three bad reasons." In New York, a teacher had some of the white students bid on their Black peers for a mock slave auction. In Tennessee, a student was given the role of Hitler in a living history assignment and was told by the teacher to end his presentation with the *Sieg Heil,* which emboldened students to respond with the Nazi salute in and outside of the classroom. Fifth graders in North Carolina were given a "tic-tac-toe" assignment with different options, including drawing or building a model of a concentration camp. They also could pretend they were children in a concentration camp and write a letter to their parents. It is difficult to imagine that educators gave these assignments. Thankfully, courageous people spoke out against each one. Change was the result. The success of their actions, along with the actions of Archer and Jordan, inspired me to write this novel.

How many more reprehensible assignments go unchecked and unreported around the world?

In our complex global environment, we will all find ourselves facing ethical dilemmas. What to do? Follow the crowd? Find a way to defend the indefensible? Or speak out? My characters Logan and Cade exemplify young people who are vocal against hate, intolerance, and racism. My novel is a work of fiction, but it is rooted in today's society.

For students, speaking out against any injustice, especially when adults are involved, can be a formidable task. But it's critical, life-changing, and perhaps even life-saving.

Here is what I hope you, dear reader, know: in darkness, be the light. Let yours be one that illuminates the world, guided by an unwavering moral compass, courage, compassion, and love. Make your home, your school, your community a place where humanKIND is welcome.

Stay strong,

Liza

ACKNOWLEDGMENTS

Thank you. These simple words fail to convey the impact and depth of my gratitude to the people who have been a part of this novel's journey to publication. Friendship, kindness, patience, faith, empathy, knowledge, wisdom, constructive criticism, and love were key elements that enabled me to complete this work. I am humbled by your generosity. It is my hope to pay it forward. If I inadvertently forgot to include you in these acknowledgments, I ask for your forgiveness.

For me, there is no other explanation for how I came to write this novel than Divine Providence, so thank you, God. The extraordinary series of events that led to meeting Archer Shurtliff and Jordan April began on July 25, 2016. High school librarian Wendy Scalfaro messaged me on Facebook, asking if I would be interested in speaking at her school. That April 2017 trip to New York changed my life. If you're interested in the full story, please visit lizawiemer.com.

Archer and Jordan, thank you for speaking out and for being my inspiration. No matter where you are or what you do, I know you'll continue to have a positive impact.

My agent, Steven Chudney, thank you for discussing the manuscript with Ralph, for changing my life with your *yes*, and for being such a positive, supportive force. It's an honor to be a ChudMate. I couldn't have a better mensch in my corner.

I am grateful to Beverly Horowitz, my editor, for her insight, guidance, vision, unwavering faith in me, and most of all for being this novel's champion. It's a privilege to work with someone so exceptional, passionate, and dedicated. Rebecca Gudelis: I only know a fraction of all you do, but it's obvious to me that you're a Wonder Woman. Thank you for your support. To my talented and dedicated Delacorte team: Shameiza Ally, Cathy Bobak, Angela Carlino, Lili Feinberg, Colleen Fellingham, Marlene Glazer, Imani Morris, Josh Redlich, and Tamar Schwartz. Jen Strada, thank you for the A+ job on this "assignment."

For interviews or assistance researching the Holocaust, anti-semitism, Fort Ontario and the Fort Ontario Emergency Refugee Shelter, or SUNY, thanks to: Professor Christopher Baltus, Reverend George DeMass, Jack and Renee Dygola, Rabbi Cheski Edelman, Rebecca J. Fisher, Professor Emeritus Alan D. Goldberg, Josh Goldberg, Elfi Hendell, Kevin Hill, Elana Kahn, Paul A. Lear, Beth Martinez, Etzion Neuer, Louise Reed, Banna Rubinow, Raizel Schectman, Rabbi Shmaya Shmotkin, Alexa Smith, Dan Smith, the research staff at the United States Holocaust Memorial Museum, Rabbi Yisroel Wilhelm.

Additional interviews:

Sarah Abrams, Erica Cameron, Hal DeLong, Molly Ellner, Liam McLean, Bill Reilly, Claudia Schneider, Amber Scruton, Ava Wales, Blair Wales, Michelle Wichman.

Lifelines and beta readers. Thank you for input and support: Nancy Angulo; Alexis Army; Martina Boone; Shirlee and Barry Doft; Danielle Ellison; Andye Epps; Mary Evers; Amy Fellner Dominy; KayLynn Flanders; Alan S. and Cathy Goldberg; Barbara and Don Goldberg; Kelly Hager; Yitta Halberstam; Laura

Harrington; Sydney Hartnett; Ana Jordan; Betsy Kaplan; Benay and Jeff Katz; Sarah Kealy; Clara Kensie; Deborah Lakritz; David and Maureen Luddy; Lizzy Mason; Rachel Muniz; Anuradha Rajurkar; Patricia Riley; Gayle Rosengren; Wendy Scalfaro; Leia, Sebastian, and Rosalie Schaefer; Sheri Schubbe; Rachel Simon; Kathryne Squilla; Marcilia Tartaglia; Payton Thweatt; Steve Waldron; Michelle Walny; Tammara Webber; Barbara Weiss; Sarah Weiss; Lynn Wiese-Sneyd; Nancy Wiese; Heidi Zweifel.

Thank you for your hospitality or for giving me a home away from home to write: Christopher Baltus, Deborah Doft, Nili Doft, Marianne Fons, Alan D. and Dottie Goldberg, Banna Rubinow, Marcy and Moishe Yavor, Write On Door County.

Special shout-outs to Silvia Acevedo, Erin Arkin, Jaime Arkin, Katie Bartow, Sandy Brehl, Mason Carnell, Terri Carnell, Jenny Chou, Phoebe Dyer, Becca Fowler, Daniel Goldin, Cade Holder, Tara Jordan, Hannah McBride, Lisa McCarthy, Dee Paulson, Amy Reale, Jerod Santek, Andi Soule.

Boswell Book Company staff, ChudMates, Delacorte Mavens, Jewish Kidlit Mavens, North Shore Library staff, The River's End Bookstore staff, SCBWI-Wisconsin.

To the teachers, librarians, students, booksellers, online YA book community, and readers I've had the pleasure of meeting in person or online. Your support has meant the world to me. Your time is valuable. I'm grateful you spent some of it with me and my words.

My Doft, Goldberg, Katz, Lahav, Meisel, Pence, Ruminski, Schmidt, Sadan, Shul, Wiemer, Zighelboim family. Last, but never least, thank you to the loves of my life: Jim, Justin and Annabella, Ezra, Bracha, and Mendel.

I took liberties with my description of Safe Haven Holocaust Refugee Center, especially with the photographs. Yankel's story was loosely based on conversations I had with Holocaust survivor, Jack Dygola. Peter Franklin's experience was inspired by World War II US Navy Lieutenant Jack Taylor's survival in Mauthausen concentration camp. In chapter thirteen of Ruth Gruber's *Haven: The Dramatic Story of 1,000 World War II Refugees and How They Came to America,* I read about the death of baby Elia (Rachel) Montiljo during the voyage to America on the USS *Henry Gibbins.* Her grieving parents were granted permission to bury her in Oswego. The tragic loss of this tiny Holocaust victim—so close to freedom—haunted me. I was determined to find baby Elia's grave, to honor her memory and her parents. When I returned to Oswego in July 2017, Jordan, Archer, and Reverend George DeMass, past president of the board of directors at Safe Haven Holocaust Refugee Shelter Museum, searched the Jewish burial area at the Riverside Cemetery. Archer found the marker sunk into the ground and hidden by soil, grass, and leaves. We uncovered it. That moment left an indelible mark on me. Cade and Logan's scene at the cemetery was inspired by that visit.

RESOURCES

ORGANIZATIONS

American Civil Liberties Union (ACLU) aclu.org, 212-549-2500,
  @aclu
American Defamation League (ADL): adl.org, 212-885-7700
  (national office), @ADL
Human Rights Campaign (HRC): hrc.org, 800-777-4723, @HRC
The Leadership Conference on Civil & Human Rights: civilrights.org,
  202-466-3311, @civilrightsorg
Southern Poverty Law Center (SPLC): splcenter.org, (888) 414-7752,
  @splcenter

WEBSITES

en.gross-rosen.eu: Museum Gross-Rosen in Rogoźnica
ghwk.de/en: House of the Wannsee Conference
historicfortontario.com: Historic Fort Ontario
safehavenmuseum.com: Safe Haven Holocaust Refugee Shelter
  Museum
ushmm.org: United States Holocaust Memorial Museum
yadvashem.org: Yad Vashem, The World Holocaust Remembrance
  Center
yahadinunum.org: Yahad-In Unum

FILMS

Conspiracy (2001)
Die Wannseekonferenz (German-language film, 1984)

Elie Wiesel Goes Home (1996)
Safe Haven: A Story of Hope (2000)
The Wave (1981)

BOOKS

Alexievich, Svetlana. *Last Witnesses: An Oral History of the Children of World War II*

Desbois, Patrick. *The Holocaust by Bullets: A Priest's Journey to Uncover the Truth Behind the Murder of 1.5 Million Jews*

Gruber, Ruth. *Haven: The Dramatic Story of 1,000 World War II Refugees and How They Came to America*

Lipstadt, Deborah E. *Antisemitism: Here and Now*

Lowenstein, Sharon R. *Token Refuge: Story of the Jewish Refugee Shelter at Oswego, 1944–1946*

Marks, Edward B. *Token Shipment: The Story of America's War Refugee Shelter, Fort Ontario, Oswego, N.Y.* (Revised and illustrated edition by Rebecca J. Fisher and Paul A. Lear)

Prager, Dennis, and Joseph Telushkin. *Why the Jews?: The Reason for Antisemitism*

Roseman, Mark. *The Wannsee Conference and the Final Solution*

Safe Haven Museum and Education Center Staff. *Don't Fence Me In: Memories of the Fort Ontario Refugees and Their Friends*

Stamper, Vesper. *What the Night Sings*

Strasser, Todd. *The Wave*

Wiesel, Elie. *Night*

PLACES TO VISIT
In the United States

Safe Haven Holocaust Refugee Shelter Museum, Oswego, New York
United States Holocaust Memorial Museum, Washington, D.C.
Fort Ontario, Oswego, New York

Abroad

House of the Wannsee Conference Memorial and Education Site, Berlin, Germany

Museum Gross-Rosen, Rogoźnica, Poland

Yad Vashem (The World Holocaust Remembrance Center), Jerusalem, Israel

ABOUT THE AUTHOR

LIZA WIEMER is a writer and an award-winning educator with over twenty-five years of experience. She is the author of two adult nonfiction books, as well as a young adult novel. When Liza isn't writing, you'll find her in the kitchen, cooking meals to share with her Milwaukee community, family, and guests.

LizaWiemer.com

Now that you've read *The Assignment,* here are some questions to think about:

* Consider your initial reaction to the assignment. When you finished reading the book, did you have a different point of view?

* Cade and Logan felt compelled to do something about the assignment. Think about what you might do if given such an assignment.

* Social media plays an important part in what happens in the book, as well as in real life. Do you see social media as more helpful than harmful? Why or why not?

* In your own life, is there a moment when you spoke up for yourself or someone else? Reflect on that time, and if you'd like, share and discuss it with a friend.

* Hate speech and actions occur in all communities. Can you think of ways to combat this antisocial behavior?

◆ One of this novel's themes is that no one should defend the indefensible. Reflect on this idea and how you can embrace this principle in your own life.